The Honeymoon is Over

Also by Keith Lee Johnson

Sugar & Spice: A Novel
Pretenses
Little Black Girl Lost
Fate's Redemption
Little Black Girl Lost 2

The Honeymoon is Over

Keith Lee Johnson

URBAN BOOKS LLC

Urban Books
10 Brennan Place
Deer Park, NY 11729

ISBN 978-0-7394-7605-5

Printed in the United States of America

Acknowledgements

To Him, who is able to do considerably more than I can ask or think, I give You thanks today and always!

To Carl Weber, my publisher extraordinaire, who has taken my career to a whole new level, I'm humbled by what you've done in a very short time. I always know what I'm going to get from you and that's your very best effort, which is all I can ask of anyone. Continued success and may the Lord God continue to rain down success upon you; may everything you touch (especially my novels, hehehe), turn to fine gold.

To Roy Glenn, who I finally met in Baltimore earlier this year (2006), thanks for being a true professional and treating me with respect and the utmost courtesy. May God bless you as much as he blesses Carl.

To Martha Weber, my editor, you did another excellent job with The Honeymoon is Over. Were it not for your thorough examination of the manuscript, this novel would not be what it is now; a tightly written piece that I'm expecting to take my career to another level by the time Little Black Girl Lost 3 comes out in February 2007. May God bless you, too.

To the beautiful and intelligent Carol Mackey of Black Expressions, thanks for accepting nearly all my novels and being so instrumental in where my career is going. It was great seeing you at BEA, by the way. May God continue to bless you.

To two of my biggest fans, Dana Bowles & Carol, who read The Honeymoon is OVER in advance and loved it. Thanks for your criticisms and accolades.

To my main man in the literary jungle, author Phillip Thomas Duck, thanks for reading this one in advance and offering your criticisms as well. Also, thanks for always being willing to interview me for my Dare to Imagine Newsletter. You do it well. Be blessed, my brotha.

Special thanks to Darryl Newsome, Dana Ingram, Rodney Vincent Allen, Tricia Olsby, and Donna Garth, all friends and most close enough to be considered family, thanks for standing in that seriously long line at Borders during the February 1, 2006, Little Black Girl Lost 2 signing. You all know you didn't have to wait that long. I could have signed your books some other time. It was a very proud moment to see you all stand there for so long like all my other fans in Toledo, Ohio. Heart felt thanks to each of you for doing that.

To Tabitha, manager of Borders Bookstore in Toledo, Ohio, thanks again for asking me to sign at your store. I know most of the people in your store thought the signing was going to be an abysmal failure, but it was your biggest signing to date. The black women in Toledo had another thing to say, didn't they?

To Torian Thornton, thanks for being kind enough, and thoughtful enough to give me a call on Father's Day! I was totally shocked, totally surprised that you called. May the Lord God bless all that you put your hands to do and may he lead you and guide you into all truth.

Last but far from least, to my dear mother, Rose Marie Murray, did you ever think your son would have six books published in three years? Did you ever think I paid any attention to your God-given wisdom? Well I did, Mom, I did. Much of who I am, I owe to your insights and a consistent belt on my backside. Thanks for waking me up in the middle of the night (on a school night) to take out trash I knew I was supposed to take out before I went to bed, or to wash the dishes for that matter. Thanks for coming up to Lincoln Elementary School and talking to my sixth grade teacher, who told you all my dirt, and then jumping down my throat about it. Thanks for sending me to church four times a week and four times on Sunday to make sure I knew that God was alive and moving in the lives of those who diligently seek his face. Thank you for loving me enough to chastise me on the regular. You'll never know what heights you've propelled me to by doing so. May God let His blessing to you, flow through me continuously and forever more.

Dedication

To the best barber in T-Town, Keith Russell, and to Ministers Eric Sherman of Victory Life Worship Center and Talmadge Thomas of Mount Zion Baptist Church, your level of success will be determined by your level of commitment.

Chapter 1

Transamerica Building
Downtown San Francisco
Monday, September 10, 2001

Ifound her silence more than disturbing. It was like the sound of a car horn blowing just before dawn, wafting down a quiet, sleeping street, making its presence felt by all who heard it. I was in my office, working late as usual. Parris Stalls, my girlfriend, had called and she sounded strange. At first, I didn't pick up on it because I was still working, shuffling papers, trying to get caught up before heading home for a few hours of much needed rest. I asked her if she loved me, but she didn't respond.

Parris was thirty-five, midnight black, vivacious, alarmingly pretty, with a wide mouth and a perfect heart-breaker smile. We'd been seeing each other for four years and planned to marry. However, lately, she'd been evasive, quiet, hinting, never saying what was on her mind.

I had dismissed it all and continued working, attempting to take the company my father started, Kennard Janitorial

Services, to greater heights. I guess I had been neglecting Parris, and that's something a man with a beautiful woman can ill afford to do. I guess I got a little too comfortable, started taking her and our relationship for granted. I guess I thought I had her wrapped around my finger tighter than a snare drum, but oh, how wrong I was. To the best of my knowledge, I was her first and only lover. Until this very moment, I had no reason to doubt her commitment to me—to us—to the life we'd been planning.

I sensed she was out of the relationship already, but she didn't know how or didn't have the guts to tell me it was over. While we held the phone in silence, me waiting for her to answer, and her, I supposed, waiting on me to figure it out, I began to wonder if she was seeing another man. Is that what she was waiting for? Was she waiting for me to ask her if she was seeing another man? My heart began to pound, my breathing grew erratic; I was scared. Was I about to lose the love of my life?

For a second or two, I contemplated asking her then quickly decided against it. If she was seeing another man, I didn't want to know. I wanted to bask in the bliss of unabashed ignorance. That would keep my heart from breaking for a few more precious minutes, a few more precious hours, or perhaps days. If she was seeing another man, I knew she wouldn't volunteer the information because she was having trouble telling me she didn't love me anymore. How was she ever going to find the strength it would take to tell me she'd found another lover?

"What's wrong?" I asked her, knowing, or at least believing, I knew already.

Again, silence occupied the space between us like a threatening thunderstorm. This time, I closed my eyes, now knowing she wanted to leave me and why. Still, the love I felt for her wanted to hear every torturous word from her. In my complete and utter desperation, I hoped if she couldn't say it, if she couldn't speak the words, it wasn't over until she did. In my foolish mind, I knew she would never say the words, and therefore, it would never be over. That's what I wanted to believe, anyway. Then, for the first time since I asked her if she loved me, she spoke.

"Since you can't figure it out, I'll say it. It's over, Nelson."

There was such finality to her words, like there was no need for me to try to hold on to what we had together. I could hear it in her tone. It was like she had been thinking about ending the relationship for a long, long time. As a matter of fact, her words sounded like the relationship had been over for her for quite some time. Saying the words only closed the casket of a dead relationship that had been prepped for burial months ago. Only I didn't know it. Or did I?

"Can we talk about it?" I asked, nearly pleading like a pathetic beggar with no means to sustain his life.

Parris took a deep breath and blew it out, her exasperation exploding in my ears. "Talk about it for what, Nelson?" she screamed. "You know why!"

"No, I don't," I said, lying, still desperate to hold on to her.

She sighed heavily into the phone as if I was getting on her last nerve. "You wanna know why?"

Now I was quiet. Chillingly quiet. Hell naw, I didn't want to know. I wanted to remain in nirvana for as long as I could.

"Because I'm sick and tired of waiting for your ship to come in! That's why!" She was screaming into the phone again. "Night after fucking night, I sit in this empty apartment, waiting for you to get me the things my girlfriends have, the things I deserve. I'm sick and tired of them living like queens and me living like a fucking pauper. I'm beautiful, Nelson! All my friends say it. They all told me to leave your broke ass a long time ago. But I didn't, Nelson. You know why? Because I tried to believe in your sorry ass. I tried to believe in you for as long as I could. And now . . . I'm going for mine without you. I hope you make it, Nelson. I re-

ally do. At least then you'll have something to show for all
the nights you work in that office."

The fear that was about to consume me disappeared and
was immediately replaced by blinding, vengeful rage. "You
stupid-ass bitch! Why the fuck are you listening to those
bitches?" I continued, not expecting an answer. "Dorothy's
man is a goddamned drug dealer! And you're okay with
that? And your other so-called friend has three goddamned
kids, all with a different daddy. None of them muthafuckas
are paying child support, and the fat bitch is pregnant again.
And you're listening to those hoes? These are your sages?
Damn! They say birds of a feather flock together, but I
thought you were smarter than that. I see I was wrong."

The line went dead.

I was about to call her back, but changed my mind as my
pride replaced my fear of losing her. I began to tell myself it
was her loss, not mine; anything to assuage my feeling of
profound emptiness. I tried to throw myself back into my
work, telling myself I didn't need or even want a woman who
listened to losers, but I couldn't. I stood up and looked out
the window of my office as the realization of the end of our
relationship washed over me. The innate pain I felt, the kind
that ruptured a ventricle in a man's heart, the kind that
pierced the soul, the kind that could never be salved, en-
veloped me, completely obliterating my sense of self-worth. I
grabbed my stomach and doubled over as though the wind
had been knocked out of me.

Chapter 2

Unable to work, unable to control my thoughts, unable to suppress my deep and abiding love for Parris, I decided that I wasn't letting go of our relationship. I wasn't giving up so easily. I loved her and I told myself that she loved me, too. For all I knew, she might have had another man, but she might not have. Whichever the case, I knew a man was behind all of this. As far as I'm concerned, when a beautiful woman decides to leave a man, especially her first lover, some other man has wormed his way into her heart.

I believed that if I put in the hours, if I committed myself to getting more and more contracts, if I pushed our business into all the major cities on the coast, I could slow down in another year or two.

It was working, too. Kennard Janitorial Services was on the move, but as a result, it created more work for me. What Parris didn't understand was even though we were bringing in more accounts daily, I couldn't spend that money on her. I couldn't even spend the money on myself. We had to put nearly every dollar we earned back into the business in order to grow and become a major player in the country.

My vision for the business extended way beyond San Francisco, way beyond California. My vision for Kennard Janitorial Services was to have contracts in every major city in the continental United States. However, that was going to involve a lot of work and lots of hours. Thinking about it now, I guess I really couldn't blame Parris for dumping me. At the same time, why couldn't she understand that riches don't magically appear overnight?

As I drove over to her Alamo Square Victorian, every good thing about her, every good thing about us, flooded my mind like a good movie, a love story you never want to end. The time I reserved a suite at the Crystal Gateway Marriott Hotel when we went to Washington, DC, came to mind. We made love every day, sometimes two or three times a day, and still managed to see all the sights and memorials.

I remember visiting John Fitzgerald Kennedy's grave and looking at the eternal flame Jackie lit. Camelot was gone, thirty years removed, and yet this touching legacy still brought tears to Parris' eyes. I hugged her and she hugged me back. From there, we walked down the stairs to a landing where they had phrases from his speeches engraved in stone for all to read. With me standing five foot nine and dwarfing Parris, who wasn't quite five feet tall, we read them all.

After remembering her height, I found myself smiling, laughing even about how sensitive she was about her stature. "I'm four foot eleven and seven eighths," she'd say with rancor, letting everybody know exactly how tall she was when people guessed her height. One of the things I loved about Parris was she stayed in shape, exercising religiously, keeping that marvelously sculpted body of hers looking like it belonged on the cover of a magazine. And as far as I was concerned, it did, along with that pretty face of hers.

Thoughts of losing her returned with the unrelenting emotional pang and fear of our relationship being over. I didn't want it to be over. I hadn't felt this emotional since my doctor told me my NBA career would never be. That was the first time I remember crying since my father stopped whipping me for breaking his rules. And cry I did. I cried so loudly that day, people visiting their loved ones left them and came to comfort me. They all knew who I was back then. I was Nelson "Skywalker" Kennard.

I was hell on the hardwood, too. They'd all seen me shoot jumpers with two or three guys hanging all over me and still hit nothing but strings. Not only could I make thirty footers consistently, I could, as they say, jump outta the gym, hence the name, Skywalker. I was awesome. Awesome! If I was anywhere near the basket, somebody was going to get slammed on, and it didn't matter how tall the player.

One time, Utah came to the University of San Francisco. They had a seven-footer who was known for blocking shots. I dunked right in his face. He was totally humiliated. The whole team fell apart after that. I scored forty and we routed those guys 120–65.

There was a serious buzz about me being the number one draft pick of the Philadelphia 76ers. Michael Jordan was still the best in the league, and the ESPN talking heads were hailing me as the next greatest prospect to come along. Just as the experts predicted, Philadelphia drafted me and offered me an obscene amount of greenbacks. And this was guaranteed money! Guaranteed!

I remember sitting at the table with my family and my best friend, Sterling Wise, who at the time was in law school at Georgetown. He and I played high school ball together and he was very good, too. We were all waiting in eager anticipation when David Stern went to the podium and announced, "With the first pick of the NBA Draft, the Philadelphia 76ers select Nelson Kennard." I was richer than rich in an instant, and within the hour, I was on a private jet to meet the own-

ership. I remember riding in a limousine to the Spectrum
and then walking into the locker room, where they already
had my name on my locker.

The same private jet flew me and my family back to San
Francisco. The plan was for me to pack all my personal be-
longings and move into a posh townhouse in an exclusive
suburb of Philadelphia that team management was renting
for me until my mansion was built. The Philadelphia brass
did everything first class. These guys even took me to a couple of sites so I could choose where I wanted to live. It was
mind blowing to go from having nothing to being able to
buy *anything* I wanted. There was no way I was going to screw
this deal up. No way!

But I did screw it up. What made matters worse was that
for years I've had to live with my own stupidity. My mom,
dad, Sterling, and everyone, even the Philadelphia brass
told me not to doing anything foolish before I was an official
76er. And what did I do? I went by the park and decided to
play in a pickup game. I had been there all day, playing ball,
enjoying my last game at the park. Just as I was about to
leave, some guys who knew me begged me to stay and play
one more game. Something in me said, "No, go home and
get ready to go."

Instead, I ignored the voice inside my head and told the
guys I'd play one last game. The game was nearly over and
we were about to win. I had the ball and the defender was
playing me too close, which told me I could go around him
and give the spectators what they wanted—a high flying slam
dunk.

My first step was lightning quick, and I went around the
defender like he wasn't even there. When the other players
saw me come into the lane, they parted like the Red Sea,
preferring not to get dunked on. However, when I went to
push off on my left leg, my knee gave out. I screamed in pain
as I felt my kneecap slide up my thigh, causing me to crash

back to earth like a duck shot out of the sky by a camouflaged hunter.

My career was over before it had even begun. Fortunately for me, the president of the school liked me and allowed me to come back to school to get my master's degree in business, free and clear.

When I turned onto Steiner, where Parris lived, I was lucky enough to find a parking space not far from her Victorian. Just as I was about to get out of the car, I saw Shenandoah Armstrong, a former basketball rival, get out of his Mercedes Benz, walk up the stairs, and ring her doorbell. What I saw next blew my mind. Unable to believe what I'd seen, I sat in my car and continued watching them, totally befuddled, totally dismantled and debilitated.

Chapter 3

As far as Parris was concerned, Nelson had finally done what she had been wanting him to do for more than six months. She needed a reason to break it off with him. Calling her a stupid-ass bitch was more than enough reason. No one had ever called her stupid and gotten away with it. She hated being called stupid. Even more, she hated being called a bitch, even though the word frequently found its way out of her mouth when referring to a difficult woman. But to be called stupid and a bitch in the same sentence, especially by a man, her so-called man, well, that was unforgivable.

Without even a second's hesitation, she picked up the phone and called Shenandoah Armstrong. Shenandoah was the man who had been relentlessly pursuing her for nearly six months, offering her diamonds and pearls, expensive cruises, pressuring her with tempting ideas of sipping cool drinks on tropical islands. These were the very things she longed for, the very things she thought she deserved. But there was a problem. She loved Nelson more than she loved the things he couldn't give her—at least that's how it was until everyone she knew began to tell her what a fool she was for not jumping at a catch like Shenandoah Armstrong. A man of means was always better, was their philosophy.

Her friends and family didn't understand what she saw in Nelson in the first place. Sure, he was in business for himself; however, he wasn't making anywhere near the money Shenandoah was making in his position as an executive with Software Unlimited. Shenandoah had the whole package: position, power, money, real estate, stock options with Software Unlimited, and thriving investments. On top of that, he was a good-looking man.

At first, she wasn't even tempted by his success, but as she listened more and more to her friends and family, without even realizing it, she began to contemplate the possibilities. At some point in the previous six months, the decision to leave Nelson for Shenandoah became all too clear.

Parris could have anything she wanted, and she was going to have everything. Nothing would be too good or too expensive now that Nelson was out of the way. After all, a beautiful woman like her deserved it. She convinced herself that she'd given Nelson more than enough time to produce. He hadn't, and now it was time to move on. The only question that remained was how would she get rid of Nelson? She couldn't just up and leave one man for another man. That's what whores did, and she wasn't a whore. At least that's what she told herself.

Besides, if she left him for no "real" reason, she would never be able to live with herself. That's when she decided to be a thorn in Nelson's side. She believed that if she was moody enough, if she was rude enough, if she was belligerent enough, if she disrespected him enough, he would do or say something that would give her reason to leave him.

Still, no matter how many times she tried to set the stage for an all-out fight, Nelson never fell into her trap, which frustrated her to no end. She needed a reason to break it off and she didn't have one. When she tried to start arguments, he wouldn't argue. When he visited her and she didn't talk, he'd fall asleep on the couch, which pissed her off.

She thought about cutting off the sex, but Nelson was a wonderful lover, and even though she wanted to him leave, the sex could stay. Finally, she decided to break it off the old-fashioned way, which was to just break it off. Now that she was free to see Shenandoah, he needed to be told she was his, mind, body, and soul, if he still wanted her.

"What!" Shenandoah screamed into the phone after seeing Parris' name in the caller ID. "I told you not to call me until you're through with Nelson, didn't I?"

Hearing the rage in his voice, the lioness that Parris had been with Nelson became a lamb. In a schoolgirl voice, she said, "Yes, Shenandoah, you did."

He screamed at her again, "Well? Did you break it off or not?"

Again, sounding like a kindergartner, the former lioness offered a demure, "Yes. It's over."

Shenandoah was positively beaming with pride. He felt like the conquering king at that moment, but continued talking roughly to her. "What did he say?" he growled. "Did he cry? Did he turn into a little candy-ass bitch and beg you to stay with him?"

Realizing Shenandoah needed to feel like he took her, rather than her giving into wanton greed, she answered, "I didn't even bother to listen to him once I decided it was you that I needed in my life. You're ten times the man Nelson is, and better looking, too."

"If that's the case, why the fuck did you make me wait six goddamn months?"

A long pause occupied the distance between them.

She raised her voice several octaves. "You think I'm a whore, Shenandoah? Is that it? You think I'm a whore?"

"Are you a whore?" he asked roughly.

"If that's what you think, maybe I made a big mistake."

"Did you make a big mistake, Parris? Because if you think you made a big mistake, you made a big mistake, okay? And I don't have the time or the fucking patience to wait around for a woman that doesn't know what the fuck she wants. Now, what's it going to be?"

His fiery words silenced her again and at the same time excited her. She found his harsh tone sexually stimulating. A campfire ignited in her private place and began a slow, steady burn.

Instead of answering his direct questions, invitingly she asked, "Are you coming over or what?"

"If I do, I'm not coming over there to talk. I'm tired of talking, aren't you?"

The schoolgirl returned and offered a sexy, "Yes."

"Look . . . I'm not for any more games, Parris. Are we going to do this, or not?"

"Yes."

Shenandoah looked at his diamond-studded Rolex. "I'll be there in thirty. And you better not be playing games. You understand?"

"Yes."

After hanging up the phone, Shenandoah acted as if he were a second grader with a crush on his teacher. Everyone had a price, he knew, and he had bought himself the prized possession. He had fought a six-month battle for the affections of Parris Stalls and won. The only thing left were the spoils, which he would plunder in thirty minutes.

He went to his bathroom, opened the medicine cabinet, and took out his package of Cialis. He put one in his mouth, threw back his head, and swallowed hard. Then he went to his bedroom closet and grabbed a twelve-pack box of Trojan condoms. He was expecting to make love to her that night, the next day, and the day after that.

Chapter 4

Upon hearing a knock at the front door of her Victorian, Parris took a deep breath, held it for a brief moment, and exhaled. The time had come to put up or shut up. She walked to the door, pushed herself up on her toes, and looked through the peephole at Shenandoah, who was standing on the porch. Before opening the door, she took another deep breath, let it out, and then opened it, offering him her heart-breaker smile.

Parris had already prepared herself for this night, having bathed and perfumed her exquisite body. While she would make love with Shenandoah, she was nevertheless nervous about the encounter because she had only been with Nelson. As a matter of fact, she thought Nelson would be the only man to enter her precious temple. But now, she had to let in a different man—a rich one.

After all, sex with Shenandoah was a part of the game. Marriage was, too, whether he knew it or not. She had drunk a tall glass of wine prior to calling Nelson, which she knew would make it easier to have sex with a man she didn't love. The wine was doing exactly what she expected it to do, lowering her inhibitions. And the bad-boy attitude Shenandoah displayed added to the overpowering stimulant.

As soon as he saw her standing there in a red negligee with a plunging neckline, the Cialis kicked in. While most of the garment she wore was sheer, he couldn't see her erect nipples nor could he see her crotch, which made the allure more tantalizing. He stepped inside the house and manhandled the petite woman like he was Genghis Khan raiding an unprotected village. And when she didn't resist, when she didn't even flinch, he kissed her hard on the lips and she kissed back, slipping him her tongue and grabbing a handful of his muscled body. While they were still in a tight, wanton embrace, Shenandoah reached out for the door with his left hand and closed it.

Parris pulled her lips away, placed her small hands on his chest, and said, "Do you want to go upstairs?" Not bothering to wait for an answer, she took him by the hand and led him up the stairs to her bedroom, where the kissing began anew. This time, hands, both hers and his, were moving, too. However, Nelson Kennard was in the room with them, even though he was only in Parris' mind.

Chapter 5

I met Parris in August 1997. My father and I had just closed the deal with the law offices of Daniels, Burgess, and Franklin. On the way out, we ran into my best friend, Sterling Wise, who worked for the firm. I hadn't seen him in a long time, and we all talked for a few minutes before getting into an elevator. When the doors opened to the lobby, I saw Parris standing there, waiting. Our eyes locked and she flashed her heart-melting smile at me. Those dimples of hers made me weak in the knees.

My father and I were pressed for time, and the brief conversation we'd had with Sterling cut into it, as we were supposed to bid on another contract within the hour. As we rushed past her, I couldn't help but to stop in my tracks and turn around. I had to see this beauty one more time. Just as the elevator doors were about to close, she noticed me looking at her, then quickly reached out and stopped the doors from shutting. The whole time, I could feel my dad's eyes on me, although he never said a word. Even if he had, it wouldn't have made one bit of difference. I *had* to talk to this woman.

The fact that she kept those doors from closing meant the

opportunity had presented itself, and I wasn't about to let this woman go without getting her phone number. As I started back to the elevator, she got off so the other people could go on without her. From our brief conversation, I found out she was a schoolteacher and very easy to talk to. We'd still be talking right now if my father hadn't come over and said, "Young lady, will you please give my son your number so we can go?" And that's how it all began.

Now, my dealings with Shenandoah Armstrong were altogether different. No friendly conversations; nothing friendly at all. It was competition from the start. We went all the way back to my basketball days at San Francisco State University. The egghead, a name I use to refer to all Stanford guys, played for the Cardinals. I would wear his ass out on the hardwood every time we played them.

Just as Parris was between us now, two decades ago or so, another woman was between us—his woman. Because she meant nothing to me, her name escaped me. She was just one in a sea of female admirers who loved hanging around the soon-to-be millionaire basketball star willing to do anything I asked. And I asked a whole lot of times, indulging my carnal passions with any and all the women I could. Even though we were kids back then, perhaps he loved his woman as much as I loved Parris.

Is that why he's here? Is it because he's got a twenty-year-old score to settle?

The porch light was on, allowing me to see everything as I sat in my car, absolutely stunned by what I was seeing. Parris was wearing the same negligee she'd worn a few years back when we were in the nation's capital. When I saw her smile at him, when I saw her look at him the way she used to look at me, my body began to shake uncontrollably. My mind raced as my heart shattered like priceless crystal.

It was my own fault that I was seeing this. I shouldn't have gone over unannounced, especially after our rough break-up. It was then that I began to wonder why women followed their men around when they thought their men were seeing other women. Who in their right mind wanted to see the person they loved passionately kissing another? Who actually wanted to see it? I sure as hell didn't, yet here I was looking at it, unable to divert my eyes. Besides, what does a woman do when she catches her man kissing or in the very act of screwing another woman? What was I going to do, knowing that I was in that very situation?

A woman would never forget the visual as long as she lived, just as I knew I would never forget what I just witnessed. Seeing them together like that would be forever seared in my mind. It could have been worse, though. She could have been screwing a fourteen or fifteen-year-old like an alarming number of teachers were doing these days. That would add insult to injury.

There could be no denying this—none. Oh my God! Just when I thought it couldn't get any worse, she was putting her tongue in his mouth. The same tongue she used to put in mine. I knew Parris, and I knew how she kissed. While I couldn't actually see this, I knew it was happening—knew it!

Out of nowhere, my mind, the same mind that had been in denial for months or perhaps years, began to reveal a truth that would lead me to an agonizing conclusion. The mood swings, the festering anger that lingered, the feeling that something was wrong even though she constantly denied it, all seemed to come from nowhere. Now I realized that her antics were nothing more than an orchestrated waltz, a sordid little script that led to the bad, very bad movie I was watching.

It didn't matter that I had done the same thing to Shenandoah more than twenty years ago. Call me a hypocrite if you want. I don't give a damn. What happened in the past was the past! This shit was fresh! And the smell of it was truly foul. I had been a fool, a buffoon, a clown, and a court jester for these two cheaters, and in so doing, crushed my dream of a life with Parris. A myriad of questions ran through my mind all at the same time. As I thought on these things, red hot anger began to simmer.

Was this the first time the lips that belonged to me touched his? It sure didn't look like it. It looked like this had been going on for a long time. The way they were kissing in the doorway for all to see, the way they clung to each other like static electricity clings to clothes, they had to have had sex—more than once. More than twice. It looked like this obsession of theirs, the fire that burned in them both, was a five-alarm blaze that no amount of water could douse.

Did they discuss me? Were they laughing at me? Were they discussing our sex life? Was he a better lover than me? Was his dick bigger than mine? All of those questions ran through my mind like an out of control locomotive. As the train of questions raced through my sensitive mind, as my heart broke more and more, a jealous rage replaced the love I felt for Parris, and dominated my unforgiving mind. Just like that, my love was devoured and swallowed whole by an unflinching desire for vengeance.

As the tears formed, I fought them back.

I was going to be strong.

I wouldn't cry. Not over a woman—not over a bitch—not over a whore! Never!

But I would kill the bitch! The whore! She broke my heart!

I was going to kill both of them.

Chapter 6

As a business owner who made nightly deposits, it only made sense to possess a weapon to protect myself and company assets. I reached over to the glove compartment, where I kept my 10mm Glock 20 and ammunition. I was going to put some serious holes in them. I was going to empty the clip in them. As I slid the magazine in and flipped off the safety, I mentally prepared myself to begin the assault. After exiting my car, I walked across the street filled with blinding rage; the kind of rage that would only dissipate when the object of my hatred lay dead or dying at my feet.

I jogged up the stairs and went to the door. Reaching out, I grabbed the doorknob and turned it back and forth forcefully. It was locked. I reached into my pocket and grabbed my set of keys. I can't begin to describe what I was feeling at that moment. The only thing I knew was that I had to get inside. In my anxiousness, I dropped the keys, causing them to clang when they hit the porch. Quickly, I picked them up and began sorting through them again. Having found the key, I slid it into the lock and turned. The door opened, but the chain kept it from opening all the way. The chain, which was so thin, couldn't possibly keep me from entering and killing them in the very act.

In my haste, I left the key in the lock and with my free hand, grabbed the door where the chain was connected, forcing it open. With the gun still in my hand, I walked up the carpeted stairs to the landing, which is when I first heard Parris' rhythmic sighs . . . the same sighs I used to hear in my ears when I pumped her hard and steady just the way she liked. Monstrous rage plagued my mind, quelling sensibilities, urging me to do what I had to do, pushing me to commit a double murder, leading me down a dark path that would mean three deaths, not two, since the voice inside my head told me to pop myself after putting seven bullets in both of them.

And I would.

I would kill everyone in the house that night.

I took the remaining five steps and edged toward them, my back against the wall. The door was open, and I listened for a while right outside her bedroom. I don't know how long, but I listened to the howling bedsprings. I listened to them moan in each other's ears with no shame for what they were doing and what this act was doing to my shattered heart, which couldn't break any more.

I didn't want them to have a chance to stop. I wanted to kill them while they were doing it and send them straight to hell where they belonged. Shortly after that, I would join them in the intense inferno. Then, once we entered the fiery gates of hell, I would shoot them both again and again, throughout eternity.

As quietly as I could, I slid the barrel back and chambered a bullet with Parris' name on it. She would be the first to feel the heat of my fury.

I took a deep breath and spun around to the entrance of the bedroom like a cop in a TV show. Even though the room was dark, I could see them. I saw them moving, pumping. I heard them groaning like they were in a state of heavenly bliss, like sex with each other was the greatest pleasure they had ever known. They were oblivious to my presence.

I stood there, frozen solid in time like a Greek statue made of granite, watching fleshly carnality, watching sinners sin. With my Glock pointed at their thrusting bodies, I tried to pull the trigger, but I couldn't. Instead, my aching heart softened, tears welled, and they fell. A river of them fell as I watched and listened for what felt to me like five minutes, but in all actuality, only a couple seconds had elapsed.

I lowered the gun, stepped back out of the room, and listened to see if they had heard me. They hadn't, I knew, because Parris was coming loudly, which drove the dagger already in my heart to the hilt. I doubled over and let the grief in my soul have its way, albeit silently.

Chapter 7

Soon Shenandoah was fast asleep and snoring. As I knew she would, Parris got out of bed and went to the bathroom. She loved the act of lovemaking, but hated the mess that resulted from it. Emerging from the room, she turned left, flipped on the light, and went down the hall to the bathroom, unaware that I was standing there with my arms folded and had seen it all. Just as I thought, she closed the door. Funny how she could make love with her bedroom door open, but made sure the bathroom door was closed and locked every time she went in there.

I walked down to the bathroom and leaned against the right side of the wall, knowing she would turn left and head back to her bedroom. I could hear the steady flow of pee splashing in the toilet bowl. Shortly after that, I heard the toilet paper roll scrolling and the toilet flush. The bathtub faucet knobs screeched when she turned them, and water splashed in the tub. Then she started humming some high-spirited tune.

How dare she be happy? She's lucky to be alive! I felt like kicking the door in and pistol whipping her to death, but I waited for her to come out. The door opened.

When she exited, she was wearing a towel that covered her breasts and came down to mid-thigh. Her hair comforted her shoulders. Damn she was fine, but she was no longer mine.

I needed to get her attention without waking Shenandoah. "Pssssst!"

"Ready for another round, baby?" she said while turning around.

She gasped loudly and nearly jumped out of her skin when she saw me leaning against the wall, gun in hand, my cheeks wet. The towel she was wearing fell to the floor, exposing her nakedness. She covered her breasts and vagina as best she could. Spontaneously, in the recesses of my mind, I could hear them making love; the moaning and groaning filled my consciousness again.

I pointed the gun in her face and uttered words from a broken heart. "Oh, how I loved you so."

Resignation defined her. She closed her eyes. I guess she knew it was over. And it was.

Just before I pulled the trigger, I remembered that I had done this very thing to Shenandoah. I had been inside his woman, pumping her hard, making her moan the way Parris was moaning just a little while ago, and knowing me, it was probably too many times to remember. Did he love her? What was her name? Did he love the woman I had bedded? If so, he couldn't have loved her as much as I loved Parris, but I bet he felt what I was now feeling, perhaps worse.

"Open your eyes," I commanded, amazed that she wasn't begging for her life, apologizing, or even crying. Shock, I guess. I don't know.

She opened her eyes and we stared at each other for a long, long time. The hallway was extremely quiet. In the distance, I could hear Shenandoah snoring, oblivious to the life and death situation playing itself out about thirty feet from where he slept like a sedated infant.

Parris stood before me, shaking like a leaf in a strong fall wind. In her state of fright, pee ran down her legs and splashed on the towel that had fallen to the floor. Tears filled her eyes and fell. She was sorry for what she'd done, I thought, judging by the look on her face.

Why are we always sorry *after* we've fucked over somebody, I wondered.

I put the gun to my head and cocked it. Just before I squeezed the trigger, Parris begged, "Please don't, Nelson. Please, please, please don't do it. I'm so sorry for hurting you like this."

Now, there's irony. I came to kill her, and she was pleading for my life?

I looked in her eyes and saw the sincerity in them.

After lowering the gun, I clicked the safety on, took a few steps closer to her, and said, "Don't ever do this to anyone again." I was saying it to myself as much as I was saying it to her because I now knew what it felt like. Reaching for her hand, I placed the gun in it.

Softly, I said, "I fucking loved you, Parris."

Then I left her standing there, holding the instrument that was supposed to take all three of our lives that chilling September night.

Chapter 8

After leaving Parris with her slumbering lover, I drove back to the office with the intent of trying to complete the work I hadn't finished. I was still numb, still shocked, still baffled by it all. Was I really going to kill myself? What if Parris hadn't begged me not to pull the trigger? I think I would have. I really do. Given the sudden revelation of infidelity, given the crippling hurt I felt, given the anguish that pierced my soul, given the sound of those two cheaters fucking each other, howling like the animals they were, given the jealousy that overwhelmed me and the subsequent anger that controlled me, and given the fact that I broke into her house, gun in hand, pointing it at the lovers, pointing it in my precious Parris' face, pointing it at my own head . . . yes, I would have. I would have blown my head clean off and ended it all.

Never again.

Never again would I love a fallible woman like this.

Never again would I allow my heart to be this vulnerable.

Never again would I trust.

I walked over to my desk, sat down, and picked up the papers I had left, attempting to do some work. The erotic sounds of Parris and Shenandoah filled my head, took up residence, and kept my conscious thoughts fixated on what I'd seen—what I could still hear in stereo. I looked at the clock. It was just after midnight. I thought, *Maybe Parris was right.* After what I had just seen, I was attempting work again. Was I a nut job or what?

I looked at the papers on my desk and blamed them for keeping me in this office for so many hours, for so many days, for so many months, causing me to neglect a relationship I had cherished, and driving the woman who was to have my children into the arms of a former rival. In a wide, sweeping motion, I pushed everything from my desk to the floor, stood up, and paced the room, going back and forth, trying to make sense of it all.

Did Shenandoah love Parris? I hoped so. At least then, in some insane way, all of this would make sense, as crazy as that sounds. I stooped down and picked up the radio I had swept to the floor with everything else, hoping it hadn't broken. I was attached to it. Parris had given it to me for Christmas the previous year.

I flipped it on and changed the channel from WJAM to an AM station playing soft classical music, which they say soothes the savage beast. After what I almost did that night, I'd say I fit into the beast category. Going over to the couch, I stretched out, closed my eyes, and tried to relax, rubbing both hands over my face and head, attempting to comfort my aching mind.

I wanted to cry again. I needed to cry again. For some reason, though, I resisted this, believing I was somehow weaker if I did. Why was that? Who made that stupid-ass rule? I had tear ducts, didn't I? I had tears in my eyes, didn't I? Why, then, couldn't I cry? No one was here but me. Who would know if I released the emotions I felt? Who would know if I wailed like an infant needing to be nursed by its mother? I had heard somewhere that tears sped up the healing process. Was that true? I had no idea, but I wanted the torturous misery I was in to go away.

Would I heal faster if I let loose and truly mourned for the first time in a long time? Perhaps it was the tears that kept me from killing Parris and Shenandoah, not her begging me not to. When the tears came in her hallway, I felt no anger when they fell. Is that why we kill women when they hurt us like this? Is it because we don't cry when we're emotionally hurt? Is it because we fight our natural inclination to cry and exchange it for another emotion—the dangerous one, the destructive one—anger?

I decided to give it a try. I decided to see if crying would somehow medicate my gaping wound. It started with a sniff and became a moan. I told myself that no one could hear me, and little by little, I let loose and wailed—loudly. When I finished, I fell asleep with the sound of classical music playing softly in my ears.

Chapter 9

My mind was still in a fog when I heard a man on the radio say, "It's been nearly three hours since United Airlines flight 175 and American Airlines flight 11 crashed into the Twin Towers of the World Trade Center. We are under attack. All flights have been grounded and the Air Force has been given orders to shoot down any planes that refuse to land . . ." It sounded like the man had said this before, like he was only reporting what everyone already knew. Was I dreaming this? I opened my eyes, and looked at my watch. It was nearly 8:30 AM, making it 11:30 AM in New York.

The first thing that came to mind was the Oklahoma City bombing. They say Americans did that one, but I was always suspicious. After rising from the couch, I surveyed the mess I'd made of my office and remembered Parris had broken it off with me and found another man. My heart still ached, but not as badly as before. Maybe the tears did help. Perhaps I was still in shock. I don't know.

I searched through the wreckage and, after locating the television remote control, hit the power button. The first thing I viewed was a plane flying low and heading into Manhattan. There was a small caption in the upper left-hand corner that read: RECORDING. I focused on the plane again and watched it slam into one of the towers. It was like a movie. It was surreal. A few seconds later, the news station played a recording of the second plane slamming into the other tower.

Damn! What the hell is going on?

Over and over again, they replayed the attack, and I still couldn't wrap my mind around it. This was actually happening. Just as I was starting to accept what I was seeing, I read the news ticker at the bottom of the screen, which was reporting more tragic news. Yet another plane had slammed into the Pentagon.

All of this almost made my personal problems appear insignificant, which they were, compared to what was happening in The Big Apple. I welcomed the diversion. I couldn't imagine what was going through the passengers' minds as the planes descended and headed into downtown Manhattan. Did they know the terrorists were going to fly the planes into buildings? I hoped they didn't. Maybe the terrorists killed everyone first. At least then they wouldn't know what was going on, I thought as I rationalized cold-blooded murder.

All of a sudden, I was glad to be alive, glad I hadn't killed Parris and Shenandoah, glad I hadn't killed myself. As I continued watching the breaking news, I realized life was just too short to be wasted on women like Parris Stalls. Nevertheless, I still felt the pangs of separation, the pulling of my flesh to be with her. I wanted it all to end, but I knew it would be quite some time before that happened. Love wasn't something I could turn on today and turn off tomorrow like it was a cell phone or something. Love . . . *my love* . . . for her was deeper than the mysteries of the universe itself; my whole being was submerged in it, and I thought hers was, too.

Yet another recording was being shown now. Helicopters had circled the towering infernos and transmitted live pictures. What I saw had taken place more than an hour earlier, but the tape was nonetheless unbelievable. I was shocked to see people still alive, hanging out of windows, no doubt screaming for help. But seeing the people on the roof had me shaking my head. There was no escape for them. A news anchor was saying that the people on the roof had probably been having breakfast at the restaurant on the top floor.

The people on the roof were on fire, burning alive. The fear and panic they must have been experiencing, knowing it was all over, had to be overwhelming. Smoke and flames were everywhere, with no place to go but down with no parachute. I turned away from the screen when I saw several of them jump to their deaths, burning as they plummeted story after story and then crashed into the unforgiving Manhattan asphalt.

Then, as if by implosion, one of the towers collapsed. As I watched the tower burn and cascade downward into a heap of rubble, I saw tremendous opportunity. People were losing their fortunes, stock prices were plummeting, and I somehow knew that even the solid companies' stock prices were going to drop to near rock bottom, too. In the midst of tragedy, a tremendous opportunity had just presented itself to the bold. I knew prices were going to keep falling because Americans were going to be afraid to fly for a long time.

I needed to speak with my banker. I wanted to see how much money I could invest while people were terrified of losing everything. Of course it was a huge gamble, but I had to play my hunch. I was going to mortgage everything; the business and our house that had been in the family for three generations. I was going to empty our bank accounts—even our retirement money. I knew I couldn't tell my dad what I was doing because he would think I was crazy, and I can't say he wouldn't be right. But chance, as they say, favors the bold. Right now, I was feeling like Mel Gibson in *Braveheart.* I picked up the phone to call my banker.

I heard someone open the door and walk in.

I looked up.

It was Parris.

She had my gun in her hand.

Chapter 10

The night before, I didn't care if I lived or died. Now, the sight of the woman I had threatened to kill with the gun she was holding scared the hell out of me. While I was still hurt by her wicked betrayal, I wasn't ready to die. Not now. Not after deciding I would risk it all to become the very thing she was looking for—a rich man. I looked at her more intensely and realized she wasn't there to kill me.

Parris was there for another reason. She was returning my Glock, but that wasn't her only reason for coming to my office. I'd known her for more than four years now, slept with her, ate with her, laughed with her, and spent long hours talking with her. So, I knew she was here to talk. For me, the time to talk was before she gave Shenandoah what I thought was mine exclusively. Talking after I saw her kissing him, after I saw her making love to him, after I heard her orgasm while he pumped her, was way too late.

I mean, what the hell do you say after that shit? I'm sorry? And what the hell would she be sorry about? I mean really. When did remorse rear its head? That's an easy one. Right after she saw me in the hallway. That's when she was sorry.

She was sorry she had been caught. If I hadn't walked in—
check that—if I hadn't broken in and cold busted her, I
guarantee she would not be sorry.

Parris handed me the Glock and said, "We need to talk."

I nearly doubled over with laughter behind that one.
What I found particularly funny was that she was serious,
which made the irony even more amusing.

"What the hell are you laughing about, Nelson?" she said
loudly and ferociously, yet not screaming. "I don't see anything funny about any of this."

I stopped laughing. "Look, ho." I was brave now that I had
the gun. "We don't have anything to discuss. The time for
talking was when you called me here in my office, yet you
held the phone and said virtually nothing when you had a
chance to tell me then that you had met someone else."

"You fucking hypocrite! Who the hell are you to judge
me? Especially since you're guilty of the same shit!"

I remembered I was still holding the phone when it gave
off a noise that sounded like an alert Klaxon, letting me
know I needed to return it to its cradle, which I did. Then I
sat down in the cushioned leather chair at my desk and
stared into her eyes.

"I have never messed around on you, Parris. Not one time,
okay? Never!"

She sat in one of the chairs in front of my desk. "So . . .
you're telling me you never messed around on any of your
women—none of them?"

"All I can say is that your conscience must be really fucking you over. You're the one sleeping with Shenandoah."

"At least I broke it off with you before I did it."

I stared into her eyes, raised an eyebrow, and said,
"Scruples? Imagine that."

"Are you saying you never slept with another man's
woman?"

That question could only have come from Mr. Armstrong,

I knew. My own sins were confronting me, but I had dealt with them the prevoius night when I let us all live to see the sun rise again. Looking at her now, listening to her try to justify her actions, made me want to heave. This was the woman I loved? It's blind, they say.

I looked into her eyes and offered, "Like a man said, I was blind, but now I see."

"You fucking bastard! Who are you to call me a whore when you used to fuck everything that moved?"

I kinda laughed at that one. This was so typical of her. In all the time I'd known her, she could never take full responsibility for anything she did. It was always somebody else's fault, or she had to somehow bring up someone else's sins to diminish her own. She was losing it, and I was amazingly cool all of a sudden. After all, I wasn't guilty of anything—check that—I was going to take my father's money without talking to him. Now I realized, though, I had better get his permission for his share.

"Yes, I did. I offer no excuses for it. None whatsoever. However, I put that life behind me a long time ago, before I even knew you were alive."

She ignored my confession and continued the foolish barrage. "So, you admit you had a relationship with Shenandoah's girlfriend in college?"

I laughed out loud. This was ridiculous. "Is this what you wanted to talk about, Parris? Who I fucked when I was the toast of the Bay City? That's what you wanted to talk about? You knew I was a star in those days, and you know what comes with that. So yeah, I fucked a lot of women. There . . . are you happy now?"

"So, you knew Anna Benton was Shenandoah's girlfriend and you still had sex with her?"

"Who?"

"Anna Benton! You don't even remember her, do you?"

"If it's any comfort to you, I don't remember any of them.

Make your point and then get the hell out of my office. I don't ever want to see you again as long as I live."

She had managed to put me on the defensive. Curious as to where this was going, I leaned back in my chair and swiveled from left to right, studying her.

"My point is that everybody makes mistakes . . . even you, Nelson. I'm sorry I hurt you and I—we, that is Shenandoah and I, want to make it up to you for sparing our lives last night."

Laughing, I said, "This oughta be good."

"I'm serious, Nelson. We want to make it up to you."

I nearly leaped out the chair after that one. "Make it up to me? You can't make it up to me, Parris! You dumb ho, don't you realize I will never forget what I saw? I could have a lobotomy, be a vegetable, and still have the visual running around in my head. Can you do anything about that? If you can somehow erase everything that happened so that I never know you or how you ripped my heart out, you can make it up to me. Now, can you do that?"

"You'd need H. G. Wells' Time Machine for that. What I'm offering is better, though. In time, what you're feeling will go away. Yes, you'll always have the memory, but the pain will disappear." She paused. "Do you have any money saved up?"

Incredulous, I frowned. "Why?"

"Software Unlimited is merging with Datatech Computers Corporation on June first of next year. It'll be a blockbuster deal. You'll be an instant millionaire."

Cha-ching! Now that definitely got my attention. I eased back in my chair and thought about the possibilities for a moment or two, then looked at her. She was dead serious. Was Shenandoah that grateful for his life? Or was this a setup of some kind? After all, this was insider trading, a federal offense.

Parris interrupted my thoughts. Having known each other for a long time, she knew exactly what I was thinking. "All you have to do is buy shares every month along with buying stock in other companies. The Securities and Exchange Commission won't suspect a thing."

I furrowed my brow. "Shenandoah has done this before?"

Without thinking, she answered, "Yes! And the SEC never even approached him."

That's when I realized God had done me a huge favor. I had planned on marrying this bitch! Damn! The night before, while tragic, was a blessing in disguise. I almost felt sorry for Shenandoah. He had stolen fruit that looked good, but was rotten to the core. They deserved each other. However, even knowing this now didn't alleviate what I was feeling inside. I still loved this woman, but in time, I believed, I would love another woman again.

"Money? Is that all that matters to you?"

"Yes or no, Nelson?"

"You wanna make it up to me? Tell me something. Since money is what drives you to do the things you do, why in the hell did you become a schoolteacher? You had to know the job didn't pay well enough for your expensive palate."

"Yes or no, Nelson?"

"Last night, you ripped me for not being financially well off, yet you haven't lifted a finger to get what you wanted. You looked to me to provide it for you and when it didn't happen fast enough, you went to Shenandoah."

"Yes or no, Nelson?

"You're going to get old one day, Parris. I hope you realize that. What are you going to do then?"

"For the last time, yes or no on the deal that I—we're throwing in your lap?"

"No! I'm not going to end up in Folsom over your greedy ass."

"Hmpf. Just as I figured. I told Shenandoah you wouldn't go for it. You're such a pussy, Nelson. You'll be broke from now on. Good luck!"

"So, this was his idea?" I said, ignoring the symbolic kick in the balls.

"After you left, we talked all night. We were both glad to be alive after what we had done to you—even though technically we were over."

"Technically my ass, bitch! The cheating began long before you fucked him. Fucking him was the culmination of the cheating you had been doing for a long time. Can you deny that you two have been having a relationship without sex before last night? Or did you hop in bed on a fuckin' whim?"

"He told me why he came after me and why he wanted to hurt you, but he had fallen in love with me," she said, ignoring my penetrating rant.

"So he loves you?"

"Yes."

"Do you love him?"

She diverted her eyes for the first time.

"Do you love him?"

She stood up and turned to leave. "We're driving to Vegas to get married. He's downstairs waiting for me."

Another dagger found its way into my fragile heart and twisted. While I didn't want her anymore, my love for her was still alive. I knew she still had feelings for me even though she had betrayed me—*technically*—and for some reason, it made me feel good. I don't know why, but it did. It was like a consolation prize.

She headed for the door.

I found myself looking hypnotically at her hind parts and shaking my head. The woman had a nice ass. A very nice ass.

She opened the door, but before leaving, turned around and said, "I still love you, Nelson. As hard as that is to believe, it's true. But I'm not about to let a little thing like love stand in the way of security and peace of mind. Shenandoah offers me all that and more. I'm quitting my job, Nelson. Shenandoah's going to take good care of me for the rest of my life. If you had your shit together, I would have stayed with you.

"When you turned down the tip, I knew you'd never be able to provide the things I need to feel secure. No wonder you fucked up your knee that day and kissed away millions. You were a fool then and you're a fool now. You have the nerve to call me a whore and to question why I became a schoolteacher. Well, you should learn a lesson from this schoolteacher slash whore. Winners win and losers make excuses. You're a good man, Nelson, but face it, you're also a loser."

Damn!

Talk about femme fatale!

Pow! Pow!

And with that, Parris walked out of my office and my life.

Chapter 11

When I was a first grader, we used to chant, "Sticks and stones may break my bones, but words will never hurt me!" Who thought of that lie? Words do hurt me. As a matter of fact, words devastate me! Words are capable of twisting the mind if one dwells on them long enough. I find it strange that I don't dwell nearly as long on positive, uplifting words; the kind of words that motivate and inspire; the kind of words that make us believe in ourselves and propel us into the stratosphere of possibilities, where thoughts, and dreams, and inspiration can and do become reality.

I kinda slumped into my chair after Parris' parting gifts blasted my pride and psyche all to hell. I began to consider what she'd said. I began to wonder was Parris right about me. Was I a loser? Should I have taken the offer to invest with Software Unlimited? I guess I still could. But was everything about money? Was everything about our innate desire to have more and more things? Was life about living lavishly, wearing sophisticated outfits, driving expensive automobiles, and blatant greed? Was greed the new god? Was greed the

American way? I didn't know, and didn't much care, but I was going for mine now, too.

I began to wonder if integrity, honesty, and truth were still virtues. I didn't know anymore. It appeared that cheating was the way to get ahead in America. The honest man seemed to get the shaft while the dishonest man got riches and the girl—*my girl*. If I had listened to my dad, if I had listened to the Philadelphia 76ers brass, I'd be on easy street, even with the injury.

I bet they can't even measure how stupid I was in those days. If they could, I'd be way below the moron and imbecile level I'm sure—a candidate for the infantry, where they put dumb people and call them heroes after they've been blown to smithereens, and then use them as poster boys to recruit more dummies to go to the front lines, where the worst kind of death is a virtual certainty. That's how I felt when Parris called me a loser.

Was I a loser? I remembered the many gung ho speeches my coaches gave after losing a basketball game. They would exhort us, quoting other great coaches, military commanders, and famous generals who had won great victories. Of all the locker room speeches I heard, only one sentence ever meant anything to me. Only one! If I'm not mistaken, I believe it was Vince Lombardi, Hall of Fame coach of the Green Bay Packers, who said, "Winning is a habit and so is losing."

Lots of people trivialize sports, but I learned plenty of lessons from them. For example, when we were losing and time was running out, if we wanted to win, we had to take some chances to steal the ball from the opposing team. That was the only way to win the game. Playing it safe was a sure-fire way to lose. Now it was time to apply that lesson to my life. I had a hunch, and now I was going to play it. I wasn't a loser. I was a winner, and a winner finds a way to win, no matter what the circumstances are. I was going to show Parris that she fucked up but good. And when she came crawling back to me, and she would, I'd take pleasure in seeing her on her knees, but I'd have no mercy.

I picked up the phone and called Grace Underwood, my banker, to set up a meeting with her for the loan. I told her how much I needed and what I planned to do with the money. She offered no resistance. I believed she'd do whatever she could to help me secure the loan and mortgage because she'd been hinting at dating for a while now, asking me to dinner or to a show at the Curran. I was always flattered by her compliments, and were it not for my commitment to Parris, I would have taken her up on the offers.

If Grace asked me out again today, I was going to say yes. I might even ask her out. That is, if she was still available. Lots of heterosexual women in San Francisco didn't have men due to the vast homosexual community that existed here, which had always been a good thing for heterosexual men.

Next, I called my dad at home. The line was ringing. I already knew his answer before I even asked the question, so I had to be savvy when I made the proposition.

"Hi, Dad," I said enthusiastically when he answered.

"Are you watching this crap on TV, son? We gotta respond to this immediately."

I thought, *Here we go.* He was about to go on a rant. My dad was in the Marines and had fought in the Korean War, special ops. He was still a crack shot, too.

"You know how this happened, don't you, son?"

I knew what he was going to say, but I played along. I was a good son. "How, Dad?"

"Vietnam!"

My dad blamed everything on how that war—check that—how that "conflict" turned out.

"When we pulled out without finishing," he continued,

"other punk nations wanted some. I told you when you was just a little biddy kid that we shouldn't have pulled out because our future was in danger. Remember, son?"

Hell naw, I didn't remember. I was sixteen or seventeen at the time. Who listened to their parents at that age? I just wanted the keys to the car. "Yeah, Dad, I remember." I thought it best to let him have his say, let him know how right he was, and then while he was feeling good, make my proposal.

"Why, it was just four years after Nixon pulled the rest of our boys out that that damn Ayatollah Khomeini and them damn terrorists took our people at the Embassy in Tehran, remember, son?"

"Yeah, Dad, of course I remember."

"And Jimmy Carter didn't do jack about it. Remember, son?"

I covered the phone and laughed silently. This was going to go on for a while. The same stuff he'd been saying for over three decades. "Yeah, Dad."

"You know what we shoulda done, son?"

"Yeah, Dad."

"What?"

I decided to speed this up. "We should have written the hostages off and went in there and killed everything that moved. Right, Dad? Everything that moved."

"Yeah, son. That sho' is right!"

"If we had, we wouldn't be in this mess now, would we?"

"We sure wouldn't."

"Oklahoma City and the first attack on the World Trade Center would never have happened because all the terrorists would know we don't play that. Right, Dad?"

"That's right!" he said, proud I had learned what he believed. "That's my boy!"

I tossed the ball back to him. My father was loquacious

and loved to pontificate about geo-political matters. "What do you think we oughta do about this latest incursion on American soil, Dad?"

"Son, I hate to say it, but we gotta go over there and make them folks behave. That means we gotta kill everything that moves."

"Everything that moves?"

"Yeah, son, everything that moves!"

We laughed uproariously.

"Now," my father began, still laughing, "what do you want? I know you called for a reason, right? What can I do for you?"

"Dad," I said, no longer laughing, "the terrorists have given us an opportunity to make some real money. It's a gamble, but I think it's one worth taking."

"What did you have in mind?"

"Uh, well, uh . . ."

"You don't sound too sure, son."

"Well, Dad, it's a gamble. As you know, with every gamble there's a certain amount of risk, okay?"

"How much money are we talking about?"

"Millions, Dad! But no guarantees."

"No, I mean how much do we have to come up with?"

"As much as we can. I'm thinking of mortgaging the house and the business and emptying our bank and retirement accounts."

My father sighed heavily into the phone. "Son, have you lost your mind? You want to mortgage everything? You want to put everything on the line and roll the dice?"

"If it doesn't pan out, we'll still have our business. We'll just be in debt. Right now, we're expanding all over California. Our dream has always been to take Kennard Janitorial Services all over the nation. I'm thinking . . . uh, well, I believe . . . I know we can accomplish this quicker by buying up as much stock as we can when the prices fall. And they're going to fall, Dad. It'll be a while before the value goes up, but it will go up sooner or later."

My father sighed softly. "Nelson . . . boy . . . son . . . how do you think your mother's going to feel knowing we've lost it all on a whim?"

"Dad, how much do you think we've lost today? People are losing fortunes because of the terrorists. Do you realize that? You're counting on money that may not be there anyway. It's going to take a while for the smoke to clear, but when it does, the whole country is going to feel like they were seriously screwed because of this. Chance favors the bold, Dad, and now is the time to take advantage of it. Think about it . . . if these investments pay off, in a few years, we'll be on easy street."

"You feel that strongly about it, son?"

"Yes, Dad."

"Since you took over the company, you've made a lot of good moves. I'm going to trust you, son. I'll meet you halfway, okay? Go ahead and mortgage everything except the house and half my share of the retirement fund. I won't risk your mother's money on this. If it falls through, she'll at least have a place to lay her head and some money in her purse. Whatever you do, don't mention a word of this to your mother. You got that?"

"Got it, Dad!"

I hung up the phone.

Wow! What a rush!

Chapter 12

My phone rang. I wouldn't admit it if asked, but I hoped it was Parris calling to tell me she'd made a foolish mistake. Call me crazy if you like, but that's how love is. Love should be classified as a sickness, a mental disorder that makes people first think crazy thoughts, and then carry them out. I really believe that. People justify all sorts of things in the name of love—even murder.

Why do people expect others to behave rationally when dealing with matters of the heart? I say this: show me a person who claims to be in love and acts rationally, and I'll show you a liar. When two people love each other and one wants to leave the other, especially if the woman is leaving the man well, you know what I almost did that night. I'll leave it at that.

I picked up the phone.

"Hello, Nelson. Grace Underwood. I'm wondering if we can have a working lunch at Pier 39. I have some errands in the area and thought we could discuss your plans then."

She didn't have any errands in the area, I didn't believe, but I didn't care. If she wanted to meet at a restaurant to discuss "business," that was fine with me. Besides, I was feeling quite vulnerable at the moment. I needed to feel wanted, and the tone of her sophisticated voice made me feel like a man again. Parris cut my balls off last night and then took the rest with her when she called me a loser. Grace's voice was like a medicated but sweet-smelling salve, taking the sting out of the castration I'd suffered.

"Sure, no problem. Let's see . . . Pier 39, huh? Do you like seafood?"

"Love it."

"How about Dante's?"

"Sounds wonderful."

I looked at my watch. "Noon okay with you?"

"Perfect."

"Great. I'll see you then."

Chapter 13

I had always found Grace attractive, but I didn't realize she was so tall, at least six feet, I'd say. Not that it would cause a problem if we decided to go out or whatever. She arrived on time, a minute or so after me. As she approached the table, she offered a friendly smile and slid into her seat across from me. Being as vulnerable as I was, I stared a bit and smiled back as I inhaled her perfume. I found myself being pulled in by the scent she emitted and her overall demeanor, which was polite and sociable.

"Been waiting long?" she asked.

"Actually, I just got here myself."

A waitress came over and placed menus on our table. "Can I get you anything to drink while you decide?"

We both asked for bottled water.

"Nelson, I insist on picking up the check, okay? It was my idea to turn this into a business lunch. Order anything you like."

"That's very generous of you. Thanks. I never turn down a free meal, especially from a beautiful woman."

Did I say that? The words came out all by themselves. Was it the perfume that swirled around me, forcing me to imbibe? Or was it the emasculation I was suffering from? Both, I think. I needed to feel strong again. I needed to feel the presence of my ego. I needed to feel my confidence course through my shaken mind again. I needed to know that even though I felt like a eunuch, I could get a woman again, particularly this woman sitting across the table from me. I needed to feel like a winner. Since I had lost a woman, I had to win another. Only a woman can make a man feel like a man, and only a woman can make a man feel less than.

Grace beamed. "Where did that come from, Nelson?"

The waitress brought us two bottles of Evian and two glasses with ice in them, setting them on the table and saving me from having to answer her question.

"Ready to order?" she asked.

I stared wantonly into Grace's brown eyes. "Are you ready?"

She stared back. The attraction was still there, I could tell. It made me feel good. I was wanted—desired, even.

Still staring at me, she said, "I'll have the Prawns Diablo, please."

"And you, sir?" The waitress cut into our transparent trance.

The first thing that came to mind was oysters. Thank God that didn't tumble out of my mouth. To be honest, I really wasn't hungry. Losing Parris had interrupted my appetite. I looked at the appetizers section of the menu. "Garlic bread and the New England clam chowder."

"Is that all, Nelson? Aren't you hungry? You can have anything you want. Really, it's no problem."

Not for food, I was thinking. *I'm hungry for attention, Grace. Can't you see the paralyzing anguish in my eyes? Aren't they supposed to be the windows to the soul? Look into my eyes. I'm a train wreck over here. I need to be loved. I need to be embraced and com-forted. Don't you realize that, Grace?*

Breaking our gaze, I looked at the waitress and said, "The bread and chowder is fine. Thanks."

I looked at Grace again, who was still staring at me.

"Well, Nelson?"

"Oh, okay. I'll get started. As I said on the phone, we want to take Kennard Janitorial Services to a whole new level. We've already branched out in Oakland, Sacramento, Monterey, and other places in the San Francisco area, but we want to move down to Los Angeles, San Diego, and the surrounding areas in the next two to three years. We're also looking at Las Vegas." When I said that, I was suddenly reminded that Parris and Shenandoah were on their way there to get hitched. I looked at my watch and tried to calculate how far away they were.

Love should be outlawed. It's too damn destructive, turning men's hearts into open graves and leaving only the shell in its wake. I looked at Grace again and continued my proposal. "From there, we want to move east, all the way to New York, Maine, Atlanta, and all parts of Florida. But that's in the grand scheme of things."

"Are you in a hurry, Nelson?"

"No, not at all. Why do you ask?"

"Well, you keep checking your watch. It makes a girl feel rushed, like you have something more important to do. Do you?"

"No, Grace. A friend of mine is getting married in Vegas. I just found out this morning. It was a whirlwind kinda thing."

"Oh, okay. A girl likes to have a man's full attention, or didn't you know that?"

"Of course," I said while pulling off my watch and shoving it into my pocket. I was doing it more for me than for her, though. I wasn't aware of how often I looked at it. The idea that every passing minute put the woman I loved closer to vowing to stay with a man she didn't love—forever for better or worse—bothered me, to say the least. Do vows mean anything anymore? Do people repeat those words only because it's an expected part of the wedding ceremony? Or do they have the mental disorder called being in love? And as such, do they believe what they're saying at the time? I wondered.

"I'm sorry for being distracted."

"Apology accepted. Now, as to your loan, I don't see a problem. You're a valued customer with excellent credit. Come in the office in the morning and fill out the papers. I'll push it through and have a check ready for you by the end of business."

"Great! Thanks."

The waitress placed our food on the table and disappeared.

"Nelson, listen. I need to be very honest and up front with you, okay? You had to know that I could have told you all of this over the phone this morning. Lunch wasn't necessary."

I offered a forgiving smile. "So, you didn't have any errands near here?"

"I did, but I only had them after you agreed to meet me, which brings me to what you said earlier about me being beautiful. You do remember saying that, don't you?"

"Of course."

"You've always been professional, even when I've hinted at going out with you. Yet today, not only did you accept my lunch invitation, but you paid me a very nice compliment, too. Were you flattering me to get the loan, or did you really mean it? And please be honest with me."

I looked into her eyes again. "The compliment was gen-

uine, just as your beauty is," I answered sincerely. I meant
every word, too.

Grace smiled again, no doubt feeling that after so many
hints, I had finally gotten the message.

"So, have you always felt like that, or did you finally notice
me because your friend is getting married?"

My eyelids lowered slowly and I ran my hand down my
face as I contemplated her penetrating question.

"It's okay, Nelson. We've all been there. I've been there too
many times to count, but I haven't given up on you men. So,
don't give up on us women, okay? There are so many good
ones out there . . . here . . . at this table . . . looking into your
eyes and finally seeing what's going on in your soul."

I lowered my head. Tears welled. "Excuse me," I said and
fast-walked to the men's room. I had to get away. I couldn't
break down like that in front of a woman. I couldn't. I had to
show some dignity, didn't I? I looked in the mirror and saw
more tears forming. I couldn't stop them from falling. I felt
so weak, so powerless. I must have been sick in the goddamn
head to even care for a woman who would do what Parris
did. Nevertheless, I did. God help me, I did.

I sniffed as my nose began to run, and it occurred to me
that this is why we men kill women. This is why we choose
anger over feeling weak. At least anger makes you feel powerful, vengeful, and destructive, almost like a warrior. But
this? Crying and shit? Fuck that! And fuck love! It ain't worth
it. Warriors don't cry; they kill. They kill everything that
moves. I thought of my father just then and laughed a little,
which alleviated the pain a bit.

I returned to the table and slid into my seat.

"You okay, Nelson?"

I forced a smile. "I'll be okay."

"I called the bank and let them know I was taking the rest
of the afternoon off. I told them I had a sick friend that
needed special care."

My smile returned on its own.

"Will you let me take care of you today, Nelson? Let me pamper you for a few days just until you feel better."

Turning her down never even crossed my mind. No way on earth was I going to turn down pampering from this woman. I'm hurt, yes, but I ain't crazy!

Chapter 14

Two hours later, we were at Grace's place watching movies from her incredible collection of films. She had everything from *Gone with the Wind* to *King Kong* (the original version) to *Imitation of Life* to *A Soldier's Story* to *Aliens* to *The French Lieutenant's Woman* to *Mommy Dearest* to *Crouching Tiger Hidden Dragon* to *A Preacher's Wife* (Denzel and Whitney) to *Scream* and everything in between.

We both loved Cary Grant pictures, and she had all of his movies, so we picked *North by Northwest*, which we had watched already. Now, we were sitting on her couch watching *Mr. Lucky* and eating buttered popcorn, with a quilt draped over us. We held hands and enjoyed the film. Not only did it feel good, it felt right, so I went with it. Not once did I look at my watch. I had escaped reality. Isn't that what films do for us? Don't they free us of our responsibilities for just a little while?

At some point, Grace gently wrapped her arm around me and pulled me close to her. I felt her body heat. Then she pulled my head to her shoulder as if to say, "Lean on me." Bill Withers' lyrics actually came to mind. Not long after that, I looked up at her, into her brown eyes, which were a clear invitation to something more, I thought. She stretched her long neck down to me and closed her eyes. We kissed. At first, it felt strange to have lips on mine that were not Parris'.

She pulled back a little and looked into my eyes. "It's okay, Nelson. I know what you're feeling."

Did she? Did she know what I was feeling? I wanted her to be Parris. Did she know that? If she did, was she telling me that was okay? How could it be? Parris was in Las Vegas having sex with her new husband. Even so, I felt like I was cheating on Parris with Grace. That wasn't right.

I opened my mouth to speak.

She placed her first and middle fingers on my lips.

Then she removed them and put her lips back on mine.

Sexual excitement surged through me as she laid me down, kissing me all the while. We gave into our desire for physical fulfillment and made love on the couch and then in her bed.

Chapter 15

The next morning, I awake to the smell of eggs and bacon. I opened my eyes. It wasn't a dream. I was still at Grace's place, still under a thick quilt in her comfortable bed, nude, but not ashamed. I thought about what had happened the last two days, but I didn't feel nearly as bad as I had. In fact, I felt pretty damn good. Grace had sweetly taken away my pain, and I was grateful.

I began to think about a relationship with her. She had said she was a good woman. Was she? So far, so good—and I do mean *good*—is all I could say at this point. But don't all relationships start off good? Is the sex, or at least the sexual attraction, the catalyst in the beginning? Sex is the easy part, isn't it? It's the relationship that gives everybody a goddamn headache! But when it's good between a man and a woman, it's really good, isn't it? And I don't mean the sex. I mean when a man and a woman click, when they're in sync. I wondered if I could be in sync with her.

Grace walked in and offered me a friendly smile. "Hey, Mister! How are you feeling this morning?" She sat beside me on the bed.

"I'm feeling so much better. Thank you for caring."

"No problem. Listen, I need you to sign your application." She handed it to me along with a pen. "I made you a big breakfast. I hope you're hungry today since you had me slaving over a hot stove."

"I am," I said and returned the signed application to her.

"I gotta go. Make yourself at home and come by the bank to pick up your check this afternoon, okay?"

"When would be a good time?"

"What about noon?"

I smiled. "That's how we ended up here, isn't it?"

"Nelson . . . hey . . . I gotta be honest with you, okay? I know the only reason you're here is because the woman you love left you for another man and married him. I have no illusions about that. I was glad to take care of you yesterday, but I won't be your rebound woman. I've been there, and I'm not going back. I want you, and I'll take you when you're ready. Some other woman can be your rebound. I understand how it goes. I'm willing to smother you with affection the rest of the week. I'll give you until Sunday to stay with me and make love with me, if you want, just like in *Pretty Woman*. After that, we have to separate."

"But I—"

"Hear me out, Nelson, please. You may not feel like it now, but you're still messed up inside about what happened the other night. I understand. Right now, after spending the day and the night with me, you feel like I'm what you need. But I'm a sedative disguised as the cure for what ails you. At some point, you'll realize that and move on, leaving me with all these incredible feelings for you. And I just can't go through that with another man. I just can't.

"So . . . I've decided to give you a glimpse of what I'm capable of giving you on a regular basis. Then, come Sunday, you have to go . . . go and do what you have to do with some other woman, or heal, or throw yourself into your work, or whatever you need to do to move on from Parris, okay?"

With sincere eyes, I asked, "Why do you care so much, Grace?"

"Because right now you need someone to help you start your new life . . . your new life without Parris. Everybody needs to start all over every now and then. We all make gigantic mistakes. By the time Sunday rolls around, believe me, the hurt you felt that first night will be long gone. You'll start to remember what a bitch she really is. The rejection you feel won't pull at your emotions like they were that night and even yesterday at Dante's, because all the things you overlooked, personality conflicts, flippant attitudes, and the fundamental disrespect she had for you will come back and replace how you think you feel about her.

"There's a problem, though. If we start something together, if we start a relationship now while you're vulnerable, you'll think you're in love with me, but you won't be. I want you to be totally free of her, and then maybe we can get together. But I won't wait around for you because you may never come back to me. I'll date other men from time to time, and if I find a man who can truly love me, I won't be available. I'm not saying this to put pressure on you; I'm just being honest. I deserve some happiness, too. Surely you can understand that, can't you?"

"Yes, I can," I responded.

"I've gotta run. While I'm gone, I'd like you to think about what I've said, okay?"

"Okay."

She kissed me gently on the forehead and then on the mouth. "There's bacon, eggs, pancakes, and fruit on the table. Since you kept me in here talking, you may have to microwave it."

"That's not a problem."

She walked toward the bedroom door then turned

around. "I put some fresh towels in the bathroom for you. Please clean out the tub after you've showered."

"I most certainly will."

"See ya at the bank in a few hours."

She blew me a kiss.

Chapter 16

I stayed in the bed for a little while, thinking about what Grace had said. I was definitely going to take her up on the offer of staying with her until Sunday. No doubt about that. I hadn't had it this good in a long time. Hell, I was due for a few days off. I had worked my tail off, expanding Kennard Janitorial Services. As a matter of fact, I was going to take her advice on seeking out other women. Anything to get Parris out of my system. Grace was right about Parris' shortcomings, too. They had already started to come to mind. I don't know why I even put up with her for as long as I did.

Her mood swings were legendary. Come to think of it, I never knew what kind of bag she was going to come out of on a daily basis. I should have confronted her on it long ago. No excuse for that. It wouldn't happen again. It was about me now. It was all about me. Parris said she was going for hers . . . I'm going for mine, too. She'd be sorry. I'd make sure of it.

I wondered if Grace Underwood was all she seemed to be. One never knows these days. What if she was for real,

though? What if she was just in the market for a good—
check that—a decent man who came home every night? I
would do that much, I knew. What man in his right mind
wouldn't want to come home to Grace? I should have
dumped Parris a long time ago and took Grace up on her offers six months before when I first met her at the bank. I en-
visioned having a nice comfortable life with her. It was
settled. In a few months, I was going to come back and win
Grace over. Hopefully, she'd still be available.

I went home and showered. It didn't make much sense to
me to shower at Grace's place and put the same clothes back
on. Besides, I wanted to pack a few things and take them
over to my new *friend's* house so that I would have my own
shampoo, toothbrush, shaving cream, cologne, condoms,
and whatnot. If I was going to spend the next three nights
with this giving woman, I was at least going to have clean un-
derwear to change into.

Later that morning, I asked my dad to meet me in the office. I'd said I had some things to discuss with him. By the
time I arrived, he was there, sitting on my couch, reading the
Chronicle. When I entered, he put the paper down and said,
"I told your mother about your plans to gamble a good portion of our assets on your hunch, son."

"What?" I shouted at him. "But you told me not to say anything to her. Then you go back and tell everything? I just got
the bank to loan us the money, Dad! How could you do that?
What am I supposed to do now? Tell them I changed my
mind? That I lied about why I needed the money? Dad, I was
counting on that money!"

My dad eased back on the couch, crossed his legs, and
coolly listened to me rant and rave like a maniac, knowing I
would tire out soon. Then he said, "Nelson, I know what I
told you, and I meant it at the time. But that's my wife of
forty-two years. A man and a woman get to know each other
real well after forty-two years."

Impatiently, I asked, "What happened, Dad?"

My father looked me in the eyes and sighed deeply, like I was getting on his nerves. I knew the look well. I'd seen that look for forty of the forty-two years he and my mother had been married, and I knew he was trying to keep from yelling at me.

He opened his mouth to speak. "Nelson, sit yo' ass down and listen for a second." His words were even and measured.

I did as I was told. Even though I was a grown man, he would always be my father. Unlike many of my contemporaries, I was taught to respect my parents from the time I was old enough to understand. I was given a set of rules by which to live in their house, and when I broke their rules, *both* of them beat my ass to show me they were together on the decision. In spite of what the talking heads of social science have to say on the subject of spanking, when the belt touched my hind parts forcefully, I learned to do what they said. So now, even at forty, I respected my mom and dad.

"Now, listen," my dad continued. "I didn't feel right not telling her what we were going to do. I called you last night to talk to you first, but you never answered the phone. I guess you stayed with Parris last night."

I cut in. "Me and Parris are through, Dad."

"What? When did this happen? I thought you two were getting married."

"I did too."

"Well, what happened, son?"

"I'll tell you about it when we get this money mess you've made settled."

My father sighed again. "Nelson, listen to me! Now look, your mother knew I was hiding something and wouldn't leave me alone until I told her. When you've been married as long as me, let's see how you deal with a relentless woman who won't let you sleep until she knows all your secrets. Come and talk to me then. Until then, shut the hell up!"

I laughed out loud.

"I swear it was Samson and Delilah all over again."

Still laughing, I said, "Well, at least Samson got laid for his trouble."

"You think I didn't, son? Oh my God! Your mother has always been good in bed—a real tiger."

"Dad, don't tell me that. I don't want to know, okay?"

"Okay, son."

"So, what's the bottom line?"

"Well, after Delilah got me to tell her the secret of my strength, she told me a few secrets too."

"Like what? And I don't want to hear anything sexual either!"

"Like she's been investing money for over twenty years. She feared one day I might do something stupid with the business and she might end up broke and on the streets, so she started studying the stock market and investing. Lately, she's been buying into a hot property called Software Unlimited. She thinks they are due for a big payoff because her broker and best friend, Claudia, told her that she heard Software Unlimited was about to get in bed with some company called Datatech Computers. Software Unlimited has a new operating system that will give Microsoft all they can handle."

My mouth fell open all by itself. So, two-timing Parris *was* trying to help me, huh? She was still a bitch, though. Should I tell my dad what I knew, or should I keep it to myself? Wasn't this insider trading? Couldn't we all go to jail for this? On the other hand, my mom was buying stock all along, wasn't she? Her broker told her. And that's what brokers are supposed to do, right? Tell their clients what investments to invest in, right?

I was going to invest in Software Unlimited for sure now, but I had to justify it in my mind to alleviate any resulting guilt. So that none of it came back on Kennard Janitorial, I would get my mom's broker to do the investing for me in my mom's name. Yes! That's what I'd do!

"Nelson," my father said, interrupting my thoughts, "did you hear me?"

I snapped back to reality. "Yes, Dad, I heard you."

"I thought you'd be happy about this."

"I am, Dad. Believe me, I truly am. You have no idea how happy I am right now."

"So, what happened between you and Parris?"

Chapter 17

At first, I thought about lying so he and my mom wouldn't think so terribly about her, but since he told me the truth, and I pretty much hated Parris' guts, I didn't give it a second thought. "I caught her in bed with Shenandoah Armstrong."

"Shenandoah Armstrong? How do I know that name?"

"He used to play for Stanford back in the day. I used to wear him out on the court, and I took one of his girlfriends, supposedly. Some chick I can't even remember. I can't even remember her name or what she looks like. Evidently, he never forgot about it. He and Parris got married in Las Vegas last night."

"Married? You're better off, Nelson. For her to up and marry the guy, it musta been going on for a long time."

"Maybe. But it's about the money, Dad. That's all it's about. Shenandoah is loaded, and we're still putting everything we make, most of it anyway, back into our business. That's how I see it."

"Wait a minute! It just hit me. You said you walked in on them? At your place or hers?"

"Hers."

"Damn! If that was your mother and some man in my bed, I hate to say it, but I would have killed them both right on the spot. I may have even killed myself. I can't imagine what you've been going through. When did this happen?"

"Monday night."

My father stood, paced the floor, and shook his head. "So, you actually walked in on it? Damn!" He stopped pacing and looked at me. "Wait a minute. If you weren't with Parris last night, where were you?"

"With Grace Underwood."

"Our banker?"

I nodded.

"All night?"

I nodded.

"You're not serious about this woman, I know, right? Or were you seeing her all along?"

"Like I got time for two women, Dad! I didn't have time for Parris and look what happened. How am I going to handle two women?"

He looked at me skeptically. "Are you sure you weren't seeing the banker? Don't lie to me. No need. I'm not going to judge you. Just tell me the truth."

"I am telling you the truth."

"The whole truth and nothing but the truth, so help you God?"

"Well . . ."

"I knew you had to be doing something, son. Women don't just lay up with men."

I looked at him and rolled my eyes. "What I was going to say is, Grace had flirted with me lots of times, but I never responded to her advances until yesterday. She told me she wanted to have a business lunch, which I knew was about her attraction to me, but since Parris did what she did, I agreed to lunch with her. I was free to have lunch with any woman I chose at that point.

"But as far as women not laying up with men . . . that may have been true in your era, but in the turn of the century—in the nineties, for that matter—women are doing the same things men have done and are continuing to do. The situation's critical, Dad. Gone are the days when you didn't have to worry about your woman or your wife. It's crazy out there. Crazy as hell!"

"You need to get a Christian woman, son. That's what you need."

I laughed at that one. "Christian women are pulling down their panties, too, Dad. Don't you know that? The whole thing is outta control."

"Not *that* kind of Christian woman. You need one that's devoted to God, son, like your mother. I don't even wonder about your mother, Nelson. Why? Because I know she's devoted to doing God's will. Find a woman like that and you'll be fine. If not, find one of those cute Muslim women that's devoted to her God. That's the only way a man's ever going to have peace of mind about his woman in times like these, especially in San Francisco, where there's not even 'he-men' in the city."

I looked at my watch. "I gotta run, Dad. I'm meeting Grace at the bank. She's supposed to have the money by now. Plus, she may want to get a bite to eat or something."

"Okay, son. If you need to talk about this, you know where to find me."

"Can you take over the paperwork and stuff until Monday? I need to get away from it all for a while."

"Sure, son. Take your time. I understand."

Chapter 18

Saturday snuck up on us more quickly than we thought it would. I was not looking forward to going back to my place, which was nice, but barren. I liked having Grace to go "home" to every night. I enjoyed having a "normal" life, a home cooked meal, watching films every night, playing board games, and talking to her. By the end of the second day, I knew I could fall in love with her. She was so right about that, which is why I knew she was also right about us parting ways for a while until I was completely over Parris—the whore.

We decided to go to the United Artists Metro Theater over on Union Street and get some pizza and pie at Amici's before returning to Grace's place. We had narrowed our movie choices to *Rush Hour 2, The Others,* and *The Musketeer.* Grace was a huge Nicole Kidman fan and wanted to see *The Others.* I opted for Chris Tucker, Jackie Chan, and Ziyi Zhang. Grace was wonderfully accommodating, much like she'd been the entire time we were together. I was at a loss for why this woman didn't have a steady man in her life.

Were her choices that slim? Whatever her reasons for being alone, I was damned grateful for her generous hospitality.

We bought our tickets for *Rush Hour 2* and were standing in the concession line when I thought I saw Parris on the other side of the lobby, standing in another line. Without thinking, I did a double take. That's when I saw Shenandoah Armstrong, too. The newlyweds kissed sweetly like they were madly in love, like they were the only two people in the theater, like this was their time and no one else's. Even though I had been happy with Grace, even though I was progressively getting over her, part of me, a very big part of me, still belonged to Parris.

I still loved her deeply. It had only been a few days and now, seeing them again—together, there in the lobby of the theater, looking like they didn't have a care in the world— my cool went from chilly to Death Valley hot in microseconds. Again, without thinking, I left Grace standing there, probably watching me, wondering where I was going, wondering what I was doing or why I didn't tell her if I was going to the restroom. Courtesy. But Grace wasn't even in my sphere of existence, wasn't even on my radar, wasn't even in my periphery of sight.

Tunnel vision. In a lobby full of people, only three people existed: Parris, Shenandoah, and me. The rest of the people were puppets on a string, mannequins, papier-mâché cutout people; stiff, lifeless, distant, and virtually invisible. In slow motion, it seemed, I moved toward them with the intent to do irreparable bodily harm. It was like an out-of-body experience, like I was watching myself move in their direction, weakened by the insanity of love, bent on destruction, powerless to stop myself, powerless to control the impulse to kill the newlyweds and put an end to their marital bliss. I was only a few feet from them now. Something was missing, but I was too blinded by passion to recognize what it was.

I guess Shenandoah could feel someone staring at him and looked my way. Suddenly, Grace's voice cut through the thick cloud of fury that saturated my evil mind. "Nelson!" I heard her scream. My senses returned to me and I looked in her direction. Grace had been watching it all and knew what I was about to do. The fact that she was still in the theater when most women would have left me there to make a fool out of myself says much about her. She stayed and tried to prevent the inevitable. Nevertheless, the inevitable would not be denied, and an all-out brawl ensued.

Chapter 19

Apparently, I had taken a fierce ass whipping. All I remember is looking at Grace when she screamed my name. When I turned back to Parris and Shenandoah, I saw his fist coming right for my eye. *Bing!* I was dazed and off balance. *Bing!* He hit me again and I fell backward. *Bing!* I went right through the glass candy case.

I woke up a few hours later in a hospital bed, my eyes swollen, my nose full of bloody cotton, and my overall pride ground to dust. But my mind kept trying to remember what was missing at the theater. I was missing something. What was it? I forced myself to think about something else. After the beating I took, I knew I had to leave Parris alone, or get some "real" help to get over her.

Fully conscious now, I could feel eyes—nagging eyes, prying eyes—staring at me. Someone was in my hospital room. I turned my head to the left. My lids went up like window shades. I saw her—Grace Underwood.

Hurt, embarrassment, and disappointment all registered when I looked into the windows of her soul. My shades closed for a second as what I had done to this wonderful woman flooded my mind. After what I had done, after how I had totally disrespected her and all she had done for me in my time of need, I wouldn't blame her if she never spoke to me again. Why should she?

Yet, here she was like the Rock of Gibraltar, strong and immutable. For those very same reasons, I knew I had to leave her alone and let her find a man worthy of her sacrificial spirit. What could I say to the woman who was there for me when I was at my lowest? I'm sorry? Was I sorry for what I had done? Of course, I was. Again, how come we're always sorry after we fuck over somebody? How come we don't think about that shit before we take them and their gifts of kindness for granted?

She opened her mouth to speak to me, the classical fool who not only ruined her evening, but quite possibly added to her laundry list of reasons why she didn't have a steady man in her life. During the seconds that passed from the time she opened her mouth to the time I heard her voice, I wondered how many men had disappointed her before me. How many men had she given her best to, only to have her best go unnoticed, unappreciated, and discarded like refuse? Parris had ripped my heart out the Monday before September 11. A few days later, I had done the same thing to Grace.

"Nelson," she said softly, "do you understand now?"

Of course, I understood. How could I not? I exhaled hard and nodded.

"Give yourself six months . . . a year, maybe. Then let a woman in, okay? Promise me you'll do that."

I looked at her, stunned by her kindness. "Why do you even care?"

"Perhaps someday I'll tell you. In the meantime, I packed your things and brought them to you. I wanted to stay to make sure you were okay before I left. Is there anything I can get you before I go?"

I shook my head.

"Well, I should go."

She stood and walked toward the door.

"Grace," I called to her as guilt overwhelmed me. She stopped and turned around. "I'm sorry. I'm truly, truly sorry."

"I know," she said then left me alone with my thoughts.

Chapter 20

"How are you feeling?"

I opened my eyes and saw a priest standing in the doorway. While I couldn't remember his name, I recognized him immediately because he was the same priest who visited me in this very hospital so many years ago when I blew out my knee.

"I came up the moment they told me you were here, Nelson."

It suddenly occurred to me that this could be all over the news because of my former status as a superstar collegiate athlete and former number one draft choice of the Philadelphia 76ers. The media loves to show how far the mighty have fallen. The thing that bothered me the most, though, was how my parents were going to feel about my latest faux pas. People always blame the parents. If I'm honest, I'd have to say I do, too, when it's someone else's kid. But this was all on me.

"Nelson," the priest called to me again.

"Sure, man. Come on in."

"Father Malloy," he said and offered his hand. "You remember me, son?"

"Yeah, man. I remember you."

"They told me you were unconscious. Therefore, I took the liberty of calling your dad. I hope that's okay."

I exhaled. "What's done is done."

I guess he was trying to bring a bit of levity when he said, "How does the other guy look?"

He probably thought that shit was funny, but it wasn't. I just looked at him and didn't bother responding.

"How do you think all this happened, son?"

"Look, man, I'm not trying to hear all that, okay?"

"Hear all what, Nelson?"

I exhaled hard and loud. "Look, man, I've had a fucked up week, okay? My woman left me and called me a loser. But what would you know about that? You're a priest. No women. You don't know what it feels like to give your heart to a woman and have her trample it under her unwashed feet, do you? All you know about is listening to people tell their dirt. That's all you know is somebody else's dirt. I'll tell you what, Father Malloy. Clean up your own house and then come see me. Try that."

"The root of bitterness leads to destruction, my son."

"Oh really, father? Then it sounds like bitterness is exactly what you need."

Father Malloy frowned. "I don't follow you."

"Maybe you priests need to get bitter so you can stop your brethren from fucking little boys in the ass. If bitterness leads to destruction, surely it can make you mad enough to stop all the bullshit in your brotherhood. As I said, after you take care of that, then come and see me about my bitterness."

"Nelson Dubois Kennard!" my mother shouted when she

walked into the room. "Don't you ever in your life let me hear you speak that way to a man of God! Now apologize!"

"I meant every damn word. Take your ass to Rome, talk to the Pope, go on television, do whatever the fuck you have to do, but clean up your own house. Then come talk to me. In the meantime, please leave."

Father Malloy looked at me for a moment before speaking. "I'm not your enemy, Nelson. Bitterness is. I'll keep you in my prayers."

And with that, he left.

"You ought to be ashamed of yourself, Nelson," my mother huffed.

"Well, I'm not. If he's a good priest, he and others like him should be ashamed for letting it go on and covering it up. Blame him. Don't blame me."

"All of this over sorry-ass Parris?" my mother said incredulously. "What's so special about her, Nelson? What? She's nothing! A nobody! Which makes you a damn fool. You let a whore twist you all up into a pretzel. A whore, Nelson! Think about that for a second."

"What's going on in here?" my father said as he entered, closing the door behind him. "I can hear both of you all the way down the hall."

"You need to get your wife in line, man . . ." I responded indignantly.

Before I could finish my sentence, my mother slapped me across the face. It stung and got my attention.

My father fast-walked over to my bed, grabbed my hospital gown, and pulled me close to his face. I saw the fury in his eyes, and while I was stronger than him, I knew that if I continued to disrespect his wife, my mother, the woman who carried me for nine months and experienced excruciating pain, he would eventually have to kill me. He was too old to whip me in a fistfight.

"Boy, don't you know that I will kill you?"

He meant that, too.

"Answer me!" he demanded.

"Yes, sir."

"Now, you get your shit together, and I mean pretty damn quick, too. All this bullshit over Parris is for the fuckin' birds. We told you she was no good, but you just had to have her. That was your decision, and you made it. Don't take that shit out on us or any fuckin' body else. You didn't listen when your mother told you this would happen. Your mother saw right through her from day one and told your dumb ass." He paused. "Now, apologize to your mother."

"I'm sorry, Mom."

After I extended my apology, he threw me back onto the bed. "Put your clothes on and we'll take you home."

"I haven't seen the doctor yet," I said.

"I just spoke to him," my father continued. "He said you'll be fine. You don't have a concussion or anything. Said he'd look in on you after you get dressed."

I went into the bathroom to put on my clothes. The white turtleneck I had worn was now stained with my blood.

Father Malloy had told me the same things years ago about bitterness and how destructive it was. I didn't listen then either. I had just pissed away millions, and no amount of counsel would console me. As a matter of fact, I was still bitter about that, too. I still hadn't forgiven myself for blowing all that money. Perhaps bitterness was why I'd blown two marriages, too. I don't know.

After putting on my clothes, I walked back into my room. "Dad, I need to take some serious time off. Can you run things while I go somewhere and clear my head?"

My father hugged me and kissed my swollen cheek. "Sure, son. Take as much time as you need."

Chapter 21

By Monday, the swelling around my eyes had gone down. My nose no longer bled, and the puffiness was no longer visible. Looking at myself in the mirror, if I didn't know I had gotten my ass whipped two nights ago, I could deny it and my face would back me up. I felt comfortable leaving the house, since only my pride was still bruised.

I needed to cash the check I'd received from Grace, who I hadn't seen or heard from since she left my hospital room, and deposit it in our business account. After that, I planned to visit my mother's stockbroker and buy as much stock as I felt comfortable buying in Software Unlimited. I was going to buy it in my mom's name as planned since she was already buying that stock. I wanted to be careful not to attract the attention of the Securities and Exchange Commission. Call me paranoid, but I wasn't going to jail for insider trading. I also opened an account for Kennard Janitorial and bought several other stocks I'd been interested in prior to the September 11 attacks. Stock prices had plummeted since that infamous day, but I believed they would rise again. In the meantime, I was overdue for a vacation, and was going to take one a long way from San Francisco.

I walked into the living room, and just as I picked up my keys, which were right next to my answering machine, I noticed I had several messages. When I got home Saturday night, I was still angry and hurt and I didn't want to speak to anybody, so I turned off the ringers on all my phones. I hit the play button and cringed when I heard Parris' voice.

You black bastard! Didn't I tell you you were a fuckin' loser? Now you know it, too, don't you? Shenandoah beat the shit outta you, didn't he? I was so turned on by the way he knocked you down and punched you in the face that I literally came right then and there. And then we hurried back to my place and we fucked, Nelson! We fucked all night long! I came so hard! Then I sucked his dick and everything! That's how turned on I was! You never turned me on like that!

Tomorrow, we're going to the police and tell them everything you did the other night, you fuckin' stalker! We're putting a restraining order out on you and you better not come anywhere near me or they'll put your ass in prison so you can get your ass kicked again. And, Nelson, you know what they do to pretty boys like you, don't you? From the way Shenandoah kicked your ass, all quick and shit, not letting you get a punch in, you don't stand a chance in Folsom.

She was laughing now.

You know what, Nelson? I hope you do bother us again so those hardened criminals can fuck you in your ass.

She slammed the phone into its cradle.

And I was going to marry her? *Her?* I was going to marry a woman that would leave a message like that on my answering machine? *Damn!* It was like she wanted to systematically dismantle what little pride I had left.

The next call came from my mother, who was just checking to make sure I was all right and if I needed anything.

That call was definitely a welcomed one after Parris' short but devastating diatribe.

From her slurred speech, I could tell Parris had been drinking a bit, but that didn't excuse any of it. Isn't it strange what former lovers can actually say to the people they were sexually intimate with? The same person who whispered sweet, honey-drenched words in my ear while I was pumping her was now tearing me apart with spiteful glee. This was totally unwarranted, especially after I let those two bitches live the other night. I was no angel and I'd used some women in my life, but nothing like this. When I was a superstar and women were all over me, we both knew it was sex and that was it. The women never wanted it to be over, even though they knew it would be. But I never pretended to be something I wasn't. They were the ones pretending because when I was on top, they all wanted to marry me, but when I blew out my knee, not one of them called to see how I was doing.

The next call came from my best friend and attorney, Sterling Wise.

"Nelson, Sterling." His voice sounded strange. "I need you to come down to my office first thing Monday morning. I saw the news the other night about the brawl at the Metro. Are you all right? Your girlfriend—"I heard papers ruffling—"Parris Stalls, has gotten a judge I know to sign a restraining order against you. The judge remembered us playing ball together and gave me a heads up. What the hell is going on, man? Call me as soon as you get this message."

Chapter 22

I hadn't seen Sterling Wise in a long time. He was in great demand after he won a nationally televised trial back in '97. As a result, our relationship drifted a bit, and it seemed like we only dealt with each other for my business contracts, which he no longer charged for, but did as a favor. Before hearing his message, I had thought of calling him, believing that if anyone could pick up my spirits, he could.

I had known him since we were kids. As Sterling mentioned in his voicemail message, we had played ball together in high school. Sterling and his brothers were all athletic, but he and William were also scholastic achievers. As a result, both received free rides to prestigious schools. Sterling went to the Air Force Academy in Colorado Springs. From there, he went on to law school at Georgetown. William got his Ph.D. in psychology from Harvard. These guys were destined to succeed. Even Jericho, the oldest brother, who turned out to be a drug dealer and gunrunner, lived like a self-made, self-crowned prince in a Cayman Islands hotel/casino he owned.

I think the last time I saw all three brothers together was at

William's wedding back in August 1999. *Has it really been that long? Have two years really passed? It seems like yesterday. I really need to get out more. And as of today, I will.*

Sterling had been a district attorney prior to going over to Daniels, Burgess, and Franklin law firm. Now, in addition to being a defense attorney, he was a high-powered sports agent, too.

I walked through the outer doors of the Wise Choice Sports Office, and then up to the receptionist's desk.

"Hi, I'm Nelson Kennard. I'm here to see Sterling," I said, smiling pleasantly.

"I know who you are, Mr. Kennard. Sterling talks about you all the time when our NBA clients are here."

"Really?"

"Really."

I smiled. It was nice to be still talked about. I was a good ballplayer in those days, but I was also arrogant, which is why I thought nothing could ever hurt me. I was Nelson "Skywalker" Kennard.

The young lady spoke again and interrupted my reminiscent moment of would-be NBA glory. "They've been expecting you. They'll be with you in a minute or two."

"They?" I purposely let my response hang in the air, hoping for clarification.

"Yes. Le'sett Santiago will be handling your case."

I'd never met Ms. Santiago, but I knew of her. Sterling had mentioned her in passing a few times, I think. Le'sett was the assistant district attorney on the aforementioned nationally televised case prior to becoming Sterling's partner. She and Sterling had a brief sexual relationship back in '97 after he got his client acquitted.

"Why is Ms. Santiago handling the case?"

"Well, Nelson, it's kinda like a doctor operating on his son or daughter. He's too close to the situation, so he gets someone he trusts to do it for him. Understand?"

I nodded.

"Now, can I get you something to drink? Coffee, tea, or Evian?"

"Evian," I answered.

"Please have a seat, Mr. Kennard. I'll get it for you."

I took a seat on the comfortable sofa a few feet from the receptionist's desk. It wasn't long before she brought me a cold twenty-ounce bottle of Evian. I cracked open the bottle and turned it up. When my head tilted, I noticed auto-graphed pictures of NFL greats, Jim Brown, Walter Payton, Gale Sayers, and OJ Simpson, all Hall of Famers, all wearing their respective team jerseys and shoulder pads. I stood and walked around the office, looking at NBA greats, Connie Hawkins, Kareem, Magic Johnson, Dr. J., Michael Jordan, Bernard King, Elgin Baylor, Isaiah Thomas and so many oth-ers. I couldn't help wondering if I would have made it to Springfield, Massachusetts, home of the NBA Hall of Fame.

"You should be up there, too, Nelson," Sterling said.

I turned around, looked at the impeccably dressed former point guard, and smiled. "You really think I could've made it, man?"

"No doubt. Not even a debate, my friend."

There were two things I really liked about Sterling. He al-ways seemed to be in a good mood, and he never let any-thing or anyone keep him from getting what he wanted—an unbeatable combination.

We embraced each other warmly, and I could feel his love for me.

"Come on into the office. Le'sett is waiting for us."

I turned the Evian bottle up again, chugged, and followed Sterling into the office. When I saw Le'sett in her plum-col-ored Versace blazer and black skirt, I wondered what was going through Sterling's mind when he let that get away. Superficial of me, I know, but this was one fine-looking Latina. From what little of it I could see, she had a nice figure, too. My eyes ran down her legs, taking in the sheer black pantyhose that covered them. Not to mention, those black-and-plum pumps were doing something to the flesh below my waist.

As we approached her, my eyes finally found their way up to her face, which was strikingly pretty. Her painted red lips were full and divinely luscious. Her brown eyes looked into mine, studying me. Did she know what I was thinking? Of course she did! All women know when a man wants to rip her clothes off and have his way with her. I could tell she was used to the kind of attention I was paying her. I suppose most beautiful women are.

She extended her hand to me and said, "Mr. Kennard, Ms. Santiago."

Ms. Santiago? What, no first name? I knew then that she was letting me know she'd seen what was in my eyes, and she was all business. Nevertheless, I looked at her left hand. I saw no ring, and regardless of the business-like introduction, she was on the market.

Le'sett spoke again. "Let's get down to business, shall we, Mr. Kennard?"

"Nelson," I offered warmly with invisible strings, hoping to move into her inner circle and become more than a client, more than an acquaintance.

Le'sett exhaled and looked at Sterling briefly, then shot an agitated stare my way. "Mr. Kennard, I'm very busy. I only agreed to listen to your side of this mess you've made as a favor to Sterling."

Hmmm, she called him by his first name. Does that mean they're still seeing each other?

"Now," Le'sett continued, "I need to ask you a few questions. Before you answer them, understand that I cannot suborn perjury."

Confused, I looked at Sterling for an explanation of what

she'd said. "That means that whatever you tell her, she has to go with that. For clarification sake, let me give you a hypothetical. Let's say some guy catches his fiancée in bed with another man." He paused and furrowed his brow. "This same guy has a gun in his possession with the intent to first kill the woman and the man, and then put the gun to his own head. If this guy tells his," he looked at Le'sett briefly and then back at me, "attorney he actually did something like that, his attorney would have her hands tied. You follow me?"

My shoulders slumped. My head tilted forward as the air in my balloon slowly deflated.

Sterling continued the hypothetical. "Now, if this same guy saw the two lovers at a theater on, let's say, Union Street, and started a brawl . . . the attorney's hands would be further tied." He paused strategically for more emphasis. "Here's the caveat for the poor bastard: If a woman was messing around on her fiancé, if she would do something that low down, then she would probably lie on the fiancé, too. And at that point, it would be her word against his. I mean, hypothetically speaking, of course."

I opened my mouth to speak.

"Mr. Kennard," Le'sett looked frustrated when she asphyxiated my words before they touched the air, "I haven't asked you one question yet."

She looked at Sterling again and rolled her eyes, like he had blackmailed her into representing me. That's when I knew she thought I was the kind of guy who probably rode to school on the small yellow bus, the one for "special" kids. And women in Le'sett Santiago's position, women who were well educated, accomplished, and fine as hell, didn't date guys who rode that bus—ever.

Le'sett began again. "On Monday night, September 10, 2001, did you use your key and enter the premises of Ms. Parris Stalls?"

I bowed my head in shame and lied my ass off. "No, Ms. Santiago, I did not."

"You didn't know Ms. Stalls was sleeping with Mr. Shenandoah Armstrong?"

Again, I lied.

"You didn't point a Glock in her face when Ms. Stalls came out of her bathroom?"

Another lie.

"And you didn't put the gun to your own head, threatening to take your own life?"

I exhaled hard after that one. Reliving this shit in the presence of my long-time friend and this beautiful and obviously intelligent woman was surreal. I couldn't believe I was going to blow my own brains out over some sorry whore.

"No," I said forcefully.

"So, the night you saw Ms. Stalls at the theater, that was your first and only suspicion that she was having an affair?"

"Yes."

"Were you going to the bathroom when Mr. Armstrong punched you in the face?"

"Yes, I was."

"And you never hit Mr. Armstrong?"

"I never did."

"Are you saying that it was Mr. Armstrong who started it all by assaulting you?"

I smiled for the first time. This thing was starting to turn against my accuser. "That's what I'm saying. I was just—"

Sterling cut in, using my former basketball sobriquet. "Sky, don't get creative, okay, man? Just answer her questions."

I looked at Le'sett, who was shaking her head slowly like I was the dumbest client she'd ever had. "Just a few more questions, Mr. Kennard. Please listen to them carefully, okay?"

I nodded.

"Even after all that Mr. Armstrong did to you, having sex with your fiancée, assaulting you publicly, you don't want to file assault charges against him, do you? You want the whole thing to go away, right? You never plan to go anywhere near Ms. Stalls after what she did to you, right?"

"Right."

"Okay. Do you swear that the statements you've given me are true?"

"Yes."

"I'll have it typed up. You'll sign it, and the whole thing goes away. No record of it will be filed against you."

Grateful, I said, "Thank you."

"Can I give you a piece of advice, Mr. Kennard?" she asked, looking directly into my eyes.

I cringed after hearing that and seeing the look on her face. I paused for a few long seconds, trying to decide if I wanted to hear what she had to say. The truth is, I didn't. I didn't want to hear it, so why did I say, "Sure"?

"If I were you, from this point forward, I would seriously consider only dating women with something more on the ball. Parris Stalls is the worst kind of hemlock. Learn something from your friend Sterling here."

Le'sett stared into my eyes for a moment—I guess she wanted me to get the message she was sending—and then she left the room. I craned my neck to watch her leave, looking at her curvaceous derriere, inwardly saying, "*I sure would like to get a hold of that.*

That's the thing about the male psyche. I was still hurt over Parris' betrayal, yet, my loins didn't know my mind had been twisted into some serious knots over her. My loins serve but one purpose, and that is to enter a beautiful woman and ejaculate. That is it. That is all. My loins pay no attention to, and are not governed by emotion. They are only driven by my deep and abiding lust. And this was why, even though I was devastated, I could not only sleep with Grace Underwood, but wanted to bed Le'sett Santiago, too. All of this just seven days after discovering that the love of my life was allowing another man to do the very thing I'd love to do to Ms. Santiago.

Sterling cut into my wicked thoughts. "Sky, I know you're hurt by all of this madness, but I've got a senior shooting guard at the University of Las Vegas that I gotta take a look at. I want you to come with me, and we're going to party in Sin City! You game?"

I heard the question, but strange as it may seem, something about Parris and Shenandoah was bothering me and it wasn't the wild sex they were having. It was the same thing I couldn't put my finger on before. What was it? I was sure I wanted to party, but I wasn't sure I wanted it to be in Las Vegas. After all, that's where the lovebirds had gotten married.

What the heck, I thought. *Why not?*

I forced Parris and Shenandoah's amour out of my mind and said, "Yeah, man. I'm game. When do we leave?"

"Tonight!"

Chapter 23

Our plane landed at McCarran International Airport at 10:05 that same night. Throughout the flight, I thought about the restraining order I'd read. It didn't mention anything about Parris coming to my office on September 11 and giving me back the Glock I had poetically placed in her hands as if it were my broken heart. Another conspicuously missing item I noticed was that she never mentioned anything about the insider trading information she gave me.

Parris was a two-timing bitch, but she wasn't stupid. She knew that if she told the police about returning the Glock, it might trigger my memory on the Software Unlimited/Datatech Computers merger. If I made it known to the proper authorities, that vital information would bring heat from the Securities and Exchange Commission. I began to wonder if she'd purchased stock. Perhaps she was thinking of keeping herself out of the correctional system. Or maybe she was concerned about her husband spending time in the very prison she hoped I'd end up in. That's probably why

Shenandoah didn't file for a restraining order and Parris did.

As we made our way to the baggage claim area, I remembered the advice Ms. Santiago had given me. I thought the advice was wise, and I appreciated her for offering it. While I would have liked to see if Le'sett was a better breed of woman, I knew I had virtually no chance with her. But still, I knew she would be in my thoughts for some time to come. When I was ready, I'd see if Grace was still interested. I hoped I hadn't blown that sweet deal. I hoped she understood that only a few days had passed since my break-up with Parris and that my behavior in the theater could be excused for that reason alone. Maybe not.

We rented an SUV, and Sterling drove us over to the Mandalay Bay Hotel and Casino. He told me Jericho, his older brother, knew the guy who owned the place, and got us the presidential suite for a few days of unrestrained debauchery.

Just before we exited the mammoth vehicle, Sterling looked at me, shook his head a little, and said, "Sky, my man, listen. There's only one cure for what happened to you."

"Oh, really," I said. "What's the cure?"

"New pussy."

I laughed uproariously and said, "You would know, I guess."

"I do," he continued, "and where we're going, there will be more than you can handle. By the time we leave, I guarantee you'll feel a whole lot better. You'll be weak in the knees, but you'll forget all about Parris Stalls. I suggest you get as much pussy as you can get. Chris Rock said it clears the mind. I agree with him."

I was laughing still, but Sterling was dead serious. I don't think he ever got over the love of his life, a woman named Vanessa Wright. In my view, the break-up was why he never married. Vanessa was his live-in lover, and had cold busted him in the act a few years ago. I didn't care what he said; he still loved that woman. Having said that, I was no fool. I planned to take his advice on this trip to Gomorrah.

"What did Ms. Santiago say about me when I left your office?"

"She thinks you're cute, but you're the typical male. You might've had a chance if you hadn't undressed her with your eyes."

"Really?"

"Hell yeah, man. You might want to give it a try when you get past your thing with Parris."

We entered the lobby, still talking, and made our way over to the private elevator and entered when the doors opened. Sterling already had the key card for the elevator and the suite.

"Are you serious?" I asked.

"As a heart attack. But give it some time . . . at least six months. And whatever you do, don't do no more dumb shit like go anywhere near Parris. If Le'sett finds out you started some more shit, you can forget about it. She can forget this incident, seeing that you just found out about the affair. Don't press your luck, is all I'm saying."

"So, you wouldn't mind me seeing her?"

"Not at all. It was only once, and there were no emotions involved. Maybe if we weren't partners, I'd go for it, but she wouldn't have me because I like to fuck too many different women. She'd go for a guy like you, if you played your cards right. She's a catch, too. She's ambitious, hardworking, got her own money, nice crib."

As the elevator ascended, we continued the conversation.

"If she's all that, why doesn't she have a man?"

"Because she's all that and lives in a city full of homosexuals. The man before me was screwing around because he had so many choices. You know how it is, man. At some point in a relationship, all the fucking you did in the beginning will cease, and then the women want a relationship and kids and whatnot. Arguments increase in frequency, and with all the free pussy in San Francisco . . . well, I think you understand. I can tell you what happened—in my view, anyway."

"What happened?"

"Her man got sick of arguing with her over little shit. He probably turned down a lot of women initially, but as the arguments with Le'sett prevailed, he finally said fuck it."

We laughed hard.

"Yeah, Sky, you know how that shit is, man. If you're arguing, guess what? You ain't fuckin', period. Most women need the relationship to be damn near perfect before they can give themselves to their men. On average, if a woman's pissed, she can't get turned on. She can open her legs, and probably will at first, but when she gets tired of you getting yours, she'll cut you off, and that's when the whole thing collapses. That's when a man starts to accept all the pussy he's been turning down."

"Why didn't he just break it off with her instead of messing around?"

"Come on, Sky. Are you serious, man?"

"Yeah, I mean, if the relationship wasn't working out, why not leave her and move on?"

"Because he was probably hoping things would go back to the way they were before the relationship became a fucking prison camp—hard labor and shit. He probably still loved her, but the relationship rarely goes back to what it was. Rarely, bruh. But a man still hopes as long as he can. In the meantime, his dick still gets hard every damn day, and he needs to get laid. His woman gives him grief and he has to go to bed with a hard one. That's why I said fuck all that a long time ago. I get me a piece whenever I can and move on."

"You seeing anybody now?" I asked.

"Yeah, man. I met this FBI agent named Kelly McPherson

back in June. Met up with her again a month or so later, and we hooked up. I'll stay with it for as long as it lasts, but I doubt it'll go anywhere because she's broke. And you know me. If a woman doesn't have her own shit, there will be no nuptials, okay? We can fuck if she wants to, but that's where the shit ends."

Chapter 24

The elevator doors opened and we exited with our bags in tow. Sterling slid the card into the slot and opened the door. When we entered the presidential suite, I was immediately struck by the luxurious décor. I smiled when I saw the floor to ceiling windows, which led to the private swimming pool. I walked through the suite, taking in all the expensive extravagance everywhere I looked.

The suite offered high ceilings, a large terrace, a spiral staircase that led to the bedrooms, a stocked bar, a fully equipped kitchen and dining room, a living room, which included a 42-inch television and a state-of-the-art stereo and entertainment center. I entered the bathroom and took in the detailed marble everywhere. It included a large sunken tub and a separate walk-in shower stall.

The doorbell rang. Imagine that. The place actually had a doorbell. I knew then that one day I was going to live like this all the time, not just one week on a friend's influence. This was real living, and I wanted it.

"Get that, man!" Sterling called down to me from his

room. "It's probably management sending up some complimentary champagne and strawberries or something."

I opened the door and saw what looked at first glance like fifteen or twenty women. All of them were striking in appearance, and apparently from every corner of the earth. Much like the Ms. Universe Pageant, they were all dressed in an assortment of expensive navy, crimson, emerald, onyx, lavender, and gold evening gowns with silk sashes identifying their countries of origin. I saw Ms. Tanzania, Ms. India, Ms. Puerto Rico, Ms. Brazil, Ms. Mexico, Ms. Japan, Ms. China, Ms. Germany, Ms. France, Ms. Switzerland, and so many others. I felt like King Solomon.

I looked them all over in a microsecond, and was immediately enraptured, snared by the flesh just south of my waist, and didn't much care because I wanted them all . . . every last one of them. Besides, after what I'd been through with Parris, I deserved this, didn't I? My lust mushroomed quickly as my desire to have them overtook me and fueled my thoughts of sexual fulfillment. I had no idea who these women were, yet I wanted to savagely enter the folds of all these beautiful women, especially if they could somehow wean me off whatever opiate Parris had used to addict me to her inebriating vineyard.

I smiled pruriently, about to invite them in, when they shouted in unison, "Nelson Kennard, we're here to cheer you up!"

Chapter 25

All of a sudden, I heard the sound of trumpets, cymbals, drums, lead and bass guitars, and the voice of JT Taylor, front man of the musical group Kool and the Gang, singing, "Oh yes, it's ladies' night, and the feeling's right." Equally as sudden, all the lovely ladies rushed me like I was a rock star and smothered me with affectionate kisses, which I didn't resist. It was ladies' night, all right. It truly was. For a fleeting moment, I thought I had died and gone to heaven.

Then I couldn't help but notice another woman, behind all the others, whose face I couldn't ignore. She was quiet, unassuming, and gorgeous, exceedingly so, the crème de la crème of the harem without question. She was dressed in a red sequined evening gown. The sash she wore read: MS. AMERICA. Her skin was dark and as smooth as the silk sash that wrapped around her shoulder and draped her inviting breasts. While I was being smothered with affection, she stood in the doorway watching it all, as if she were waiting for me to come to her. She smiled at me. I assumed it was an invitation to the sweet intimacy her beauty offered and I craved. I didn't hesitate.

"Excuse me a second, ladies," I said and left them where they stood.

I almost bowed before the majestic queen who was holding an envelope. She handed it to me and I took it, but continued my unblinking, wanton stare.

"Open it," she said, shattering the silent barrier between us.

I opened the envelope, took out its contents, and began reading.

Sky,

My wife and I heard about what happened, man. She suggested I send these ladies to cheer you up. The gesture is symbolic in that it is designed to give you a tangible representation of the cliché, There are plenty of fish in the sea. Please accept our gift of pleasure in your time of grief. They will be at your beck and call for the rest of the week. If you need them longer, let me know, and I'll take care of it.

All our best,
Jericho and Pin

"I see you got the letter, huh?" Sterling asked after coming over to us.

I turned around and looked at him. He was holding what looked like a very expensive bottle of Cognac. I turned the bottle around so I could read the label—Courvoisier. "Yeah, man," I said. "These are call girls?"

"Not just call girls. Top of the line call girls. The kind you couldn't afford if you only had ten thousand dollars."

"Ten thousand dollars? And I have all of them for a week?"

"Uh, we, man. We have them for a week. What are you waiting for? Let's get our party on, man!"

I took Ms. America by the arm and escorted her into the suite where the "beauty contestants" were completely nude and already engaging in the kind of debauchery that was still criminal in some states. Standing there, watching it all, listening to the erotic murmuring of delicious sex acts, we joined them and they ravaged us both until the heat of sunlight singed our naked bodies through the tall tinted glass.

Chapter 26

Parris and Shenandoah were in bed, naked and engaged in a sexual act that was usually reserved for couples who had become very close, couples that trusted and had complete faith in one another—cunnilingus. Shenandoah had found a comfortable position on the bed, placed her legs on his shoulders, and flicked her spot, but her body didn't respond. Her moans didn't come forth and fill the room like they once had when the torrid affair began six months ago.

The erotic sounds she usually emitted stimulated his need for fulfillment, stoking the fire of his anticipatory release. Nevertheless, he kept at it hungrily, yet tenderly, lapping and slurping her juices, believing she would eventually respond and then he could get what he wanted—fellatio.

When it came to oral sex, Parris was a professional. She knew how to take Shenandoah to the peak of excitement without pushing him over the edge. She was capable of doing this for over an hour without getting tired. As a matter of fact, she enjoyed giving her man anything he wanted. Knowing that she pleased her man in bed was something in which she took immense pride. When she gave of herself sexually, absolutely nothing was forbidden.

Shenandoah knew he had to give to get, and so he picked up his pace, determined to get her involved in the work he was putting in. But nothing was happening, and he was getting tired.

"We need to talk," he heard her say firmly.

He exhaled hard. He knew what she wanted to talk about, and he didn't want to, not now, not ever.

"What, Parris?" he asked softly, restraining his frustration, seeing this interruption of coitus as female strategic manipulation. If she wanted to talk, why didn't she want to talk before they started kissing, before they started caressing, before they got naked, and definitely before he tasted her fruit? Hoping to complete the sexual interlude, he quelled his inner screams of foul play.

"I can't get into this, Shenandoah. I just can't. Not unless we talk about it."

Shenandoah believed talking before sex was a woman's ultimate weapon, because no man—no matter the background, no matter the ethnicity, no matter the religion, no matter what color his skin was—wanted to talk when he was naked, in bed, and about to enter his woman. Only women wanted to talk at that time, because they knew sex was the bartering chip.

Sex was Parris' way of getting his attention, because if she let him in, if she let him pump her, if she let him spew his seed in her, in his blissful peace, no "real" talking would occur. She would no longer have any leverage. If a man wanted to finish what she allowed him to start, he would have to bend to her will, which made her weapon of choice so effective. She had tried everything else to get his attention.

As a matter of fact, she had been moody, despondent, and disrespectful, hoping to provoke an argument that would eventually lead to what she wanted. It was the same tactic she'd used on Nelson, and the man before that, and the man before that. When these weapons failed to get results, she simply closed her legs. This final trump card hadn't failed her. She would have used it with Nelson, but he was her first lover, and she enjoyed the sex too much. Shenandoah, however, was only average in the sex department, so she could cut him off and wouldn't be missing much.

"Fuck!" The word seemed to burst forth from deep in the pit of his belly and catapulted up through his throat. "Why do we have to talk about this shit now?"

Chapter 27

She raised her head off the pillow and looked down at Shenandoah, who was still between her legs, looking back at her, scowling. "So, you think it's shit, huh? You didn't think it was shit when you tried for months on end to pull me away from Nelson, did you? You didn't think it was shit when I let you fuck me that first time when Nelson busted us in the act, did you? You didn't think it was shit when you kicked Nelson's ass at the Metro Theater and we came home and fucked all night, did you?

"But now, six months later, it's shit. Six months later, sex with me is the equivalent of shit, huh? Even though it's shit, you still want me to suck your dick, don't you?"

Parris was right. After everything she said, he still wanted a blowjob. Shenandoah exhaled hard.

Parris pushed herself away from his face and pulled the sheet over her sensational curves, feeling naked all of a sudden, exposed. "Are you a man, Nelson?"

Shenandoah raised his head and looked her in the eyes. "What the fuck did you just call me?"

Parris realized she'd called him Nelson, but that was just a slip of the tongue. She had been with Nelson for four years. Anybody could have made that mistake, she rationalized. Calling him Nelson wasn't even all that important. The questions posed were. "I called you by your name, and don't try to change the subject."

"You called me by your ex-man's name while we were about to fuck, and I'm not supposed to notice that shit? I'm supposed to pretend you didn't call me by his name? I'm just supposed to answer your questions?"

"And that's another thing I hate!" she said, on the verge of screaming. "I hate when you call what we're about to do fucking. I've told you and told you and told you it makes me feel like a greased hole. It makes me feel like a goddamn sperm receptacle, yet you continue to use that awful word to describe our intimacy."

Totally frustrated because he knew there would be no sex now, let alone the much anticipated blowjob, he decided if she wanted to talk, talk he would. "Why do you keep bringing up his name? Do you compare me to him? Do you fantasize about him when we're fucking, Parris? Is that what you do?"

Parris exhaled hard and deliberately. "I just asked you for the billionth time not to use that word as a description of what we do in bed, Nelson! Shit! Show me some fucking respect in my house and in my damn bed! I'm sick of this shit! Sick, sick, sick! All you want to do is lay up. I want to start a family. When are we going to start a family, Nelson?"

"How fucking dare you call me by his name, not once, but twice in the span of twenty damn seconds!"

"Are we going to start a family or not? Yes or no?"

"Do you still love Nelson, Parris? Just answer me that! Yes or no?"

She exhaled hard again. "Why are you so jealous of him?" she asked through clenched teeth. "I'm here with you, not him. I'm giving myself to you, not him."

"You wanted to talk, I'm talking. It's a simple question. Do . . . you . . . still . . . love . . . him?"

She stared at him. "It's a simple question? So, what are you saying? I'm stupid? Are you calling me stupid, Nelson?"

"You got one more fucking time to call me Nelson, hear? One more fucking time!"

"Please. What are you going to do, beat me?"

"Don't think I won't. Keep pushing me and you'll see what I'll do. Now answer my goddamn question! Do you still love him?"

"Taking me from him isn't enough for your fragile ego? Since that decision hasn't convinced you that I want to be with you and not him, since you're so damn jealous of a man I haven't seen or heard from for six months, what's the point in staying together, Shenandoah?"

"Are you going to answer the question or not?"

"You answer me first, and then I'll answer you!"

"You sure you want to know, Parris?"

When Shenandoah asked her that question, when he coldly looked into her eyes and asked her if she wanted to know, she knew the answer. She stared at him for a long minute, her lips tightening, her anger boiling, only seconds away from a volcanic eruption.

"You never planned to marry me, did you? All the sweet talk, all the promises were empty poetry, blank pages of a novel yet to be written." She shook her head and screamed. "I can't believe I fell for your bullshit!"

"Believe it," Shenandoah said calmly.

His words, the bitterness in them, the unflinching stare, sent a chill down her spine and made her shiver. She wrapped her arms around herself, seeking comfort from what had become a brutal reality. She felt like such a fool, having left Nelson for the unfeeling monster lying at her feet. Her eyes welled. When she saw him fighting the uncon-trollable urge to burst into hilarity, she kicked him in the face with the heel of her foot, and he fell backward onto the floor. A loud thud filled her mind.

"How dare you?" she screamed. "How fucking dare you laugh at me?"

She saw his head rise slowly until she could see his face, which had a look of both anger and surprise. Surprise because he didn't believe she had the gumption to kick him in the face and off the bed; anger because she had actually done what he didn't think she had the guts to do.

He screamed, "You little bitch!"

"I got cha bitch, you fucking bastard!"

Shenandoah stood up and looked down at her, his erection a memory. "So, answer my question. You fantasize about him, don't you?" He paused and reflected for a second or two. "You're fucking him behind my back, aren't you? Admit it, you little slut. You fucking whore!"

"Can you handle the truth, little boy? 'Cause I'll sure tell it. You want the truth?"

"Yeah! I want the truth!"

"Yes, I fantasize about him. I even pretend you're him when we make love. I should've never left him for your sorry ass! You're just a bunch of talk, a helium balloon full of gas and not much else! No substance. That's all you are. You can't even fuck, to use your word! At least Nelson knew how to fuck me. He might have been broke, but he could fuck me for hours. He didn't have to get on his knees and eat me out to satisfy me like you, you weak dick bastard. I see why he took your woman in college so easily. If he fucked her the way he fucked me, that explains it all. Can't say I blame her, either.

"And truth be told . . ." She calmed down a bit and became reflective. "If you hadn't hit him when he wasn't looking, he would have kicked your ass at the theater and you know it. If he had kicked your ass that night, I would have gone back to him because he would have at least proved that he still wanted me. Before you ask, yes, I would have given it up to him that night instead of you, you lying-ass, sneaky-ass bastard!"

Her last words to Shenandoah sent him into a rage. He fast-walked around the bed and slapped her. Then he grabbed her by the throat, lifted her off her feet, and punched her in the face as if she were a man. The blows dazed and disoriented her, but somehow, in some twisted, maniacal way, the physical confrontation stimulated him and made him brick-hard again. Feeling like a conqueror who had just raided a village and killed all the men, he threw her on the bed and tried to enter her, but she was dry.

Parris tried to stop him, but he was too powerful. "No! Stop!"

It was like Shenandoah was possessed or something. She looked in his eyes and saw a wild, crazy, vacant look in them, like he was being controlled by another being, like he was powerless to stop himself. She hit and slapped and clawed, but Shenandoah wasn't going to be denied. He wanted fulfillment and was going to get it from her even if he had to take it.

Parris stared into his eyes and said, "You tryin' to prove you're a man?"

He ignored her and moved himself around until he found her opening and forced in the tip. The anticipation of being all the way in forged him ahead until finally he was there, right where he wanted and needed to be. Soon, she began to lubricate, and he sloshed around until his seed left his body and spilled into hers. Satiated, he withdrew himself, got off her, and put on his clothes, looking down at her the entire time.

He said, "Why don't you go back to him, you little whore? Maybe he'll take you back."

And with that, he left her weeping on her bed.

Chapter 28

I was sitting in my family room, sipping Courvoisier from a tall, thin glass of crystal, getting a nice buzz, thinking about a few things I wanted to change in my life with the new money I was making from my investments and the expansion of my business, when I heard someone knocking at my door. I looked at my watch; one o'clock in the morning. I wondered who would be coming to my house at this hour. What kind of emergency could it be? Those late telephone calls and late night visits always made me nervous because usually it meant something bad had happened. I hoped nobody had died. I set my glass on the table, stood up, and made my way over to the door.

For some inexplicable reason, Sterling came to mind as I made the short trek to the door. It had been six months since I'd seen him; six months since we spent that crazy week in Las Vegas with all those beautiful "contestants" of the Ms. Universe Pageant. With both our careers on the upswing, making us incredibly busy, Sterling and I drifted apart. It's not something we planned, and it's not that we didn't care for each other. It's just that successful people are busy people. Sterling's career as a sports agent was going through the roof, and I have to say that my career was taking off, too. All the hard work I had been putting in was starting to pay off in the accounts receivable department. I'd been able to expand to Fresno, San Luis Obispo, Santa Barbara, and Los Angeles, the deals I had been working on for months before Parris, the whore, "technically" betrayed me.

While I had a great time with all the lovely ladies and spending time with my old friend, if I was being honest with myself, I had to admit that I still loved Parris. The feelings I had for her weren't nearly what they used to be, but they were definitely real, and it pissed me off because I wanted to be over her by now. Love was for crazy people, I'd concluded. Not the nut job that belong in an asylum, but the regular, everyday people like you and me.

I must have been crazy because I loved romantic love. I loved the euphoric feelings that flooded my mind when I first met a woman I was attracted to. I loved those early conversations when I spoke to a woman over the phone in low, romantic tones. I loved her response to my words and my responses to hers. Is that wrong or crazy?

Life would be perfect if those feelings never changed, but they do; especially when life's circumstances throws its unpredictable curve balls at your head at supersonic speed. Romantic love eventually dissipates and turns into disagreements, leading to arguments, leading to separation and divorce. Moreover, even when it's all over, love, the cruel master that it is, reminds you of all the good times you couldn't remember when the relationship began to get old and soured.

Of all the "contestants" that came to the presidential suite that night so many months ago, I only connected with Ms. America, the woman who had given me the note from Jericho and Pin Wise. I paid her for her delightful company for a month after the Las Vegas weekend. Her professional name was Plenty. Over the months that I've been seeing her, she'd come to like me, and finally told me her name was Rachel Radcliff and that she was from Toledo, Ohio. The story of how she became a working girl was an all too familiar one.

She wanted to be like actress Katie Holmes, who was also from Toledo. It may have happened for her, too, but she'd made the mistake of getting off the bus to spend a couple of days in Las Vegas before going on to Hollywood. At eighteen, she was young and impressionable, and fell in with a pimp named Shaggy for eight years. One night, while sitting at a bus stop waiting for Johns to pick her up, Jericho's limo stopped, and he offered her a much better deal than Shaggy. The way she tells it, Jericho did a Vito Corleone and made the pimp an offer he couldn't refuse, wanting her to work for him instead.

I knew I had to stop seeing Rachel because I was becoming too attached to her. And she was becoming attached to me. She stopped charging me after the first month. It was the kind of relationship I needed at the time to help me cope with what I was going through as far as my feelings for Parris were concerned. She met a need. Sure, the relationship was physical, but it was more than that.

It was hard to have a relationship without the entanglements, without the emotions, without the drama that comes with a loving relationship. It was my escape, my fantasy, my dream world, where everything between a man and a woman was Garden of Eden-like—perfect. I guess it was the same for Rachel. With me, she was just a woman seeing a man without the "transaction" of currency.

I knew it was time to move on with my life, so I cut it off with Rachel. It hurt her, but it had to be done. This wasn't going to be a *Pretty Woman*, Julia Roberts/Richard Gere kind of thing. Loved the movie, but it was a movie, okay? I wasn't about to marry a prostitute and have babies with her. No way! I needed something real, not a fantasy. During the months that I'd been seeing Rachel, I never neglected Kennard Janitorial Services, but that's what I told her. I think she knew I was lying. On the contrary, business was good, great even.

With the business taking off the way it had, and the money starting to roll in from having so many outlets, I had to hire several managers to rid myself of the stress of having to deal with everything on my own. It was getting way too big for me. As a matter of fact, I was able to pay off the loan I'd gotten from Grace Underwood's bank in record time.

In all those months, I never once called or visited Grace. I was too embarrassed to see her again after what I'd done at the Metro Theater. When I paid off the loan, instead of going to the branch where she worked, I went to another to avoid looking in her eyes and remembering I had not only embarrassed her, but I had gotten my ass whipped in front of her. Call me crazy. Call me an egomaniac or whatever. It's a guy thing. You can't take an ass whipping in front of your wife, your fiancée, or the woman you're on a date with. Losing a fistfight didn't necessarily make me weak; it did, however, make me feel weak, and no man wants to feel weak.

I was forty, twice divorced, childless, and now a millionaire five times over. In the next few months, I was going to close a few deals in the Los Angeles and San Diego areas. When you're broke and trying your damnedest to pull yourself up by your bootstraps, nobody will take your calls. But once you've done it on your own through hard work, initiative, commitment, and perseverance, suddenly you can get any-body on the phone.

When I made it to the door, I flipped on the porch light and pushed the curtain aside. I was stunned when I saw Parris standing there with her head bowed, deliberately re-fusing to look at me. What the hell did she want? Why was she here? My first thought was to turn off the light and go back and finish my Courvoisier, but my curiosity got the better of me. I stared at her, refusing to open the door until she looked at me, until our eyes locked. Eventually, she raised her head and looked into my eyes. When I saw the bruises on her face, my heart melted and I opened the door.

Chapter 29

Without her saying a word, I knew what had happened—at least I thought I did. This was the day I had been awaiting for six months. I wanted her to come crawling back to me so I could reject her with venomous glee. But it wasn't happening the way I wanted it to. I wanted her to somehow learn that I was now the rich man she had always wanted, but couldn't wait six more months for it to all happen.

I wanted her to find this out, realize what a fool she was, so I could figuratively kick her right in the teeth. I wanted her heart to ache like mine had, and she had ruined all my plans by coming over in the middle of the night, all bruised and beaten with a contrite heart. As much as I had thought and dreamed of this very moment and how merciless I would be, I couldn't do it. When I saw the tears falling, splashing down on my hardwood floors, I felt her pain. Imagine that! I was the damn victim in this, yet I felt sorry for her?

See what I mean about love? This shit is insane!

I led her to the family room and offered the whore a glass of my very expensive Cognac. We sat down, her on the couch, me in the La-Z-Boy recliner. I sipped my drink and watched her, almost angry with her for stealing my triumphant jubilee. This was supposed to be my time to shine, but I couldn't seize it and still call myself a human being. So, I became a friend and waited for the words that would surely come. Given enough silence, the victim always speaks, and often tells all. I knew I had to be patiently silent for as long as it took.

So, I sat there, sipping my Cognac, waiting for the inevitable. As I watched her, as I stared at her unceasingly, something began to happen inside me. Was it the Courvoisier, or was it the fact that this whore was still absolutely stunning even with the bruises around her eyes and cheekbones? I think it was both. I think the Courvoisier and her beauty had ensnared me.

Parris was midnight black, and I always had a thing for dark-skinned women. I don't know what it is, but the blacker the better. I've heard people say, "The blacker the berry, the sweeter the juice." Is it true? Or have I bought into a cliché? Perhaps the cliché has become a self-fulfilling prophecy of sorts. I don't know, but looking at her now, I was drawn to her rich, smooth, Hershey's chocolate skin. It felt like velvet when I used to touch it. When I started to throb, I knew I was in trouble, but I couldn't help myself.

Then, like magic, she began speaking, and didn't stop for fifteen minutes. "I tried to leave Shenandoah," she had said, "and he beat me up and raped me."

Floored by this revelation, I said, "You tried to leave? What do you mean? You mean you were going to divorce him?"

After those questions, she completely fell apart, and like a sudden violent thunderstorm, she let all her anguish gush forth like she had been holding it back for more than a decade.

"We never got married, Nelson," she revealed with genuine sorrow. She looked at me, tears splashing down like raindrops. "He used me! He used me like I was nothing! For six months, he kept promising to marry me and he never did, Nelson. He never did! When I told him I wasn't going to have sex with him anymore until he at least gave me an engagement ring, he beat me up and took it. I feel so worthless. I feel so violated. I'm so sorry for hurting you, Nelson. Now I know how you must have felt. Can you ever forgive me for what I did to you?"

Her penitent plea touched me. I didn't want it to, but it did. Then I remembered what she said about the engagement ring she never received. It triggered a realization of what had been bothering me for the longest time. It was the ring! When I saw her at the Metro Theater, she didn't have a wedding ring on then either. I remained silent, contemplating my feelings for her, which were overwhelming at the moment. Wave after wave of emotions bombarded my heart and forced me to say yes to her plea for clemency.

When I granted the pardon she so desperately needed, she ran over to me and threw her arms around me. In just a few minutes, I had forgotten every bad thing she'd ever done to me. I had forgotten how she deliberately and recklessly hurt me. I had forgotten that she called me a loser to my face. I had forgotten that she married another man—I believed she had, anyway. Because I had forgotten these things so easily, before I knew it, we were kissing passionately and ended up in bed. The sex between us felt so right, so fulfilling, until she began to moan in my ear as I pumped her.

Chapter 30

Parris' moans somehow sobered me from the nefarious opiate of love unrequited. It was as if a light had suddenly come on in my inebriated mind. Hearing her moan, hearing how enraptured she was by our physical joining, spontaneously and emotionally removed me from our love-making, and like a vivid vision, put me in her house six months ago when I had my Glock in hand, climbing the stairs, listening to her erotic sighs. I stopped pumping her and literally snatched myself out of her drenched sheath. Suddenly, I remembered it all like it just happened seconds ago. The anger I felt was back with a vengeance, and now I would be merciless.

"What's wrong, baby?" Parris panted when I got out of bed and started putting my clothes back on.

"Baby? You got a lot of nerve coming to me, crying about the way your man treated you. Not one time in six months did you apologize for what you did, did you?"

"Yes, I did," she said without remorse.

"When did you apologize, Parris?" Then it came back to me. "Oh, you mean when I had a gun in your face? Is that when you apologized? When you were under duress? You think that's an apology?"

She slid out of bed and sauntered over to me. Hubris defined her pretty, dark face. Kissing my glistening chest, she said, "So, we're not going to finish what we started?"

I pushed her away, and she fell onto the bed. I found the whole act nauseating now. "You mean am I going to finish fucking you like I used to? Hell naw! Get your ass up, put your clothes back on, and get the hell out of my house!"

She looked at me like she couldn't believe I was actually talking to her like the whore she was. "You really want me to leave?"

I couldn't believe how arrogant she was. Then it occurred to me that she had set up this whole scene. The tears may have been real, but it was her intent to come over to my house, get me into bed, and somehow foster some crazy obligation on my part, but I wasn't having it.

"Get the fuck out, bitch!"

"Bitch?"

"You heard me, bitch . . . ho . . . slut! They all describe who and what you are!"

Parris yawned and slid back into bed. She pulled the comforter over her shoulders and said, "It's too late for me to go home by myself. I'll just stay the night, and tomorrow we can talk about all of this. Now, get in bed so we can go to sleep."

I laughed after that one because she was dead serious. I said, "Get up, get out, and don't come back!" I walked around to the other side of the bed, where her clothes were. I picked up her panties and bra, and threw them in her face. "Put them on! Now!"

She swung her feet to the floor and sat up. "We need to talk, Nelson. I know you still love me."

"I don't love you!" I screamed.

She laughed. "You mean you don't want to love me. Isn't that right, Nelson? You don't want to love me, but you do.

And I never stopped loving you, either. I never did." She slid into her panties, put her arms through her bra straps, and hooked it in the front. "Remember when I left your office that day? What did I say?" She didn't give me a chance to answer. "Didn't I tell you I still loved you? Didn't I? Well, I never stopped. I thought I would eventually get over you, but I didn't."

With hot rancor, I said, "I don't give a damn if you do love me. Whatever love you *think* you have for me only underscores what you did. You loved me, but you weren't committed to me! You loved me, but you couldn't wait for the deals I was putting together to come through! You loved me, but you called me a loser! You loved me, but you fucked another man! You loved me, but you sucked another man's dick, Parris! Damn!

"Do you think I could ever in my life forget that shit? Do you think I could ever get that visual out of my mind? Don't you know that every time I kissed you, I'd see his dick in your mouth? But the visual wouldn't stop there. Do you think I could ever stop the images of your head bobbing while you sucked him? From there, the visual would only worsen because I'd see you enjoying it all while you sucked him!"

Chapter 31

While I was still speaking, I remembered the major drug bust that made the national news a couple of months after we'd broken up. "Remember your friend Dorothy and her drug dealing boyfriend? Remember throwing that bullshit in my face about all the gifts he was giving her? The cops busted him again. Now both their asses are doing serious time. And what about your other fat-ass friend? You know the one. The one that keeps popping out babies by different men. I bet that bitch is pregnant again by yet another man.

"But these are the bitches you listened to. These are your trusted allies? You couldn't wait for *my* ship to come in. Isn't that what you said in my office six months ago? Well, my ship came in, Parris. Maybe you were in the way. Maybe God was lookin' out for a brotha and waited until your money-hungry ass got out of my life!"

She patiently waited for me to finish my longwinded tirade and then calmly said, "You were right about Dorothy and Sheniqua. I should've never let them talk me into leaving you for Shenandoah." She smiled and continued. "So, your ship finally came in, huh? After all the work you put in, you really deserve it, Nelson."

"I know that, bitch! Too bad you couldn't wait a few more months. You could've had it all. Instead, you threw me over for a rich man who fucked you over. Now you're running back to me?"

Softly, she said, "Give me another chance, Nelson, please. Let me make it up to you. I'll do anything you want. Let me show you."

When she started to unhook her bra, I picked up her clothes, grabbed her by the arm, and dragged her to the living room. Then I sat her down on the couch. "You want another chance, ho? Listen to this tape and then tell me why I should even consider that shit!"

I searched through the messages until I found the one she'd left me that night after the incident at the Metro Theater. I hit the play button on my answering machine. It beeped and then played the profanity-laced message she'd left me after Shenandoah kicked my ass.

You black bastard! Didn't I tell you you were a fuckin' loser? Now you know it, too, don't you? Shenandoah beat the shit outta you, didn't he?

As the message played, I watched her reaction to her own hate-filled words, wondering what she was thinking. The tape continued.

I was so turned on by the way he knocked you down and punched you in the face that I literally came right then and there. And then we hurried back to my place and we fucked, Nelson! We fucked all night long! I came so hard! Then I sucked his dick and everything! That's how turned on I was! You never turned me on like that!

Upon hearing this, Parris diverted her eyes from me to the floor and then her head tilted forward; finally, some skeletal evidence of shame from this Jezebel. I should have been enjoying this triumphant moment I'd been waiting for, but I wasn't. I felt no pleasure at all, only hatred, which fueled my desire to continue the merciless annihilation. On the contrary, I was still hurt by it all, but this needed to be done. If for no other reason, so I could move on with my life.

The tape continued.

Tomorrow, we're going to the police to tell them everything you did the other night, you fuckin' stalker!

After that statement, she didn't want to hear any more and hit the stop button.

I said, "That's all right, Parris. I know what it says word for word." I began to recite each word, like I was on HBO's *Def Poetry Jam*. Stanza after stanza, I let her own words rip into her flesh until they touched the marrow of her wicked bones. Every word I spoke was like a javelin piercing her black heart, and I continued the barrage until she heard every word she'd said to me. Having finished the devastating salvo, I stared at her, looking at the guilt that was about to consume her.

She looked at me for a fleeting second and covered her face with her hands, as if she couldn't believe she'd left me that message. Or maybe she couldn't believe I actually kept it for all these months. I don't know. I'm just glad I kept it because if I hadn't, she could deny it all. With enough persuasion, and my desire to have sex with her, I could probably deny she said those vicious things to me, too. This is yet another reason why I say love is a mental disorder and should be labeled as such.

Tears fell again. "I was drinking that night, Nelson."

"And you think that makes a difference? A drunken mind speaks its sober thoughts." I paused for a second and remembered what hurt more than anything else she had said. I continued purging my soul as if my words were a therapeutic salve for my emotional heart. More of what I felt, the words I had suppressed for what seemed like an eternity, needed to be disgorged if I was ever to be totally free of her. "You sucked another man's dick, Parris! Damn! Then you had the nerve to call me and tell me about it! Am I supposed to forget that shit—ever?" I didn't wait for an answer. "Let me ask you something. Did Shenandoah hear you leave me that message?"

She nodded reluctantly.

"I see."

With genuine curiosity, she asked, "You see what?"

"That's when he lost all respect for you, you dumb ho! You left me for him because he had money. That was your first mistake. Next, you gave it up to him the same night. Mistake number two. After that, you called me and left that message, and he hears it all. Mistake number three. And to top off, everything you did, you showed no sexual restraint with a man you didn't know that well and had no papers on. Mistake number four.

"You know what he thought of you after that phone call? He thought you were a cold, ruthless ho. But see, he still wanted to fuck you. He figured he would keep fucking you until he'd had enough. He may have had feelings for you in the beginning. I don't know. He may have even wanted to marry you, but when he heard you gleefully rip me over the phone, he knew you'd do the same thing to him someday.

"And he was right, because as soon as he beat your ass and raped you, instead of going to the police like you did after the incident at the Metro Theater, you brought your whorish ass over here, willing to give me the same pussy he took. The same pussy he'd taken an hour earlier."

After I finished ripping her a new one, something disgusting entered my mind. I had two rhetorical questions now. "Did you even wash yourself before you came here? Or did you just throw your panties on and run over?" She looked at me and rolled her eyes as if the questions were ridiculous. I continued the barrage of howitzers, launching yet another devastating hydrogen bomb. "Now, you tell me, what kind of woman would do some shit like that?"

Innocently, she said, "So, there's no chance of us reconciling?"

I laughed out loud. "Put your clothes on and leave."

While Parris quietly finished putting her clothes back on, I went to my bedroom, grabbed her shoes, and threw them at her feet. "Hurry up, bitch!"

She put on her shoes and stood up. "I love you, Nelson. I always have and I always will. Nothing I can do about it. But this ain't over. You're mine. You hear me? You're mine. Contrary to what you believe about me, it's not about the money. I thought it was. I even let my so-called friends talk me into going after a man with money. Foolish on my part, I know. But now I know better, and without a doubt, it's about the love I have for you that never diminished."

I'd had enough of her arrogance. I grabbed her by the arm and dragged her to the front door. I opened it and shoved her out of my house and onto the porch. In a measured, even tone, I said, "You broke my heart, Parris. You shattered my heart."

Just as I was about to return to my Cognac, I heard her shout, "This ain't over, Nelson! You're mine!"

I ignored her and went to my bedroom. I pulled the sheets and pillowcases off the bed and put them in the trash. Then I put fresh linen on the bed and went to sleep.

Chapter 32

I woke up the next morning thinking about what had happened between Parris and me the previous night. I thought about all of it and realized that the only way I could really move on was to confront her on what she had done to me. Now that I had confronted her, I thought I could finally have a new relationship. It was time to get serious about a "real" relationship with a "real" woman. The only name that came to mind was Grace Underwood.

I liked Grace, but she wasn't as dark as I like my women. I guess that's not enough of a reason to cross someone off "the list." Trivial, I know, but I like what I like. I believed Grace was a good woman, and I'd be lucky to have her. I wondered if she was still interested. She said she wouldn't wait for me. I wondered if she'd found someone else to watch movies with. I hoped she hadn't, but the truth was, six months was a long time, and she could be in a deep relationship by now.

I looked at the clock on my nightstand; 6:15 AM. I'd made up my mind. I picked up the phone to call her, but then hung it up. This was something that should be done face to face. Besides, I didn't want to give her the chance to hang up on me before I had a chance to tell her how I felt. After all, I hadn't called her in six months. I could have at least called the woman, if for no other reason than to thank her for being there when I needed someone to comfort me. She had been there for me when I was at my lowest point, and I hadn't even bothered to call.

I decided to go over to her place and ask her if she was still interested. I knew she had to be at work by nine o'clock. I also knew I was taking a chance because another man could be there, but it was a chance I was willing to take. Unlike seeing Shenandoah going in to Parris' house that crazy night when I actually considered blowing my own brains out, I didn't love Grace, and if I saw something like that, I could move on without the drama and the profound sense of loss.

I was excited about seeing Grace again, and what I had to say to her couldn't wait. I got up, showered, shaved, and threw on a pair of navy slacks, a cream-colored turtleneck, and my favorite suede jacket, then headed for the front door. I grabbed the keys off the table where my answering machine was. I saw the red light blinking. I had three un-heard messages. I figured they were from Parris. It was probably another one of her profanity-laced diatribes that I didn't want to hear at the moment.

No way would I let her spoil the mood I was in. I was feeling good for the first time in a long time. I was about to let Grace know that I was ready to begin a relationship with her if she was still interested. The last thing I wanted was to hear Parris' apologies or finger pointing. I was in a good mood and wanted to stay in a good mood. I tossed the keys in the air, caught them, smiled, and put them into my pocket while walking out the front door.

As I drove over to Grace's place, I thought about all the re-lationships I'd observed over the years, including my own. I was twice divorced. That doesn't happen unless both people screw it up. Then it occurred to me that most relationships were not ideal. I got the feeling that happiness was as fleeting as the wind; it could not be grasped and held onto. With the exception of my parents, none of the couples I knew were "happy." Even my parents had their days when they went at it like cats and dogs.

The awakening to this phenomenon started six months ago, before Parris and I broke up. I remember sitting in restaurants, having business lunches or dinners with clients I was determined to woo, and being distracted by the conversations that sliced and diced their way into my business dealings. I overheard lots of people, particularly husbands and wives, talk openly about their sex lives, and learned that they were almost nonexistent, which was probably why so many people were having sex outside of their "committed" relationships. I guess what bothered me is that they saw nothing wrong with it, which blew me away.

Most of the people I overheard talking about this said they were having fabulous sex before they got married, and couldn't explain what happened after saying "I do." Both men and women said they had no plans to have sex outside of their "committed" relationships, but for reasons none of them could articulate, their relationships started to disintegrate shortly after the marriage began. Couples that lived together said they didn't start seeking sex outside of their relationship until years after they started "playing house."

I remember thinking, believing, and actually being grateful that I had someone like Parris, who was committed to me come hell or high water. Oh, how wrong I was! As I contemplated on these things, I started having second thoughts about talking to Grace. Relationships in the twenty-first century are nuts.

I began to question my motives. Did I really want to start something with Grace, or did I think she was safe? Did I think she wouldn't hurt me? What was really going on in my head? After much thought about this, I concluded that I was just afraid of a new beginning, a beginning that could be full of promise.

I finally made it over to Grace's place, but the street was lined with cars, no place to park. Fortunately for me, a woman was about to pull away from the curb. I waited until she left then parked in her vacated space. Just as I was about to pull the door handle and get out of my car, my cell phone rang. I checked the caller ID, thinking it might be Parris. I never changed my cell number, even though we'd broken up, so I figured it was her, but it wasn't.

The ID read: WISE CHOICE SPORTS, along with one of Sterling Wise's many numbers. I wondered why Sterling was calling. I figured he must be back in town again. And knowing him, he might have wanted to take another trip to Sin City for another week of unrestrained debauchery. The last time I talked to him, he told me he was flying to Washington to see FBI agent, Kelly McPherson, the woman he'd told me he was seeing the first time we went to Las Vegas a few months ago.

"What's up, man? Long time, no hear," I said.

A female voice responded. "Mr. Kennard, this is Diana, Ms. Santiago's personal assistant. She's been trying to reach you. Can you hold for a moment? It's very important."

"Yes," I said with trepidation, thinking, *What the hell happened now?*

While I waited, I looked at Grace's front door and saw her and a man hugging each other. Had he been there all night? My heart sank a little, but it was far from breaking. I was only disappointed she had moved on, but at the same time, I was happy for her, too.

I didn't really look at the man who was leaving. All my attention was on Grace and the flannel gown she was wearing. It was the same one she had worn when I spent the week with her, which evoked fond memories of her and me together: the movies we'd watched, me pouring out my soul to her, and the love we'd made. I sighed at the thought of what we shared and how golden those few days were.

My focus was still on the gown, and I remembered thinking I didn't find it sexy at all when I first saw her wearing it. It seemed to me like something someone's grandmother would wear. My focus then shifted to what she was doing. I watched her watch the man get into his car and pull off. Only then did she close the door, which led me to believe their relationship was serious.

"Mr. Kennard?" Le'sett asked, cutting into my thoughts about Grace and what I had blown with her because of Parris.

"Yes."

"I've left you several messages. Didn't you get any of them?"

I remembered the blinking light on my answering machine.

"Uh, no, I didn't."

"You need to get to my office as soon as possible," Le'sett went on.

"What's this all about?"

"I don't want to get into this on the air. Get in here immediately!"

The phone disconnected.

Chapter 33

I started the car and pulled away from the curb. From what I saw, Grace had moved on. I can't say I blamed her, either. It had been six months. What I can't figure out is why she was even on the market in the first place. Usually, all the good ones are taken early, leaving the best of the worst to sort through.

Oh well, I wish her the best. I hope it works out for her.

If anyone deserved happiness, Grace did. Besides, maybe I needed a little more time before I jumped into another relationship anyway. The last thing I'd want to do is hurt her again if I found out later I wasn't ready, I concluded.

Thirty-five minutes later, I walked into Ms. Santiago's office. She was sitting behind her desk, and she didn't look happy; even so, she did look good—very good, in fact. For a brief moment or two, I forgot all about her puzzling phone call, thinking, *It ought to be a crime to look that good. Damn!*

Sterling told me months ago that I had a chance with her, but looking at the scowl on her face, even though it was very becoming, I knew whatever chances I may have had were gone. I thought so, anyway. Nevertheless, since I had obviously blown my chances with Grace, I was going to see if Ms. Santiago had any residual interest.

"Sit down, Mr. Kennard," she ordered.

Defiantly, I said, "I think I prefer to stand, Ms. Santiago."

"Suit yourself," she said gruffly. "Where were you last night?"

I suddenly remembered the last time I was in her office, when Sterling explained what suborning perjury meant. I knew I had to be very careful because it appeared that, with Sterling gone, Ms. Santiago was fresh out of favors for him. I knew, or at least believed, that she was looking for a way out so she wouldn't have to defend me, if that was why I was there.

I said, "Why do you ask?"

Ms. Santiago exhaled hard and deliberately. "Mr. Kennard . . ." She paused and took in some oxygen, "I'm your attorney. You can trust me."

I rolled my eyes and said, "Can I, Ms. Santiago?"

She leaned forward and looked me in the eye like she couldn't believe I didn't trust my own attorney. "What makes you think you can't?"

"I don't know. Perhaps it's the way you treated me the last time I was in here. Perhaps it's that legal term. something about suborning perjury and all that jazz. Maybe that's it. Or maybe it's the fact that I have to call you Ms. Santiago instead of using your first name. What do you think, *Ms. Santiago?*"

She swiveled her chair from side to side, watching me, studying me, trying to figure out what kind of game I was playing with her. Finally, she said, "I'm a professional, Nelson. I had to work hard to get where I am. I'm beautiful, and that makes men think they can take certain liberties they would not take with a male attorney or a female attorney who . . . let's see, how shall I put it . . . ? Someone who doesn't stimulate their loins the way I do. All a woman has is her reputation, and while I think you're an attractive man, a lot of my clients are. I don't date my clients because it's unethical, and I really don't have the time for men like you. Now, can we move on?"

"Men like me?" I growled.

"Yes, men—like—you," she said with stone-faced resolve.

Curious, I asked, "What's that supposed to mean, *Ms. Santiago?*"

She exhaled hard again. "Men who always pick the wrong woman. Men who can't look past my looks and see me for who I truly am and what I bring to the table besides sex. Men who love women who don't love them for some insane, inexplicable reason. Men like that rarely know what to do with a real woman. Shall I go on, or can we get down to business?"

I found her commentary quite stimulating. I wanted to know what she meant by a "real" woman. I sat down and leaned forward. "Sure, we can get down to business, *Ms. Santiago.*"

"If I allow you to call me by my first name, will you promise me that you'll keep the conversation on a professional level?"

To win a war, one must win battles. It felt good to win a small victory, which was getting us on a first name basis. From there, a film and dinner might not be that far away.

To answer her question, I said, "Promise."

"Okay then, where were you last night?"

I frowned, wondering where she was going with this line of questioning, silently praying Parris hadn't gotten me into more trouble. I said, "At home. What's this all about, Le'sett?"

She ignored my question. "Were you alone?"

I really didn't want to answer that question; not that I had anything to hide—check that—I did have something to hide. I wanted to pursue something with Le'sett, and I didn't want her to know that last night I was having sex with the same woman who had tried to get a restraining order on me; the same kind of woman she had described as one who doesn't love a man. I couldn't have her thinking I was one of those guys and still get her to take me seriously as a man with real potential.

"Why do you ask?"

Again, she ignored my question while simultaneously studying my reactions to her penetrating interrogatories. "When's the last time you saw Parris Stalls?"

Chapter 34

I knew I was in trouble when Le'sett asked me when I'd last seen my ex-girlfriend. What kind and how much trouble, I wasn't sure. I sat there, thinking, going over it all in my mind.

When Parris went home—check that—did Parris go home? If she did, was Shenandoah waiting for her? Did they get into it again? Did she tell him we were fucking? If she did, did he kill her or something? Is she still alive? I hope so, because at least I won't be looking at murder charges. What the hell happened when she left my place?

I looked Le'sett right in the eyes and said, "She came by my place last night. Is she okay? Has something happened to her?"

Again, she ignored my question and persisted with the spine-tingling interrogation. "Did anything unusual happen between you two?"

"Unusual?"

Still looking me in the eyes, never even batting her lashes, she asked, "Did you invite her over?"

I didn't like where this was going. I felt like I was being

questioned by the police and not my attorney. Something bad had happened to Parris the night before that much I knew. Was I about to be blamed for it?

Feeling the pressure, with a straight face, I said, "I'm not saying another word until you tell me what this is about."

"Fair enough, Nelson. I'll tell you what this is all about. Parris Stalls was raped last night."

Relieved, I finally breathed again. "Oh, that," I said. "Does she need a witness or something? I don't see how I can help her. I wasn't there. She told me about it, though. That's all I could testify to if she needs me to. I'll be glad to tell the cops how she looked and what she said when she came to my place last night."

Le'sett continued studying me. "So, what happened? Tell me about it."

"She came by my house, bruised and a little swollen. She told me that Shenandoah Armstrong had beaten and raped her."

Still watching and judging every answer by my facial expressions, it seemed, she asked, "Why do you think she came to you with this information?"

"She had this crazy notion that we could get back together since it didn't work out with him. Is she okay?"

Le'sett leaned forward, resting her elbows on her desk, and asked, "Did anything else happen last night, Nelson?"

I didn't like the way that question sounded. And I certainly didn't want to admit we'd had sex, albeit sex interrupted. I was planning to make a move on Le'sett, and I didn't want to come off like a cold-hearted snake. I didn't want her to think I could have sex with Parris and then the next day make a play for her. But wasn't I doing that very thing?

I said, "We got into an argument."

Le'sett leaned back in her chair, laced her fingers, and rotated her thumbs rapidly, one over the other. "An argument, huh?" She furrowed her brow. "What did you two argue about?"

"She wanted to get back together, and I didn't want to." I sounded so noble, so much like the gentleman I wanted her to believe I was.

She didn't miss a beat when she asked, "Did you two have any kind of sex together?"

"Huh?"

She exhaled hard, and said, "It's a simple question, Nelson. Did . . . you . . . have . . . sex . . . with . . . her?"

I cut my eyes to the left. "Uh, no."

"I'm so glad to hear you say that. Now I can tell her attorney that you have no objections to a DNA test."

I tilted my head toward the floor. *What the hell did Parris do when she left me last night?* Then her last words to me flooded my mind. *This ain't over, Nelson! You're mine!*

I looked at Le'sett and said, "What do they have?"

Le'sett swiveled her chair from left to right, still studying me with her eyes. "So, you did have sex with her?"

"Yes, but I stopped and got up." After my admission, I felt like a complete fool for allowing those words to roll off my tongue because it was so unbelievable, even though that was exactly what happened.

Who in their right mind would believe a man could be in the throes of passion and stop before climaxing? I'd done what Shenandoah had done, as far as having sex numerous times with a woman I didn't particularly care about, but I made sure I got mine before I pulled out. I'd had sex with my ex-wives and couldn't stand either one of them; all because I needed to satisfy the monster that swung just below my waist. Keeping it soft literally meant keeping it manageable, so I gave it what it wanted, what it needed, what it demanded. It was in charge in those days.

"So, you're telling me you smoked marijuana, but you didn't inhale?"

I didn't like the Bill Clinton comment. It aggravated me, and I heatedly said, "I'm telling you, I loved this woman and she broke my heart. Okay? When she came over and I saw the bruises, I felt sorry for her. Okay? I have a heart, okay? She was looking like I'd felt for months, and I don't know . . . I felt something for her again, okay? I suppose you never loved anybody months after that shit was all over, huh?"

"I'm not being accused of rape, Nelson. You are." She shook her head and continued. "So, you felt sorry enough to have sex with her, Nelson? Is that what you're telling me? You had sex with the same woman that left you for another man; the same woman that filed a restraining order against you? That woman, Nelson? That's the woman you had interrupted sex with?"

If I didn't know before, I knew then that Le'sett thought of me as the kind guy who rode to school on the short yellow bus.

Deflated, I said, "What did she say?"

"She went to the police after she left your place and claimed you raped her. I used to be an Assistant D.A., and one of my contacts called and told me about it early this morning. I called you several times."

"What are we going to do?" I asked desperately.

"It depends on what she wants."

Confused, I frowned and said, "What do you mean it depends on what she wants?"

"What happened last night, Nelson? Tell me everything that happened and maybe I can keep you out of jail."

I flew into a rage and yelled, "Jail? For what? I didn't do anything wrong! Shenandoah raped her, not me!"

"Let me say for the record that I hate women who do this kinda shit, and I'd love nothing more than to get this bitch on the stand and rake her gold-digging ass over some white hot coals. Even though the prosecution would object, I'm sure I could bring up how she left you for Shenandoah and all sorts of things. However, they have three things going for them. One, my sources say she was definitely raped. Two, you admitted you had sex with her, which means that even though you didn't inhale," she paused for emphasis, "there'll be DNA evidence, pubic hair and probably semen. Three, she hasn't accused Shenandoah of anything."

I shook my head, thinking, *I should have just fucked her like she wanted and maybe I wouldn't be in this shit.*

"Any chance they might find Shenandoah's DNA?"

"What difference would that make, Nelson?"

I flew into a rage again. "What difference would it make? He's the one that raped her, not me!"

Le'sett shook her head again, which made me feel stupid as hell. "Don't you understand that this is a woman scorned? Having his DNA in her can be easily explained. She could simply say she had sex with Shenandoah last night and that would easily explain his DNA. And Shenandoah, what's he going to say? 'Yeah, I raped her'?"

"But she came to my house, Le'sett! How do you explain that?"

"You don't understand women, do you, Nelson?"

I just stared at her.

"She could say you asked her to come over to talk about things and that she was still confused about who she wanted between the two of you. So, she went over to your house at your request to try and sort it out in her mind. You two argued when she told you she was going to stay with Shenandoah. She'll then say that you said something like if you couldn't have her, no man could. And at that point, you raped her."

"You've gotta be fucking kidding me!"

In a dry voice, Le'sett said, "I wish I were."

All of sudden, I got a brainstorm. "What about phone records? Can't we check my phone records on something like this? I never called that bitch not one time even after we broke up! Not once!"

"Yes, we can check the phone records, but it would only look worse for you."

"How? I never called her from my home or my cell. So, tell me. How can they prove I called and asked her to come over at one o'clock in the morning?"

"They don't have to prove it, Nelson. No phone records of you calling her makes it look like you planned the whole thing. It will look like you didn't use your own phones so it couldn't be linked to you. It'll look like you couldn't get past the relationship and tried one last desperate plea to get her back. And it'll make her look like the angel who hurt a man and was doing one last favor of hearing whatever he had to say, with every intention of making sure he knew there was no chance of you two ever getting back together. Besides that, I would be willing to bet she went to a pay phone and called herself just in case we looked into it."

"You've gotta be fucking kidding me! This is insane! This bitch would go that far to get back at me?"

Le'sett took a deep breath and exhaled. "Like I said, you don't know women very well, do you? Now, tell me what happened last night . . . all of it. I might be able to figure something out, or you're through. Remember the previous problem with a restraining order? The justice system isn't looking the other way anymore when men batter women."

"But you told me there wouldn't be any record of that."

"There isn't, but her attorney will subpoena the judge who signed it and the clerk who typed it up. You see what I'm saying, Nelson?" She paused briefly before continuing. "Now, let's hear it all."

Chapter 35

After I told Le'sett every single detail of what happened the previous night, which was embarrassing as hell, she called Parris' attorney and scheduled a settlement meeting to see how much Parris was seeking in damages. I didn't see any other way out of the mess I had made. With Kennard Janitorial Services' tentacles branching out all over California, the last thing I needed was a sex scandal that would make the local and perhaps the national news; especially after the incident at the Metro made the local news.

I guess it's true. Nice guys finish last. If I hadn't let her in, if I hadn't allowed myself to feel anything for her, if I had just slammed the door in her face, I wouldn't be in this mess. But after all she'd done to me, I still had a heart of compassion when I saw her bruised face. Well, no more. After we settled this case, I was through being Mr. Nice Guy! Fuck 'em and leave 'em! That was my new motto for the foreseeable future.

The meeting was set for three o'clock in the Daniels, Burgess, and Franklin law offices, Sterling's old firm, located several floors down from Wise Choice Sports. Ironically, four years ago, I landed the contract to clean their offices and had spoken with Sterling on my way out, just before the senior partner fired him. Hopefully, this snag won't cause too much of a problem and lose Kennard Janitorial the small but profitable gig. I would have to layoff a few people if they dropped the contract. Hopefully, it wouldn't come to that.

Le'sett and I walked into the glass-walled conference room, where Parris, her attorney, and a stenographer waited, and took our seats opposite them. As much as I hated to admit it, Parris, with the exception of the bruises, looked good in the lavender business suit I'd bought her a few years back. It was obviously a ploy to play on my sympathies. I inhaled the Design perfume she was wearing. I bought that too.

The suit, the perfume, and the way she was rhythmically opening and closing her legs was doing something to the flesh just below my waist. Having been with her for four years, I knew she was sexually aroused. That's why her legs were moving like that. And she knew I knew. We locked eyes. Then she flashed that smile of hers, showing all those pretty white teeth against her velvet-like mahogany skin, telling me she knew I was sexually aroused, too.

When I sensed that both our lawyers were watching us look wantonly at each other, I looked at her attorney. He was a young man, which told me the firm he represented obviously thought this was a slam dunk case, leaving the more puissant attorneys free to handle the complicated cases. Upon realizing this, I became so irritated that I thankfully lost my erection.

I felt Parris' eyes on me again and returned the probing stare. I began to think that Parris wasn't sexually stimulated because I walked into the room. She was sexually stimulated because she was enjoying this. She was enjoying having me over a barrel, and the fact that I was still physically attracted to her. I looked at Le'sett and found her staring at me like she was jealous. She probably wasn't, but maybe I wanted her to be.

"Are we on the record, counsel?" her lawyer began.

Le'sett nodded to the stenographer.

The young lawyer began by mentioning the name of everyone who was present at the meeting, the date, and why we were there. The stenographer typed every word he said. I saw the paper edge forward, but the machine was completely silent.

Parris' lawyer continued, saying, "Here's what we're seeking in damages." He slid the paper face down over to Le'sett.

Damages, I thought. *I'm the one damaged in this, not her.*

Le'sett looked at the paper, kept her cool, and said, "Come on, Nelson. We're out of here."

She had briefed me on this before we left her office. No matter what they asked for to make this problem go away, no matter what the paper they slid us read—check that—no matter what the extortion note read, we were going to leave and try to negotiate a much smaller figure. That's why she picked up the paper, not I. She told me it would be some outrageous sum and there was no point in seeing it in the meeting, because if they somehow saw in my eyes or body language that I was willing to pay the amount asked for, they wouldn't budge.

I was nearly to my feet when Parris sweetly said, "Nelson, there's a way out of this."

I looked at Le'sett. We expected this, too. We both sat down again.

"We're listening, Ms. Stalls," Le'sett said.

Parris looked arrogantly at Le'sett and said, "This is between Nelson and me, Ms. Santiago. I prefer to speak to him directly, if you don't mind."

We didn't plan for this new twist. Le'sett looked at me and shrugged her shoulders as if to say, "What have we got to lose?"

I looked Parris in the eyes. "I'm listening."

Her young attorney looked at Le'sett and said, "All of this is off the record, Ms. Santiago."

Le'sett nodded to the stenographer, who was quietly sitting at the other end of the table. The stenographer stopped typing.

The young attorney looked at Parris. "You have the floor."

"I need to speak to you alone, Nelson," Parris offered sincerely.

I looked at Le'sett.

"It's off the record, Nelson," Le'sett said. "Maybe you two can work this out on your own." She kinda laughed and winked.

Our attorneys and the stenographer left us alone.

The moment she heard the door close, Parris began the negotiations. "First of all, I meant it when I told you I loved you last night, Nelson. But you forced me to do this. I want us to get back together."

I bit down hard on my tongue until I felt pain, so I wouldn't blurt out something to antagonize my nemesis even further.

"We can reduce the five hundred thousand I'm asking for to two hundred and fifty thousand, if and only if we finish what we started last night."

I bit down again when I heard the sum she sought.

"That's not negotiable," Parris continued. "Now, if you want to walk away from this Scot-free, that's going to take a lot more doing. I want a fourteen-day cruise with just you and me. On this cruise, we will have sex, and we will try to work this out. If, after the cruise, I haven't convinced you that I really do love you and want to be your wife, you don't owe me one penny."

I couldn't hold back any longer. "So, what you're saying is, for one fuck, I get to keep two hundred and fifty thousand of my hard earned money. If I pay for a cruise someplace, I not only have to fuck you regularly during the fourteen-day stint, but I have to sincerely try to work out our problems. Or I could opt for the third option and just pay you the whole five hundred thousand. Is that about right?"

"Plus my attorney fees," she said sweetly.

I was faced with the humiliation of a very public trial or having sex with Parris for two weeks. Sounds like a no-brainer, I'm sure, especially since I wouldn't mind plowing through her private orchard anyway, but what about unwanted pregnancy? If she were to get pregnant, I was looking at eighteen years of support. Eighteen damn years! What about my dignity? What about my manhood? She had turned me into a eunuch once, and now she was threatening to do it again. What about plain old pride?

As if she were reading my mind, Parris said, "Five hundred thousand or the sex we both want. It's a gift, Nelson. Take it, enjoy it, and throw me away like the whore you say I am."

That's when I found my resolve. Standing up, I said, "You'll have your money by the end of business tomorrow." Then I turned to walk out.

Parris called out to me. "You must really hate me, huh, Nelson? I'm letting you off the hook for a small, microscopic price. To be clear, I'm offering the good sex I know you want. Why won't you take it?"

I turned around, facing her, and said in a shaky voice, "As much as I wanted to take that deal, as good as sex was between us, I can't. And here's why: You left me for another man, Parris. You fucked him! You sucked him! And then, to show me just how evil your heart really is, you called my home and told me about it. If that wasn't enough, you then accused me of raping you when you know damn well it was

Shenandoah Armstrong who both beat and raped you last night. When I think I've seen it all, you extort five hundred thousand out of me, the very money you left me for because I didn't have it six short months ago. How am I ever supposed to forgive and forget that, Parris—any of it?"

With that, I left the conference room.

Chapter 36

Three months later
June 2002
After the Merger

Parris was sincere when she said she loved Nelson, but she wasn't about to let the five hundred thousand she'd extorted from him stay in his bank account. She had somehow convinced herself that Nelson owed her that money. After all, she had given him four years of her life, which is how she came up with the amount she wanted. Even though they never even lived together, she brazenly charged Nelson one hundred and twenty five thousand dollars for each year she stayed with him when he was broke—a very fair sum, in her mind.

When Nelson walked out of the settlement meeting, Parris knew it was over. If he could feel something for her the previous night, if he could embrace her, kiss her, and enter her body, he still felt something for her, she believed, which is why she offered him the sex they both wanted and less money. It was a huge gamble on her part, but if she could just get him on a fourteen-day cruise, if she could get him into bed night after night, she could persuade him to give her another chance, and she would have access to all his money. And of course, she saw nothing wrong with this kind of thinking because she loved him, and a wife has access to her husband's bank account.

Now all she had was Nelson's money, which she began to spend immediately, purchasing a new Mercedes Benz, and redecorating her Victorian townhouse, making it a state of the art technological marvel. She also bought as much stock as she could in Shenandoah's software company, hoping she wouldn't attract attention. Unfortunately, her greed caught up with her in her classroom, in front of her students.

"Ms. Stalls," the principal called out after knocking, then opening her second grade class room. "Uh, these men . . . uh . . ."

Two men pushed their way past the principal and entered the room.

One of the men said, "Parris Stalls, you're under arrest for insider trading," grabbing her arm and turning her around.

When she saw the shock on her students' faces, how surprised they were at what they were seeing, she knew they didn't understand how their model teacher, who taught them not to break the law, was now being arrested right in front them. She lowered her head to the floor and wept aloud as they cuffed her.

Later that day, while still in custody and sitting alone in a mirrored room for several hours by herself, she thought of the man she still loved . . . Nelson Kennard. As far as she was concerned, this was his fault. If he had just been reasonable and given her another chance, she would have been a virtuous wife and an excellent mother to the children she always wanted to give him.

As she sat there waiting for her captors to question her, she began to formulate a plan to get out of the mess she was in. She knew giving back the money wouldn't be good enough, so she thought now would be a good time to settle the score with Shenandoah. He had used her voluptuous body for six long months. When he'd had enough, he told her he wouldn't marry her. And then he took one last piece against her will, and she hadn't forgotten that. She was now going to pay him back for that by sending him to prison.

The door swung open, and the same young man from Daniels, Burgess, and Franklin law offices walked in and took a seat across from her. "You're looking at seven years plus a stiff fine, but I can get you two and a half. One year if you can give the Feds a name, but you forfeit all the money you made on the stocks you bought."

Without a second's hesitation, Parris said, "Shenandoah Armstrong. He's an executive at Software Unlimited, and he's been doing this kind of thing for years."

Later that same day, Shenandoah was arrested, too. While in custody, he told on thirty other people, and those people talked. By the time it was over, the Feds had arrested over five hundred people for insider trading.

Chapter 37

A few days later, at Parris' sentencing, Judge Keenan, who was usually merciful, was in a foul mood. The scowl she wore looked as if it were permanent. Keenan, an African American, was a long time friend of the Wise family, particularly Sterling, as they had attended Georgetown law school together fifteen years earlier. Judge Keenan's father, who was also a judge, had gotten Sterling's older brother, Jericho, into Berkley University, his alma mater, over thirty years earlier. Sterling had told the judge about Parris Stalls and how she had extorted half a million dollars from Nelson Kennard. So, when Judge Keenan took the bench and banged the mallet on the gavel, she was set on sentencing Parris to the whole seven years.

"Do you have anything to say, Ms. Stalls?" Judge Keenan asked.

Parris and her young attorney stood, and she began speaking. "Your Honor, I'm very sorry for my actions. I willfully broke the law to make money. I offer no excuses for my behavior. I am at your mercy."

"That was an eloquent speech, Ms. Stalls, but that's all it

was. I don't see, nor do I sense any contrition—no real sorrow for anything you've done. Had you not been caught, you would not be sorry. Getting caught is the only thing that prompted you to say what you did; that and your attorney's urging, no doubt. Since you have already made a deal with the district attorney's office, I cannot give you what you deserve, which in my judgment is the full seven years, no parole. However, the facility you serve your time in is at my full discretion. Tell me, is this the first crime you've ever committed? Have you ever defrauded another person for profit before this crime?"

Parris looked into the judge's eyes and said, "No, Your Honor. I've never defrauded anyone for profit, and I would never do something like that, not even to my worst enemy. The truth is I was greedy. Greed is why I'm before you seeking mercy."

Judge Keenan exhaled loudly before saying, "Are you sure this is your first time committing a crime for profit?"

Without a second's hesitation, she said, "Yes, Your Honor. I'm sure."

Judge Keenan picked up her mallet and pointed it at Parris. "I will ask you one last time. Have you ever done anything remotely like this in your life?"

Her young lawyer and the assistant district attorney looked at each other. The district attorney shrugged her shoulders and shook her head, having no idea what was going on.

The young attorney spoke to the judge. "Your Honor, may I have a moment with my client?"

The Judge folded her arms and said, "You may."

In hushed tones, the attorney said, "Is there something you haven't told me?"

"No," Parris said.

"Are you sure? She's giving you every opportunity to tell her now."

"So what? She can't give me more than a year, and I'm not going to bust myself out. Fuck that! I'll do the year and I'm out."

Judge Keenan said, "Don't indulge the court's patience any longer. For the last time, Ms. Stalls, have you ever done anything like this before? Anything at all? If you have, you best tell me now."

"No, Your Honor. I have not."

Judge Keenan shook her head, sighed heavily and said, "One year in the Norrell Prison facility. You will begin serving your time today." She slammed the mallet on the gavel.

"Your Honor," the young attorney began, "this is a white-collar crime, and you've condemned my client to a year with some of the worst women criminals in the country. This is outrageous!"

Judge Keenan pointed her mallet at the attorney and said, "One more word and you'll spend the week in jail." Then she waited for the attorney to say something, and when he didn't, Judge Keenan returned to her chambers.

Chapter 38

That very evening, Parris Stalls entered the Norrell Prison facility along with nine other women. Cat calls and profane solicitations, promises of illicit lesbian sex acts, rang out and echoed off its drab gray walls.

"Oh, look at the little one, y'all. That's gon' be mine!" a woman standing on the third tier shouted.

"Not if I get her first!" another woman shot back. Uproarious laughter filled the prison, and the cat calls continued.

The next morning, at breakfast, the woman who had shouted to Parris from the third tier approached her while she forced what the Norrell facility called food into her mouth and down her throat.

"Me and the girls was just discussin' you. We all think you got a smokin' body. One thing we didn't know about you is your height. How tall are you, schoolteacher? What . . . about four feet five?"

Parris looked the woman up and down, squinted her eyes, sucked her teeth, and with disdain said, "I'm four-eleven and seven-eighths."

The woman talking to Parris was tall, easily six feet two inches in height, and weighed about 170 to Parris' muscular 110.

The woman continued, "Me and the girls made a bet."

Parris knew this day was coming; the day when one of the women would approach her and try to turn her into a lesbian. She knew she was an easy target because of her size and good looks. As far as she was concerned, now was as good a time as any to show everybody what she was made of. She had been beaten and raped by a man. She wasn't about to be forced to have sex with a woman.

Before responding to the tall woman, she lifted her carton of orange juice to her lips, tilted her head back, and took a deep swallow. Afterward, she looked at the woman and said, "Oh, really? And I bet an educated ho like you bet every dime you had, didn't you?"

Suddenly, the buzz of friendly conversation that filled the cafeteria fell silent. The woman talking to Parris was the leader of a rape gang called the Double Deuces. They had turned out nearly every woman at Norrell. Lesbianism was a way of life, and rarely did any inmates escape this fate. Either the women were lesbians when they came in, or the gangs turned them into lesbians before they left.

Parris turned her orange juice carton up, tilted her head back once more, and swallowed.

The tall woman said, "I love a feisty woman. Makes me slippery as hell. Now, here's what I bet. I bet that you could lick my pussy while standing completely erect."

The other prisoners were beside themselves with laughter.

The guards watched it all, saying nothing, doing nothing, knowing what was going on between the two women. Limited anarchy was a form of control in the corrupt prison. The warden and the guards knew, and gave the gangs plenty of room to operate as long as peace prevailed. Once the new arrivals understood who was in charge and what was expected of them, they easily fell into a routine and didn't cause any problems.

Parris said, "Oh, I can definitely do that, but not with you." She attempted to take another swallow of her orange juice.

The tall woman slapped the carton out of her hand. Juice ran down Parris' nose and she choked a bit, coughing uncontrollably for about ten seconds. While she was still coughing, the tall woman hiked up her prison dress and exposed her white prison-issued panties. The inmates were beside themselves with glee, cheering her on. With her thumbs, she eased her panties over her wide hips, down her thighs, over her knees, and let them drop to her ankles.

She gracefully stepped out of them, as if she were Dorothy from the *Wizard of Oz* stepping out of her ruby red shoes, and left them on the floor. Then, while Parris was still coughing, she pulled up her dress again with one hand, grabbed Parris by the back of the head with the other, and forced Parris' face into her crotch. Uproarious laughter filled the cafeteria again.

The guards watched and laughed, too.

Furious rage swelled in Parris as the sweaty smell of the tall woman filled her nose and disgusted her. For some reason, thoughts of the night that Shenandoah raped her flooded her mind. She remembered it all as the tall woman grinded and pumped her face amongst unrestrained laughter and cheers. Parris could actually smell Shenandoah's cologne. She could almost feel him entering her and pumping her hard until he softened.

Flashes of what happened at Nelson's house replaced the images of Shenandoah. As far as she was concerned, he, too, had used her, stuck his tool in her, pumped her, and made her remember what it was like when things were good between them. The sensation his tool provided almost made her forget the brutal rape, but he snatched away the throbbing pleasure-giver when she was on the verge of erotic bliss.

Now, here she was, in prison, and yet another person sought to take what was hers and use it when and as often as she pleased with little to no regard for how Parris felt about it—right in front of everyone. The humiliation of having her face forced into another woman's smelly vagina was the last damn straw! Parris opened her mouth and found the tall woman's spot, gave her pleasure in front of the entire cafeteria crowd, who cheered mindlessly at the spectacle. Then, she bit into the women's swelled pleasure center until blood flowed into her mouth.

The women watched in shock and awe as little Parris Stalls viciously gnawed into the woman's sensitive flesh like a rat into wood. An agony-filled scream bounced off the walls and danced in the minds of all who watched the savagery, unable to move, yet unable to look away. The power of the scene, the raw nature of it, held them in their seats like a David Copperfield disappearing act.

Just as Parris knew the tall woman would, she swung her fist at Parris' head. With each impact of the stinging blows, Parris bit down even harder, shaking her head as she gnawed, growling like a ravenous wolf, until the woman's knees began to buckle from the agony. Parris released her, balled her fist, and hit her would-be rapist, who was now doubled over and clutching her badly bleeding flesh, in the face with a wicked uppercut. The woman stumbled backward a few feet, attempting to regain her balance, but couldn't. As she fell, she hit her head on the corner of a table, which sunk into her skull, killing her instantly—shades of David and Goliath.

As the tall woman's blood poured out of her head, the inmates banged their fists on the table, stomped their feet in a synchronized cadence, and shouted as if they were in a Roman Coliseum, having watched the long-awaited vanquishing of a ruthless, horrible foe. "Schoolteacher! School-teacher! Schoolteacher! Schoolteacher! Schoolteacher! Schoolteacher!"

Parris picked up the woman's panties, walked over to her dead body, and stuffed them into her mouth. She turned to walk away, but then, as if she was overcome by anger, she turned back and kicked the dead woman in the face.

And thus, the new queen of Norrell was born.

Chapter 39

After spending seventy-two hours in isolation, Parris was back in her cell, lying on her bed, quietly weeping so no one could hear. She had three days to cry by herself, but three days didn't even come close to the time she needed to reconcile with what she had done to the woman who threatened to turn her out.

Even though Shenandoah had taught her about insider trading, which ultimately led to her incarceration, she blamed the man she loved—Nelson.

She had made it so simple for him. All Nelson had to do was take her on a cruise and make love to her, which is what he wanted anyway. Then, she wouldn't have used the money to invest in Software Unlimited. Without the money he had paid to rid himself of her, she wouldn't have been tempted to buy so much stock all at one time, which sent up flares the Securities and Exchange Commission could not ignore.

She remembered how he looked at her in her attorney's firm's conference room. She could see the lust in his eyes. She remembered how he'd showed her compassion when she went to him the night she was raped, and how quickly they ended up in his bed.

Though she had tried and tried, she couldn't figure out why he pulled himself out of her when only moments before, he was enjoying the sex they both missed. She believed he still loved her. Otherwise, why was he so upset the night they joined? And why was he still upset in her attorney's office? It wasn't just the money, she thought. Somehow, his last words to her magically reverberated in her mind like sound waves.

How am I ever supposed to forgive and forget that, Parris—any of it?

She then realized it was the humiliation that made it easy to pay her off, even though he wanted to slide inside her familiar sheath. He was weak, she concluded. Otherwise, why did he let a woman push him around? A little woman, at that.

Now that she had killed someone, she blamed him for that memory, too. For three days and three nights, in the quiet, in the dark, in the filth of isolation, bitterness sprang forth and took root, yet she loved him nonetheless—a thin line.

She was glad, too, because bitterness would make her strong and harden her against what was to come. She had killed a gang leader, and surely, there would be reprisals. She couldn't afford to be weak, not right now, not while she was in Norrell. She would have to defend herself again to survive, she thought. And when she'd paid her debt to society, she would seek out Nelson and make him come to his senses. That's when she began formulating her plan to win him back, if possible. If that didn't work, coercion was always an option.

He paid once and he'll pay again, she thought.

"Hi, schoolteacher," someone said in a pleasant female voice.

Parris lifted her head to see who was intruding on her space and time of contemplation, especially since she was thinking of ways to get Nelson back. The woman looking down at her was pretty, but a bit on the frail side. Parris thought she could take her easily if it came down to another brawl. Besides, the woman was probably afraid after what she'd seen in the cafeteria three days earlier.

Parris decided to flex her newly acquired muscles by saying, "Get lost, bitch!"

"I'd love to get lost, but unfortunately, I can't. I've been assigned to this cell as your property, and you own the rights to me."

Unable to believe her ears, Parris said, "My what?"

"I'm your slave, schoolteacher," the woman said in a matter-of-fact tone. "I'll do whatever you want, whenever you want. I'll keep the house clean, iron your clothes, get your meals for you, and pleasure you whenever you want."

Parris kinda laughed, unable to accept the words that had entered her twin portals. The woman before her was a nut; she had to be to accept slavery as a way of life. Even if she was forced into lesbianism, who, other than a crazy person, would call themselves a slave so cavalierly?

"Please don't laugh at me, schoolteacher," the woman continued. "Please take what I'm saying very seriously. You're in a different world. You don't know the rules. You don't know how things work in this hell they call Norrell. If you want to get out of here alive, you had better learn to play the game."

"The game?"

"The game, the life, whatever you want to call it. The women here are more vicious than any woman you ever thought was your enemy. If you don't listen to me, we'll both be dead before the end of the week."

Parris sat up and looked the woman in her dark eyes, wondering if this was some sort of trick. Was the woman sent to her as a plant? Was she there to spy and report back to her friends, letting them know when Parris was most vulnerable? She wasn't sure. She needed more information. "Who are the 'they' you speak of?"

"The Double Deuces. You killed their leader. No matter what, they have to do something, or the other gangs will think they're weak and more women will die. Everybody's depending on you to keep a war from happening, and the only way to do that is to listen to what I'm telling you. You must let me be your slave. Everyone has to know I'm your mistress, and they have to know tonight, or we're both through. Do you understand?"

"Why are the women depending on me? What can I do?"

"Schoolteacher, you gotta understand that all the gangs are at war with each other. There was a truce until you killed the leader of the Double Deuces. There needs to be a balance of power. Once the war breaks out, the killing will be indiscriminate. And the guards won't stop it until most of us are dead or close to it. They'll watch us stab each other, they'll watch us tear each other apart, and do nothing to stop it because they have families and their priority is to make it through the day and get home in one piece. They won't risk their necks to keep a few lesbians alive."

Parris stared at her, trying to discern whether she could trust the woman who wanted to be her slave. Then it occurred to her that she didn't even know her name. "What's your name?"

"Whatever you name me," the woman said. "I'm yours to do with as you will. If you want to stud me for credit, you can. I can get you a lot of credit because I'm in high demand."

Parris shook her head, still stunned by the offer of having her very own slave. The thought of it was completely preposterous. Was this woman actually offering to prostitute herself if Parris wanted her to? She wondered what kind of upside down world she was in. Then it occurred to her that Judge

Keenan had given her three chances to avoid this place. She wished she had taken the judge up on her offer.

Parris didn't know that if she had confessed to extortion, which would have been a violation of the agreement she signed, Judge Keenan, at the behest of Sterling Wise, would have been well within her rights, and added to Parris' sentence. She still would have been in Norrell, only longer.

"What's your name?"

"Tracy."

"Okay, Tracy, explain the rules to me."

Chapter 40

When I learned of Parris' and Shenandoah's incarceration, I was happy they had finally gotten what they deserved. Nevertheless, I was still very bitter about what she did, accusing me of raping her and extorting more than five hundred thousand dollars from me when you add in the attorney fees. He raped her, she raped me, now they were both probably being raped. I wouldn't normally wish that on anyone, but somehow, those two being in prison, which was where she had threatened to put me, seemed fair, as if there was actually justice in America.

More importantly, I was finally free of all the emotional entanglements that kept me longing for Parris. Over the days and months, I realized why I had been so attached to her. It was the sex and the love I felt for her, combined. That's what I believed, anyway.

With all the money I acquired from the Software Unlimited/Datatech Computers merger, I knew I had to be very careful with women. So, I made a radical decision. I decided I wasn't going to have sex anymore until I was ready to get married to a worthy woman.

At first, abstaining from sex was extremely difficult. Sex was like an addictive drug. A fiery rage, which was my body's demand for sex, boiled deep inside me after I made the decision to abstain. It's funny now when I look back on it. All by themselves, my eyes kept finding breasts and butts of all shapes and sizes. It's like they were everywhere I looked. Seven days into my commitment to abstinence, I was feeling seriously deprived. I needed my "medicine" badly. The funny thing about it was that this wasn't my first time going without sex for seven days. I'd gone much longer than that before. What the hell was happening to me? Three weeks into it, I wanted to bed just about every woman I saw. It didn't matter how she looked. I was in trouble—a lot of it.

My first thought was to hook back up with Rachel Radcliff, the glamorously beautiful, high-priced prostitute I'd met in Las Vegas and was seeing on and off for a while. I didn't want to get attached to her again, so I hired some local "professionals" to meet my needs. I had even convinced myself it was better in the long run. Call girls served a public need, my need to get laid, to be exact. That way, when I took women out, sex wouldn't constantly plague my mind. I wouldn't have to fight the internal struggle of my sexual desires. I would be in control, which was essential if I was going to find the right woman.

So, I hired a beautiful, high-class escort to take care of my sex problem. The next thing I knew, I was hiring escorts, two and three at a time, having wild sex with them nearly every night. Obviously, the escort thing wasn't helping matters. While I was bedding them every night, I didn't bother to seek out eligible women to date and perhaps marry. That meant I had to go cold turkey or run the risk of getting physically attached to someone and then find out later it wasn't going to work. The idea of going completely without sex was daunting to say the least, but it was something I knew I had to do. So, I suffered through a long withdrawal—six months.

During that six-month period, I didn't date at all. I couldn't. Sex, sex, sex . . . that's all I could think about. Instead, I threw myself into my business. Without even realizing it, each day I went without, I became stronger and stronger until I was in complete control. I still had a desire for sex, but I didn't *have* to have it. Feeling it was safe to start dating again, I let every woman know up front that I was abstaining from sex.

"I admire that," they all said, but disregarded my self-imposed celibacy and tried to bed me anyway.

I must have broken it off with more than twenty women when I realized it wasn't going to work. I was just starting to trust myself, and if a woman couldn't maintain her chastity when I had suffered through what I thought was a long withdrawal, I knew she wouldn't be able to commit to me alone. In other words, when the sex got old, she would simply find another man to screw.

I guess that's okay when you're broke and have nothing to lose except the woman you love, but when you're worth thirty million and live in California, you lose the woman you love *and* fifteen million dollars. And I just couldn't see myself forking over half my fortune, which was still growing, especially after being extorted for half a million dollars and change.

So, I was firing potential mates left and right, kicking fine women to the curb at will. Just before I dropped the bomb on them, I always wondered if I was getting rid of the wrong one. Then each one of them would say, "Nelson, I hope you find what you're looking for." Translation: "If I'm not what you want, nobody is." These famous last words were the personification of hubris. And when they said them, I knew I did the right thing for both of us. I wasn't trying to be nasty; I was only protecting myself and my fortune. Can you blame me?

The majority of the women who found me attractive were

good- looking, but they were broke as hell. It turns out these broke women were a bunch of losers who saw me as an easy way to riches, and I wasn't having it. They wanted a man who had something on the ball, whether he had money, position, prestige, or an exceptional education. In other words, the man had to be much better off than she was. Translation: the women I was dating at the time wanted the extravagant life I could give them, not me. Which reminded me of something I had learned in a social studies class many moons ago: Women marry up; men marry down. However, I was about to change that dynamic.

I needed something real in my life, and I didn't want to marry the kind of women I was dating. I started thinking more like them. Why should I date a woman who has nothing to offer me? If women wanted what I had to offer, I wanted something more than sex out of the deal. As crass as it sounds, I could get sex whenever I wanted it, just like a woman. When you have money, sex finds you. You don't have to seek it.

Very few of the women were bringing anything to the table, and those that did, for a variety of reasons, our personalities tended to clash. I didn't bother trying to work it out with these women because I knew I'd only end up being miserable—her, too. The only thing worse than being broke and miserable was being rich and miserable.

Chapter 41

More than over a year had passed, and I wasn't any closer to finding a worthy woman to be my mate for life. I was nearly ready to give up until Sterling sent me an invitation to a business "Nite Out" in San Francisco, which was a special gathering of black professionals from the state of California who came together to network. I was definitely going. I had one intention—find a woman to marry. I thought it would be a lot easier with hundreds, perhaps thousands of black businesswomen at this event. I was going to find the needle in the haystack, the triple threat, a woman with brains, a thick financial portfolio, and incredible beauty.

The event was being held at the Westin St. Francis Hotel in San Francisco. I thought it would probably be my last chance to find the woman who would have my babies. I didn't know if I could remain a nonsexual being forever. This gathering was going to be the opportunity of a lifetime. In my heart, I knew I'd find my wife there. I was very excited; so excited, in fact, that I had my tailor make a new tuxedo just so I could make an immediate impression on some dark-skinned lovely who would end up being my bride.

There I was, all five feet nine inches of me, dressed in a black tux, offset by a red velvet vest and Ascot tie, looking for the woman I was going to marry. I must have talked to a hundred women, giving them my business card and taking theirs. Then I saw a familiar face in the crowd, and she was drop-dead gorgeous. It was Rachel Radcliff. I figured she must have been working in the hotel or something and slipped in to check things out. Plus, I was thinking that if I ended up leaving empty- handed, I could always make an appointment with Rachel, because I wasn't about to spend any more lonely nights at home.

I stared at her from across the room, admiring her beauty from afar. She was talking to some guy I'd never seen before, so I waited until he left and walked up behind her.

"Hi, Rachel," I said.

The woman turned around. It wasn't Rachel, but from across the room, she looked just like her. Up close, she looked like her, too, like they could be sisters, but I could easily tell them apart. She was wearing a black skirt suit, white blouse, black pumps, and a Paula Abdul smile.

"Oh, sorry about that," I offered. "You look just like a friend of mine from Vegas."

I started to walk away.

"I'm sorry I'm not Rachel, Mister . . ."

"Kennard," I finished her sentence, giving her the answer she sought.

She offered me her hand. "I'm Jamie Stansfield. Nice to meet you. Do you come to these things often?"

I took her soft hand in mine and shook it. "This is my first one."

"Mine, too," she said.

I made small talk for a bit, while I thought of an excuse to get away from her. She was attractive and all, but she reminded me too much of Rachel Radcliff. That bothered me for some reason, even though she wasn't Rachel.

But when I turned to leave, she said, "What's your hurry?"

"Well, I thought I'd mingle a little more."

"Aren't you out of cards? I saw you passing them out to half the women here."

Jamie Stansfield was aggressive. I got the feeling she knew what she wanted. I liked that about her. The ice I was encased in began to melt. As we talked, I found myself more and more attracted to her. I wanted this woman. Thankfully, I remembered my objective and harnessed my passion.

We went outside to get away from the crowd, and talked for a while. When we felt the chill of the San Francisco air, we exchanged business cards. It turned out that Ms. Stansfield was one of the best independent anesthesiologists in the country. Impressive. Very impressive indeed. She had also graduated from Columbia University, magna cum laude. I learned quite a bit about her during our conversation.

I couldn't wait to call her to learn more, but I would. I figured a month would be sufficient. When we went back inside to warm ourselves, I excused myself to go to the restroom and when I came out, she was surrounded by what looked to be about twenty men. I would have gone over, but the brothas were all up on the woman. I never understood why men hovered over beautiful women like vultures, waiting to eat their flesh.

I had found what I was looking for, so I left. Jamie stood out in a crowd, and I knew there would be a line around the corner trying to get her. I counted the days, marking off each one with a black marker. Twenty-six days passed, and out of the blue, Ms. Stansfield called my office.

Chapter 42

I hate to admit it, but I played an innocent little game with her. I didn't want her to think she could get me on the phone at her convenience, so I told my receptionist to take a message. Why the games? If I wanted an educated woman who was not only beautiful, but also had her own money, why play games with her instead of going for what I wanted? The truth of it is this: Ms. Stansfield could have any man she wanted. I wanted her to want me, *for me*, period.

The night we met, we had both asked some very straightforward questions about each other. I learned that Jamie Stansfield had been divorced for six years, had a daughter attending Georgetown law school, lived in Sausalito, and was pulling down more than four hundred thousand dollars a year. Everything I was looking for, right? What was I waiting for? Again, Jamie could have any man she wanted . . . and there were a lot of them all over her. I couldn't really blame them, either. Not only was she pretty, but she had the rich chocolate skin, too. Damn! Who wouldn't be all over that?

If Jamie realized she hadn't found any real prospects that night at the Westin St. Francis, she might be more receptive to the man who didn't call her immediately, looking for a quick roll in the hay. Anyway, she left her home number and wanted me to call her later that evening. At first, I was pumped. Then my heart rate slowed down as it occurred to me that her call could've been pertaining to business. No romance.

At about seven o'clock, I called her home, hoping she would be there. I didn't want to leave a message on her answering machine.

"Hello," she answered. Her voice was refined, smooth, and sexy.

"This is Nelson Kennard," I said in a businesslike tone, "returning your call."

"What kind of game are you playing with me, Mr. Kennard?"

"Excuse me?"

"I thought we made a connection that night at the Westin St. Francis. Was I mistaken?"

Silence.

"I know you're there, Nelson. I can hear you breathing."

I was quiet because I didn't know what to say. She was being so forward, not that I was intimidated, but I was a little stunned. "A game?"

"Yes, a game. And you haven't answered my question."

"What question was that?"

She exhaled into the phone. "Was I mistaken? I waited as long as I could for you to call me and you never did. I assumed you saw all those handsome gentlemen talking to me that night and moved on. I considered not calling you, but then I thought, why not call him? It's allowed these days, isn't it?"

Hesitantly, I said, "Yes, it is."

"Good, because I wouldn't want to pass up a good thing, would you?"

"So, you're a good thing, Ms. Stansfield?" I asked the question for one reason only. I wanted to see if she was going to tell me that she was this great woman and how she couldn't find a "good" black man . . . blah, blah, blah. She didn't know it, but if she had tried to convince me that she was this fabulous woman, like so many others had before her, I would have headed for the hills. To me, any woman who has to tell a man she's a great woman probably isn't, especially if she doesn't have a man.

"You'll have to be the judge of that, Mr. Kennard."

"When can the day of judgment begin?" I asked, relieved she hadn't tried to persuade me.

"How about tonight? I can meet you at the Compass Rose restaurant in an hour or so. And Nelson, please, no games, okay? If you don't want to meet, please say so. I'm a big girl. I can handle it."

I liked Jamie Stansfield right off. She was obviously intelligent, witty, and aggressive. But more importantly, she had her own shit. "In an hour," I said with a laugh. "No games, either. Just so you know, I'm practicing celibacy. I haven't had sex in a year. Is that going to be a problem?"

"Celibacy, huh? In that case, maybe we shouldn't meet at a hotel restaurant."

For a moment or two, I thought she was serious. Then she laughed.

I laughed, too.

Chapter 43

Six months later, we were madly in love. We were spending nearly all our free time together, which wasn't much, since she was always in and out of surgery and I was still expanding Kennard Janitorial Services east. A busy schedule notwithstanding, my life was new and special. I looked forward to the five-minute phone calls between surgeries, the late night conversations that went on much longer than either one of us could afford due to our busy schedules. I had forgotten all about Parris and Shenandoah. They weren't even in my memory banks anymore. Jamie was the only woman who occupied my mind now.

I was very happy, but it was a real struggle to remain celibate. We needed to spend some uninterrupted time together, somewhere far away, someplace where our office and cell phones couldn't reach us even if Islamic Fundamentalists detonated a nuclear device. I'm exaggerating, of course, but we really needed the time away from everything and everybody who knew us.

Even though we were both busy, we were our own bosses, which meant we could take the time to go on a long vacation together. To celebrate our six-month anniversary, I decided to take Jamie on a thirty-day cruise from Los Angeles to Sydney, Australia. I booked the penthouse suite of the Sapphire Princess. It ended up being an expensive trip, costing nearly forty-five thousand dollars, but it was something I definitely wanted to do—Jamie, too.

The penthouse was lavishly decorated, affording us every amenity, with room to move without bumping into each other. The first night, after dinner, we danced for what seemed like hours. Then we went out on the sundeck, sat in recliners, held hands, and chatted. It was breathtaking to see the heavens from the deck of the Sapphire Princess, surrounded by nothing but sea and a cloudless, star-filled midnight sky. After an hour or so, we went back to the penthouse and relaxed.

Jamie put a romantic CD she had burned in the stereo carousel and we went out on the veranda, where we drank Courvoisier and chatted a little more as we floated on the South Pacific. Twenty minutes later, Donnie Hathaway and Robert Flack's "The Closer I Get to You" filled the suite. I took Jamie by the hand and led her back inside, where we danced to the romantic tune. The next song was Skyy's "It's Real Love." The chorus seemed to be perfect for what I was feeling.

Don't be afraid of the way you feel.
Open your heart and you'll see . . . it's real love.

We looked into each other's eyes. Electricity. The words had gotten to me. The whole night was magical and perfect. I loved this woman. I kissed her. A light, teasing kiss at first, but then we got caught up, pulled in by our desire to become one flesh. My mind was telling me to stop, and I had the strength to do so. I wasn't so far gone that I couldn't stop myself. A year ago, I would have been powerless, but now, I was still strong, still in complete control of my body.

The moment was right and I wanted this. So did she. So

we plundered each other savagely, recklessly, evoking erotic desires and exquisite sensations. After we finished, as we basked in the glow of physical love, I wondered if it was only that good because I hadn't made love in eighteen months. Then I thought, so what? We were in love. That's all that mattered. We made love every day, sometimes two or three times a day. By the time we left Los Angeles, which was our port of call, I knew Jamie Stansfield was the woman I was going to marry.

On the plane back to Los Angeles from Sydney, I asked her to marry me. She accepted. I know it wasn't the most romantic way to ask for a woman's hand in marriage, but that's how it happened. When we landed, I rented a car and drove to Cartier on Rodeo Drive in Beverly Hills and bought Jamie a ten-karat Trinity solitaire diamond with three gold rings to express my commitment to her. The colors were yellow—faithfulness; white—friendship; gold—love.

Jamie was completely overwhelmed. It was going to take some doing, but we were going to try to plan a wedding in six months. We were going to be married at the Westin St. Francis Hotel, where we met.

Chapter 44

A week after Jamie and I flew in from Sydney, Sterling called and asked me to take him to the airport. He was going to Washington, DC, again, supposedly to work on a contract for one of his clients who played for the Redskins, but I suspected he was going to see his FBI bed partner, Kelly McPherson, again.

When I walked into his office, Sterling was sitting in the chair behind his desk, facing the window, looking toward the Golden Gate Bridge. He swiveled the chair around and faced me with an enraged look, like he could kill someone. I wondered what had happened, hoping the news wasn't as serious as the expression Sterling wore.

"Sit down," he said somberly.

Concerned, I said, "What's wrong, man?"

"Sky," he began, using my nickname, "I got some bad news, bro."

"What's wrong?" I repeated.

"It's ya girl, Jamie Stansfield. I had her checked out when you left the country. All that shit you were telling me about her is bullshit, man."

Stunned and confused, I said, "What do you mean? And why were you checking on her?"

"It never hurts to check people out, Sky, especially when they're too good to be true; particularly when you're considering marriage and you're a millionaire thirty times over."

"I never told you I was going to marry her."

"You didn't have to. It's easy to spot a man in love. And the way you talked about her, I was suspicious. Do you remember me telling you that Kelly's partner is a woman named Phoenix Perry?"

I nodded. I remembered Sterling had told me that Phoenix Perry saved his life in the summer of 2001 when a lethal assassin named Coco Nimburu tried to kill him.

"Well, Phoenix's husband is a private investigator," Sterling continued, "and I hired Keyth to check Jamie out. If I hadn't found anything, I wouldn't have said anything. But I did. Jamie Stansfield is a fraud. That's the bottom line."

His penetrating words felt like a butcher's knife had been plunged into my chest. Nervously, I said, "What are you saying? She's not an anesthesiologist?"

"Her being an anesthesiologist is the one scrape of truth in all of this. The woman's got a gambling problem, a drug problem, and a sex problem. To top that shit off, she's deeply in debt. I'm talkin' way over her head. Debts you're going to have to absorb if you marry her."

Sex problem? For whatever reason, even though I had heard every word my friend had said, sex problem were the only words that stuck in my mind. I had been having great sex with Jamie on a regular basis for over a month. As far as I was concerned, there was definitely no problem.

I looked Sterling in the eyes and said, "What kind of sex problem?"

"The worst kind. She's messing around on you, bro."

I sat there, thinking while staring at the floor as the reality of his words flooded my mind. Finally, I said, "I suppose you've got proof of this?"

"Live and in living color," he said, picking up a DVD and tossing it to me.

I caught the disc. Instinctively, I said, "What's this?"

"There's enough evidence on the disc for me to tell you to get an AIDS test immediately. I know you love this woman, and this isn't the easiest thing for me to tell you, but if I were you, knowing what I know . . ." He paused for a long moment. "I would not look at that disc. Take my word for it."

It turns out he didn't really need a ride to the airport after all. He just needed the excuse to get me into his office so he could drop the bomb on me man to man, face to face. I have a lot of respect for the way he handled it, too.

I've learned over the years that most people don't want to hear the truth or don't tell it because the truth causes problems. The truth makes people angry and resentful. In fact, the truth often causes the recipient to resent the person who told them a truth they didn't want to hear. Ignorance is truly bliss for them, I guess. Me, I'd much rather know and deal with it as best I can.

I left Sterling's office dazed and confused. On my way home, I tried to reason it all out. Was Jamie messing around? If she wasn't, why would Sterling lie? What was on the disc? Deep down, I knew what was on it.

Once home, I sat on the couch in my den, lightly tapping the disc on my knee, debating whether I would slide it into my DVD player. I picked up my big screen remote and hit the power button. Then, I went to the player and slid in the disc. What I saw forced the breath from my lungs as my body felt as though it was imploding.

Chapter 45

The woman I loved and was going to marry had snorted two lines of cocaine and was having unprotected sex in her bedroom with some guy I didn't recognize. Hearing about infidelity is one thing, but to witness the object of your affection in the raw getting buck wild and loving it takes that shit to a whole new level—you feel me? The room spun and I slumped against the couch, my eyes glued to the screen. It looked like my fiancée was starring in a pornographic film.

I had deprived myself of sex in hopes of finding a woman who believed in the same values, and ended up engaged to a straight up HO! I looked at the date and time the film was recorded and realized that what I was viewing had happened almost as soon as I dropped her off when we returned from the cruise. Sterling's private investigator must have wired her house when we were out of the country. Just when I thought it couldn't get any worse, the man started giving Jamie orders.

"Turnover, goddammit! I'm going to take you from the back." Before I knew it, Jamie was on her knees, with her exquisite ass in the air, ready for rear entry. My mouth dropped.

As the man thrust himself inside my fiancée, he said, "Did Nelson give it to you like this on the Sapphire Princess?"

He knows who I am? What the fuck is going on?

The man continued talking. "But this is *my* pussy, ain't it?"

"Yes, yes, oh, yes," Jamie answered, gasping, strangling the sheets as he pumped her ferociously.

When she answered him, his thrusts became more powerful. The man snarled and his face twisted into an angry mask each time he pumped my fiancée, as if he was jealous of the sex we'd had together on the ship. Jamie's body surged forward from his forceful thrusts.

"Hell naw, bitch!" The man screamed at her. "Say that shit! I wanna hear the words, goddammit!"

"This is your pussy," she gasped while thrusting her body backward to meet his tool. "Get it. Get your pussy. Get all of it."

Two minutes later, she came loudly, and I realized she had never climaxed with me on the ship—not one time. I froze the film at the point when my fiancée was coming, closed my eyes, and wept for what seemed like an eternity.

While I wept, I thought of Parris and Shenandoah for— the first time in a very long time. The whole thing was replaying in my mind again, and I was powerless to stop it. I had gone without sex for a year and a half, had learned to control my body, but I had no control over the images that coursed through my mind and made me feel like the loser Parris had called me so many months ago.

Chapter 46

Three hours later, I woke up, still on my couch. I opened my eyes and saw Jamie's face frozen on my television screen, her expression twisted as she had what looked like an incredible orgasm. I was still very much injured by her diabolical betrayal. What kind of woman could go on a thirty-day cruise with her man, make passionate love to him every day, accept his hand in marriage, and moments after being taken home, open her legs to another man?

I picked up the DVD remote to shut off the picture. I had seen more than enough. I accidentally pushed the play button, and the nightmare began again. That's when it occurred to me that Sterling had said she was a fraud. I watched Jamie and the man collapse on the bed, exhausted from their vigorous activity. Thank God it was over. A few minutes later, when their breathing slowed, they talked.

"So, how much is that ring worth?" the man asked.

"One hundred and twenty-five thousand," Jamie answered.

"Yeah, he's a sho' nuff fool, ain't he? You musta sucked his dick for him to spend that kinda money on you." Jamie didn't respond. The man snatched her by the hair, and forced her to look at him. "Did you suck his dick?"

"No, baby," Jamie said. "I only do that for you. You know that."

The man still had his hand in her thick hair. He pushed her head down to his genitals, and she took him into her mouth. I shook my head and exhaled. Don't ask me why, but I couldn't turn off the film. The engagement ring I had given her sparkled as she lovingly caressed his thighs and stomach. I just sat there, dumbfounded by what I was seeing. Jamie Stansfield, my beautiful fiancée, the love of my life, was giving what looked like world-class head.

I've had blowjobs before, so I know the difference. She didn't blow me, but she was blowing this guy like *he* gave her the damn ring. What bothered me even more was that she never even washed his genitals before taking him into her mouth. *Damn!* Five minutes later, the man came and she swallowed. That's when I ran to the bathroom and threw up violently. As I was coming back to the den, I could hear them talking again.

"So, how was Nelson in bed?" the man asked.

"Pathetic . . . a real loser. I almost felt sorry for the fool. In six months, I'll be rich."

"You fuckin' bitch!" I screamed at the screen. "Rich, huh? We'll see about that shit."

I called Sterling at his office, but his receptionist told me he was on his way to Washington, DC. I called him later that evening on his cell and told him I needed the number of the investigative firm that had gotten the goods on Jamie. Drew Perry Investigative Firm was the name of the agency, and Keyth Perry headed the organization.

Chapter 47

I called Jamie and told her I thought we should cool it on the sex until our wedding night, reminding her of my eighteen-month celibate lifestyle prior to making love to her. The bitch sounded relieved. I guess that's when the seed of killing her was planted in my heart and started to grow. After finishing the conversation with Jamie, I called Suzanne Mays, my doctor, and made an appointment to be tested for AIDS.

Over the next two weeks, as I waited for the results of my test, I plotted my revenge. I was going to teach Jamie Stansfield a lesson she would never forget. In the meantime, I made it easy for Jamie to see her boyfriend. I decided to get out of San Francisco for a while and went to the San Diego office to heal, but it never happened. In fact, I became hard and callous, immeasurably bitter about it all. Part of the bitterness I felt had much to do with what Parris and Shenandoah had done. I thought I had moved on, thought I had forgotten her wicked betrayal, but I hadn't.

I watched my fiancée's porno flick over and over until I could watch her have sex with another man and not feel a thing. I was completely numb. Jamie had ripped my heart out and served it to me like she was Hannibal Lecter.

My mind turned into a block of ice. I had become the living personification of Antarctica. Killing her was going to be so damn delightful. Hell, they oughta give me a fucking medal. Murder was a simple task if you hated the person enough. Getting away with murder, well, that took meticulous planning. Accounting for everything that could possibly go wrong was nearly impossible. But I was going to do it. I had six months to figure out how. Somebody had to hold these greedy hoes accountable for their actions. Unabated anger and bitterness were the catalysts that had driven me to this ultimate conclusion.

I considered flying Keyth Perry out to San Diego for the weekend so my fiancée could "play." I wanted to meet him and arrange 24/7 surveillance on Jamie. I wanted to know it all, which would strengthen my formidable resolve to kill her. But it occurred to me that I had to keep him out of it as much as possible, since I was going to commit cold-blooded, calculated murder.

Jamie was in Vegas at the Mandalay Bay Hotel and Casino, probably with her boyfriend, getting cash from the credit card I had given her to pay for the wedding. So, I contacted the Alex Jefferson Investigative Firm in Las Vegas to arrange the surveillance.

Jefferson faxed proof of Jamie's debts to my hotel suite. She owed over six hundred thousand dollars, nearly twice what she earned in a year, and was still spending like there was no tomorrow. She must have believed I would quietly pay the debt. After all, she had me wrapped around her finger, didn't she? Another fax printed and slid into my incoming faxes basket.

Next, I turned on my laptop and opened my AOL account. Jefferson had emailed me several photographs of Jamie buying drugs and snorting cocaine. He assured me that he could tap her cell so I would be able to listen to her calls live.

I could tell Jefferson wanted to ask me why I didn't break it off. He wanted to know why I was going through all of this. But he never asked, probably because I was paying him a bundle. Why piss off the goose laying the golden eggs?

The reason I refused to break it off is because the shit was personal. I was going to fuck her up.

Chapter 48

Two weeks later, my doctor dropped a hydrogen bomb on me when she revealed I had the virus. That cinched it. Jamie Stansfield was living on borrowed time, but I wanted her to go on playing me for the fool, and I was going to make it incredibly easy for her. I was going to be out of town a lot. Who could blame me? I couldn't stand to be in the same room with her. Overnight, I became an Oscar-winning actor. Jamie had no idea I knew all of her dirt—at least I thought I knew it all until I viewed the latest pornographic film.

Jamie's latest erotic exploits showed her having a threesome with two men I had never seen, which meant Jamie was not only playing me, but she was playing her boyfriend, too. *BITCH!*

After hitting the pause button, and with no loss of appetite, I made a Sara Lee smoked turkey breast sandwich on wheat with melted cheese and Hormel real bacon bits sprinkled on it.

I had become a wall of granite.

My heart couldn't break anymore because I had no heart.

I poured myself a glass of apple cider, dropped in two ice cubes, and went back into the den, where I ate my sandwich and continued watching Jamie do two men at the same time. One man was taking her from the rear while she gave world-class head to yet another man and swallowed.

No tears—I just shook my head.

By this time, I couldn't wait to kill her.

And I knew just how I was going to do it, too.

Chapter 49

A week later, I called Alex Jefferson from my den and told him I no longer needed his services, knowing full well that in six months I was going to murder my fiancée. I figured that if I pulled him off the case now, if the cops ever questioned him, he could tell them I knew about the affair she was having, had told him I'd confronted her, and that we worked it out, making Jefferson and his people a dead end for the cops—that is, if they even suspected foul play.

What I had in store for Jamie was truly diabolical. Stored up anger and bitterness can do that to you if you give into it, and I did willingly. I gave into it wholeheartedly, and shortly after, my mind started thinking of creative ways to end her miserable life. For the first time, I understood why Parris did what she did. Le'sett had told me I didn't understand women, but I now knew, or at least had some understanding, of a scorned woman and what she was capable of. If I somehow got caught, the world would know what a scorned man was capable of, too.

As for Parris, I wanted to kill her, too, even though I un-

derstood how bitterness motivates a person. But killing
Parris was out of the question. As a matter of fact, if the police ever suspected I had killed Jamie, Parris would be my
unwitting stooge. She would tell the police that I had caught
her in bed with another man and was about to kill them. She
could also be subpoenaed and made to testify about the five
hundred thousand dollars I had to pay her to keep my
"good" name.

She would swear on a Holy Bible and tell the jury that I
chose to pay half a million dollars to get her out of my life
when I could have paid considerably less if I had only given
her a two-week cruise and had sex with her. Then, after
she'd served her purpose, after she had unwittingly done my
bidding I'd kill her, so she couldn't fuck over any other men.
Parris would join Jamie Stansfield in the hereafter, if there is
such a place.

My lawyer would argue it was an act in the heat of passion
when I entered Parris' house that night with my Glock after
I had seen her kissing another man. Having seen her kissing
him, having seen and heard her making love to the man,
Le'sett would argue that I *did not* commit the crime. And
since I didn't commit the crime in the heat of passion, when
I didn't have thirty million dollars to lose for doing so, why
would I do it now when I had so much to live for?

In her closing argument, after summing it all up, after
making the jury see I would never do such a thing, that I
would never, ever kill anyone, let alone the woman I just
married, Le'sett would probably ask them to put themselves
in my position that night, and ask which one of them could
have stopped himself from killing Parris Stalls and
Shenandoah Armstrong on the spot.

A jury of my peers would easily conclude that the same
man who could have killed in the heat of passion but didn't,
would not coldly plot the murder of a woman he planned to

spend the rest of his life with, knowing she had fooled around on him, when he could have simply walked away from the relationship. Why would I marry her just to kill her on our honeymoon? This wouldn't make any sense to the jury, would it? It was so perfect; so very perfect indeed.

Chapter 50

As my phone rang, I looked at the caller ID. It was my doctor's office. I let it ring a few times as I considered not answering it. What could she possibly want now? I had accepted the fact that I had the AIDS virus. Suddenly, it occurred to me that she may have settled on the treatment that would keep me alive while I dealt with all my enemies. I picked up the receiver and cheerfully said, "Hello, Dr. Mays. I bet you're calling me to discuss the treatment, right?"

"Mr. Kennard, this is Dr. Mays' office calling," the receptionist said. "Can you hold for a second or two?"

"Sure," I said.

A few seconds later, my doctor picked up the phone. "Mr. Kennard, this is Dr. Mays."

There was a long pause.

"Well . . . uh . . . uh, I've got some . . . uh, rather good news."

I remained quiet and listened.

"Uh, well, it turns out we made a mistake. Your test was mixed up with another patient's test. You don't have the virus. Isn't that wonderful news?"

"Yes, thank you, doctor," I responded in a voice absent of emotions, then hung up.

I didn't even smile when I heard the "good" news. I didn't give a fuck if I had the virus or not. I was going to fuck Jamie Stansfield up and that's all there was to it. I was that bitter about what she'd done and planned to do. I was going to be cold, calculating, and extremely violent.

I had been going over every detail, writing them down and keeping my plans for murder in a safe at my house that only I knew the combination to. Before I set the deed in motion, I planned to shred all the papers and burn them in my fireplace, leaving no trace that they ever existed.

The phone rang.

Once again, I looked at the caller ID. To my surprise, it was Grace Underwood. At first, I wasn't going to bother answering, but my curiosity got the better of me.

What could she possibly want after a year and a half? Then I thought, *Maybe she's free. Maybe she wants to give me another chance after all this time.*

After how I'd embarrassed her, I thought the least I could do was take her call.

"Hello, Grace," I said, faking cheerful glee. "How are you?"

I wanted to be as careful as possible. I didn't want anyone to be able to say I was ever in a foul mood if the police came questioning them. I wanted everybody to think I was the happiest man on the planet. Sterling thought I was nuts for even considering marriage after what he'd seen on the DVD, and tried talking me out of it. He was going to make an excellent witness, too—that is, if the police ever suspected me.

I could tell Grace was smiling when she said, "Caller ID is a marvelous invention, don't you think?"

I forced myself to smile, too. People can always tell when someone is smiling over the phone. "Yes, it sure is. How have you been? I always wondered what happened to you."

"Really? I've always wondered the same about you."

Still smiling, I said, "I came by your place after that incident at the Metro Theater, and I saw a man coming out of your home. You had told me you wouldn't wait for me, and I figured you didn't. I never figured out why a beautiful, intelligent, giving woman like you was alone in the first place. But I also knew that for those same reasons, you wouldn't be alone much longer. To be honest, I knew I wasn't ready for a relationship with you, and was kinda glad you'd found someone. You deserved it, especially after that incident."

Grace remained quiet for a long, uncomfortable moment.

"If you feel that way, why don't you come by? I'll fix you dinner and we can watch *Pretty Woman* again. How does that sound? Also, I have something to tell you."

"You mean to tell me you're alone again? That guy must have been a colossal idiot to let you get away. I thought you would be married by now."

"I've been married before, Nelson. My husband was a *very* good man. He died about two years ago, six months before I started working at the bank."

A part of me wanted to call off the hit and take Grace up on her offer, but I was so angry and so bitter that those two emotions now controlled what was to become of me. As much as I wanted to say, "I'll be right over," the words couldn't find their way out of my mouth.

Instead, I said, "Grace, I'm engaged."

I heard her gasp.

Then she offered me an insincere, "Congratulations," followed immediately by, "Uh, Nelson . . . uh . . . my dinner is burning. Can I call you back?"

"Sure," I said, knowing I would never hear from this woman again.

Chapter 51

Poor Jamie Stansfield. She must have thought that all she had to do was consummate the marriage, live with me for a few months, and then take half my shit. Well, I wasn't having it. I had fooled Jamie for six months, had her believing we were going on another thirty-day cruise. She told me she would handle the wedding plans and I could handle the honeymoon. Imagine that. She was going to let *me* handle the honeymoon. The bitch had obviously forgotten that this was *my* money, not hers. I was going to give her a honeymoon, all right.

Jamie spent two hundred thousand dollars on our wedding, which took place at the Westin St. Francis, and I must say it was a marvelous affair. Three months before the nuptials, I flew to Miami and bought a warehouse near the airport, where I put the equipment I'd need—overalls, a spade shovel, a jackhammer, cement mix, a big screen TV, DVD player, and an array of tools I was going to torture her with before I killed her.

After our plane landed, I rented a car to drive to the

hotel. On the way, I said to my blushing bride, "Did I ever tell you about the warehouse I purchased down here?"

"A warehouse? Why did you do that?"

"Kennard Janitorial is still expanding, sweetheart. I thought it would be smart to have our own warehouse and have a centralized operation that supplied all our people."

"Sure, let's see it," Jamie said, falling into my trap like a rat going after what he thinks is free cheese. "And then we can get to the hotel and take care of business. I know you gotta be horny as hell by now." She laughed.

Bitch!

Jamie had no reason to be suspicious. I was an Oscar-winning actor, remember? Better than Sidney Poitier, better than Morgan Freeman, and definitely better than Denzel Washington. They would all have been envious of my performance, I'm sure.

On the way to the warehouse, Jamie's cell rang. I grabbed my phone off my hip and hit a six-digit access code, which cut into Jamie's cell and allowed me to hear everything. *Yes, yes, yes, modern technology. I love it!* You can't get away with anything these days. I hit the mute button and pretended someone was on the line with me, just in case she was paying attention. I didn't want to take the chance of spoiling my little surprise to come. I was loving every minute of this farce, this elaborate, yet inane drama.

"Hello, Mom," Jamie said.

"You miss me, baby?" a man said to my wife.

I couldn't believe that shit. The muthafucka had called my wife on her honeymoon? See, now, that was grounds to kill his ass, too. But I was going to let him live because my wife gave him permission to totally disrespect me. If she had tried to break it off and he kept pursuing, that might be different. In other words, he couldn't have sex with her if she didn't want him to. He asked and she opened her legs. That's the truth of it.

But why did Jamie even have her cell phone with her? She didn't bring it on our first cruise. Why bring it now? Was he really that damn important to her that she had to talk to him before we even consummated our marriage? This bitch couldn't even go on her honeymoon with her millionaire husband without making sure she spoke to her lover before she got on the fucking ship!

I'm so going to enjoy killing this ho!

"I love you, too, Mom," Jamie said.

It's a good thing I didn't have my gun with me. I honestly don't know if I could have stopped myself from committing the acts going through my head when I heard my wife tell her boyfriend she loved him. I felt like pulling out my Glock and shooting her right in the face, but I smiled. It was almost time to accept my Oscar.

I parked the car and we went inside the warehouse my heart thumping feverishly. When Jamie saw the big screen television, she turned around to ask me something, but I hit her with a left hook, knocking her out cold. I caught her before she hit the ground.

I wouldn't want her to die from hitting her head on the cement floor. That would have been too quick. Jamie had to suffer for the game she was playing. By the time she regained consciousness, I had taken off her clothes and hung her from the ceiling by her wrists—her ankles strapped together, so she couldn't kick me. She was naked and, I hate to admit it, very desirable.

Chapter 52

My desire to slide inside this beautiful temptress, to get caught up in the wet heat of her body, to howl as each stroke intensified my pleasure, and then to bask in the glow of an explosive release almost overpowered rational thought—almost. As I looked at her now, this vision of perfection, naked, vulnerable, and precious to be sure, I was enticed by her perfect, perky blackberry nipples. Her lush inverted triangle exposed and tantalizing was like a magnet, pulling my lust to the surface, unveiling the very core of my carnal existence—I wanted her. I was drawn by her sparkling brown eyes as they returned my gaze.

"I see you've awakened. You must be wondering what this is all about."

"Nelson, are you outta your fucking mind?" Jamie snapped. She suddenly realized she was tied up and nude. Her jaw ached. "Are you crazy?"

I pointed a remote at the big screen I had delivered and set up a month ago, and pressed the power button. Then I hit the DVD player's power button and hit play. When Jamie saw herself on the screen, fucking her boy-toys, she closed her eyes. At that moment, she knew I was aware of all her scandalous dirt. I picked up a battery-powered stapler and walked up to her.

"You know what this is?" I asked.

Her eyes filled with what looked like unimaginable terror. She nodded.

Calmly, I said, "If you don't watch the screen, I swear to God I'll staple your eyelids to your forehead." She opened her eyes. "Now, watch the ho on the screen. Isn't that you, Jamie, fucking and sucking two guys? Later, you can watch yourself doing lines with your boyfriend."

"You invaded my home? My home, Nelson? My fucking bedroom?"

"Bitch, please. This ain't even about your right to privacy, okay? This is about you pretending to be in love with me so you can take half of my shit, okay, bitch? That's what this is about! All right?"

Jamie quickly changed her tune and offered what almost sounded like a sincere apology. "You're right. You're right. I'm sorry, Nelson. I'm so sorry," she whined pathetically tears streaming down her cheeks and falling onto her exposed skin. "It was the drugs. The drugs made me do those things. The man you saw me doing lines with is my dealer. You gotta believe me, Nelson. Please! I'm hooked, baby. Help me get the drugs out of my system. Check me into a rehabilitation clinic. Can't your friend Sterling get me into his brother's clinic?"

"How come you bitches are always sorry after you fuck somebody over?" I fast forwarded the picture and then froze it when it showed her boyfriend. "So, you say this is your pusher? He's not your boyfriend?"

She lowered her eyes, suddenly embarrassed. "Yes."

"So, you fuck your pusher? Now, why on earth would you do that, Jamie?"

"I'll tell you all about it, okay? Just please listen to me, okay? Wait until I finish, okay?"

A Vincent Price-like laugh roared from someplace deep inside me and found its way out of my mouth. I said, "I gotta hear this shit." I sat on a table, crossed my legs, and let them swing back and forth. "Go ahead, Jamie. Let's hear this bull-shit story."

"It's not bullshit, Nelson! It's the truth! I swear it!"

I laughed again. "Get on with it, bitch. This oughta be a doozy, too."

"Are you going to listen to me?"

I folded my arms and did my best impression of Chris Rock. "Get on with it, bitch!"

"Well, can you at least let my feet touch the floor? This is uncomfortable, hanging by my wrists like this."

"I don't give a fuck how it feels! Get on with the story, or I'll start the work I'm going to perform on you now!"

"Okay, Nelson. You don't have to yell! I knew him in high school and he's always had a thing for me. He asked me out a bunch of times, but I always turned him down. Actually, I was very mean to him. He came from a very poor family and had to wear the same clothes to school all the time, which made him an easy target."

I shook my head and said, "You gotta do better than that, Jamie."

"This is the truth, Nelson! I swear to God! Now, are you going to listen to me, or not?"

I looked at my watch. "Get to the point! I'm on a tight schedule!"

"I'll speed it up then. When I went to Columbia—"

"You mean that was true? You actually went to college?"

"You don't have to be so fucking sarcastic, Nelson!"

"Listen, you simple-minded ho, you better get something in your head. When you finish this ridiculous story of yours, I'm going to kill you. The only reason I'm listening to your

bullshit is because it makes me feel good to see you squirm."
I pointed the remote at the DVD player again and fast forwarded. "Look at this, Jamie." I hit the play button.

Jamie watched herself tell the man in the picture that she
was going to be rich in six months and said, "I can explain
that too."

I doubled over with laughter. "I just bet you can, can't
you? Liars always have an explanation for the shit they do to
people. Go ahead. Explain that shit." I continued laughing.

Jamie stared at me defiantly. "As I was saying, when I was at
Columbia, I had to work my ass off. I had two jobs and I
barely slept. That's how I got started on the drugs in the first
place. I wasn't the only one, either. The competition was intense, and lots of us started taking speed to cope with our
hectic schedules. I'd be up for days at a time, working, studying, and going to class . . . trying to get ahead. Some of the
rich kids had it made."

"Ah, here we go with the 'woe is me' bullshit again. Now it
comes. It's everybody's fault but yours, right? The rich had it
so easy, right? A poor black girl was just doing the best she
could, right?"

"The white girls were doing it, too, Nelson. They were the
ones who got me started."

She said those words matter-of-factly, like it made one bit
of difference to me what any of them did. This was about her
vain attempt to fuck me over, period. I didn't give a damn
who started her on the drugs. Bringing white girls into it
only reaffirmed my resolve to kill her.

I said, "Now I get it. The white girls put a gun to your head
and said, 'Drop these pills and you'll be up for a week to
study for your exams.' Am I right?"

Jamie sucked her teeth. "You're an asshole, Nelson. You
know that?"

I couldn't help but laugh. Lord, I was going to enjoy this.
I hopped off the table and removed a red shop rag from a

workbench to display pliers, forceps, a scalpel, a butcher's knife, and other sharp instruments.

"Jamie, look at my new toys. We're going to have so much fun playing with them. But first things first," I said and picked up a pair of garden scissors. I grabbed a folding chair and stood on it so I could reach her ring finger. "I want that $125,000 diamond I gave you, and the easiest way to get it is to take your finger, too. You shouldn't have eaten so much salty food at the reception, honey. The ring might have slipped off. Are you ready? Here we go."

A piercing scream comforted me.

Chapter 53

"Wait! Nelson, wait! Please! Don't cut my finger off! Let me finish the story, please!"

I stepped down from the chair and backed off. "Finish . . . the . . . fucking . . . story. No pit stops, no detours, no bathroom breaks. Just finish the muthafuckin' story so I can kill your good-for-nothing ass and get to my hotel to rest."

"Okay. Well, I got hooked on the speed. It wasn't real bad or anything. I didn't need a pusher or anything until after the hospital administrator sent word down that drugs were missing."

I hopped back up on the table and let my legs swing again. "You were the one stealing the drugs, huh?"

"Yes. So, you believe me?"

I just looked at her.

When I didn't answer, Jamie continued. "Well, I knew they were watching everybody, and I wasn't the only person on staff using. I swear I wasn't. There were doctors and nurses hooked, too. Anyway, there was an orderly who was supplying the staff who used. When I found out who it was, I tried to get him to tell me who his supplier was."

I frowned. "Why? Why didn't you just buy from him?" Was I actually starting to believe this ho?

"Nelson, I knew at some point everybody at the hospital was going to get caught. I knew I couldn't be a part of that bust when it happened, and it did."

"And they didn't bust you?"

"No, because I never bought from the guy."

"So, how did you get hooked up with the pusher then?"

"I followed the orderly to the 'hood and that's when I spotted Sherman."

"Sherman? Is that his name?"

"Yes. When the orderly left, I went up to Sherman, and of course, he started hitting on me. I brushed him off and he got pissed, but he still sold me what I needed. Over time, I needed more and more and more. I was spending everything I made on cocaine. Then he tricked me into getting my drugs on credit. Before I knew it, I was over twenty-five thousand dollars in debt to him with no way to pay, which was exactly where he wanted me. And you know what he wanted me to do then, don't you?"

Damn! This bitch actually had me feeling sorry for her. I was losing my resolve to kill her.

I said, "So, why were you talking about me like that, huh? Explain that shit!"

"Nelson, what could I do, huh? When he learned we were getting married, it turned him on to know that he was still getting his piece whenever he wanted it. Besides, everything on the screen was scripted."

"Scripted?"

"Scripted. It was a sex game. When he said certain things, I had to say certain things, too. It turned him on, but I hated every minute of it. I swear."

"Now that's bullshit, Jamie!" I hit the fast forward button and showed her the scene where she had the incredible orgasm. "Explain that shit, Jamie!"

"Nelson, I faked those for his pleasure."

"Listen, I know when a woman has an orgasm. Come on!"

She laughed a little and said, "I guess you never saw *When Harry Met Sally*, huh?"

I stopped and thought for a moment, trying to remember the film. Then it came to me as if I was in the theater, watching Meg Ryan and Billy Crystal in the restaurant scene. Next, I watched as Jamie put on the same kind of show as Ryan, complete with a fake orgasm.

I shook my head, stood to my feet, and began a slow, steady pace, thinking about what I was about to do. Suddenly, the anger was leaving and Grace Underwood was coming to mind. Was she still available? Was she still interested? Did I still have a chance with her? Soon, my thoughts returned to Jamie.

"What about doing two guys at one time? What about that, Jamie?"

"When Sherman learned that I was going to marry a rich man, he wanted me to do even more weird shit. He told me if I did two men at the same time, he would take twice off what I owed him. It was so fucking humiliating, but what could I do? I had gotten in way over my head, owing him nearly two hundred thousand dollars because of the interest he charged for late payments."

"He didn't want to get you deeper into debt so he could bleed me dry?"

"No. It wasn't even about the money with Sherman. Don't you remember what I said? I had humiliated him in school and he liked me. It wasn't about money at all. He wanted to have me and humiliate me, too. He'd already had me. You saw the film. He wanted me to feel like I made him feel."

She turned to watch me as I circled her.

"Look at me, baby. You know you want me. I can do things to your body you've never imagined."

Her voice was low, seductive. the fear was gone from her large, dark eyes. Most people trust in money, but Jamie Stansfield trusted in her magnificent body and the sweet heaven between her legs to keep her alive. She also thought of me as the typical male who was controlled by the wrong head.

I stopped pacing and looked at her. "How much do you owe him?"

"So, you believe me? You're not going to kill me?"

I shouted, "How much do you owe him?"

"I still owe him a little over a hundred thousand."

"So, why were you using the credit card I gave you for the wedding expenses? Why didn't you take that money and pay him off?"

"I did. I paid him what I could, and then I got sponsors to donate flowers, my dress, and lots of other things."

"You expect me to believe that?"

"Women do it all the time, Nelson. That's why their ads were in the program our ushers handed out. The sponsors get exposure, and we get the free stuff, but I owed another hundred thousand to the Mandalay Bay for gambling debts." She thought for a second and laughed. "At least they comped my suite."

"Why would you gamble when you were already over your head in debt and having sex with Sherman?"

"That's what I was trying to tell you, Nelson. Drugs do that to you. They make you desperate. They make you think there's an easy solution, but it's never easy. It's—never—ever easy. All I did was get in deeper and deeper and deeper."

"Why did he call you on your cell phone, Jamie? Tell me that. Why did he call you on your fucking honeymoon?"

"How did you know about that?"

"Don't worry about how, but I listened to it all . . . every single word. Now, can you explain that?"

"Yes. It was a part of the game. He wanted to call me before we got to our hotel. I said no at first, but Sherman is so twisted that he said he'd take off ten thousand dollars if I took my cell and played my role. I hated doing it, but I was trying to get him off me. And I didn't want to take more money from you than I needed to. I wanted to be free of him."

More tears came.

"So, you admit you were going to take my money to pay off your debts?"

"Yes, but I was going to pay every dime back. I just needed to get him off my back."

"What about your drug habit?"

"Now, that was going to be hard, but I was going to tell you after about six months and check into Sterling's brother's rehabilitation clinic. I was hoping you loved me enough to understand. I thought we could try working our marriage out, if you did."

I shook my head and kinda laughed.

She had an answer for everything.

Chapter 54

Bitterness and anger fled. My sanity returned to me. I had been a complete and utter fool. I should have just dumped her a long time ago. I could've had Grace and been happy all these months. I could have stopped it all when she called and asked me to come by for dinner. I decided to call her. I flipped open my phone, scrolled down to her name, highlighted her home phone number, and hit the talk button. She answered.

"Hello."

"Grace." I spoke her name so desperately, like I was completely lost, like only Grace could save me. With sincere humility, almost like a child, I said, "I was wondering if you were still interested in dinner and watching *Pretty Woman*."

"I thought you got married."

"It's a long story. Are you interested? Please say you are."

"Yes, I am, but—"

"Okay. I'll explain everything when I get back."

I pressed the end button and looked at Jamie, feeling the guilt I should have felt when I planned her murder.

I said, "I'm going to do you a big favor. I'm going to pay

your debt and I'm going to pay for your stint in the rehab clinic, but you and I are done. We're getting an annulment. Don't even think about trying to fight it. I'm moving on with my life, and you can move on with yours."

"I love you, Nelson. Can't we try?"

"No," I said and cut her down.

As she dressed, she asked, "When did you find out about me and Sherman?"

"A week after we returned from Sydney."

"And you never said a word? You just played me like that?"

"Just like that. A woman scorned ain't got nothin' on me."

"Would you have killed me?" she asked while we were walking to the door.

"Yes, I would have—brutally—and slept like a baby."

"Okay, well, I guess I deserve your harsh tone after what I did, but could you tell me something?"

"What?"

"Who is Grace? An old flame?"

I opened the door, and was about to answer when I saw Parris standing there. She had a gun in her hand.

"Nice to see you again, Nelson. I told you, you were mine, didn't I?"

Now *I* was scared. "How did you . . ."

Parris smiled. "I'll never tell. I do wish you had killed the bitch, though. I guess I'll have to do it for you."

Pow! Pow!

And just like that, Parris shot Jamie in the head. Jamie's lifeless body fell to the ground, which horrified me. Then Parris looked at me and said, "See how simple that was. And guess what, Nelson? It's your gun. You should have changed the locks at your place."

Chapter 55

I was too stunned to talk. I just stood there, frightened out of my wits. I looked down at Jamie and saw the two holes Parris had put in her forehead. I was there and I still didn't believe it. The strange thing was, in my anger, in my bitterness, in the heat of blind rage, I was willing, and would have killed Jamie myself, but looking at her, seeing her vacant eyes staring toward the sky absolutely unnerved me.

I was so moved by the coldness Parris displayed that I began to wonder if I could ever kill anyone. I couldn't do it in heated passion, and I couldn't do it in cold blood, either. But Parris didn't have a problem with it. Prison must be something else, was all I could think at the moment, because I would have never thought she was capable of doing what I had seen a few seconds ago.

"Now you have a choice, Nelson. I can leave you here on your own or I can help you bury her inside like you planned all along. But, if I help you with this, I expect us to finish what you started that night I came by your place. And I expect to do it before we get rid of her body. And just so we're clear, I expect nothing less than marriage for helping you with this shit."

I looked at Parris. She was very serious about what she'd said, wanting me to fuck her in the warehouse near a dead body. *Damn! This bitch is crazy as hell.* She didn't look crazy, though. As a matter of fact, she was as calm and as calculating as I was—even more so. I could tell she meant every word. What the hell was I going to do now? I had just called Grace and told her I was going to be with her.

"How did you know I'd be here?"

"I'll never tell."

I looked at Jamie again. "Have you been following me? Is that how you found out?"

Parris screamed, "What's it going to be?"

I was still staring at a very dead Jamie Stansfield when I heard her screaming at me, which snapped me out of the fog I was in.

"I'm not marrying you, bitch!" I yelled.

"Suit yourself," she said and turned to leave, heading toward the car she apparently drove all the way from San Francisco. "I'll make sure the police find your gun, and I'll let them know about your little plan to kill Ms. Stansfield here, who, as you can see, is quite dead already."

"Wait a minute," I called to her. "Let me think about this a second."

"Take your time," she said, placing her free hand on her hip and staring at me. "No matter how you slice this pie, you're through, Nelson."

"How did you find out about this?"

"Are you deaf?" She paused, waiting, I suppose, for me to answer. When I didn't, she said, "Decide. What's it going to be?"

"You expect me to get it up after you've killed someone right in front of me?"

I sounded just like a little bitch begging for his life, when just a few minutes ago, I was in charge and sounded like I was the Emperor of Rome with the power of life and death in my thumb. A gun in the hand of a rival can humble a person real quick.

"I most certainly do. I'm ovulating and I'm horny as hell. You're going to get me pregnant tonight, and I'm going to have your baby. So, you do whatever you have to do, but get it hard and keep it hard because you're *going* to do this, or else I'm outta here. I'm sure you have some sort of plan. Maybe you can get out of it, but you know I know about this. And you know I'll expect to be paid handsomely for my silence. I love you . . . I want you . . . but if I can't have you, I'll take your money instead."

"What happened to the five hundred thousand I gave you? That wasn't enough?"

"I redecorated the Victorian. You're going to love the place. Bought a Benz, too." She looked over her shoulder at the vehicle. "The lawyer's fees and forfeiture of the stock I bought ate up the rest. I'm broke again. Listen, you're running out of time. Someone could drive up this lonely road at any time and see her body. Last chance. Yes or no?"

"Yes," I mumbled under my breath.

"I didn't hear you," she said teasingly.

"Yes, goddammit! Shit!"

Parris laughed victoriously. "That's what I thought. I'll grab her legs."

Chapter 56

When I bent my knees to grab Jamie's torso, I heard a high-powered rifle shot crack the silent night and ricochet off the warehouse. I looked at Parris, who had a surprised look on her face. Then she fell forward and landed right next to Jamie. Believing I was next, I hit the ground and lay there for at least twenty minutes before it occurred to me that Parris had an accomplice who would no doubt be sending me a blackmail note.

My cell played a portion of the 1972 Main Ingredient classic, "Everybody Plays the Fool," letting me know I had a text message. I looked at it. It read: DO THE RIGHT THING.

I was nervous as hell because two women were dead and someone had seen everything, and then sent me a message confirming they had firsthand knowledge of it all. Who was it?

Now I had to go through with my plan as if I had actually killed Jamie and payoff my blackmailer for the rest of my life because I wasn't going to jail over this. Hopefully, I'd be able to find the blackmailer and kill him before he bled me dry. That was the only solution I could come up with to get out from under all of the craziness.

I thought about Grace and what she had offered months ago, and wished I had as much control over my emotions as I had over my body. If I had, I wouldn't be in this mess.

I picked up the women one at a time and took them into the warehouse. I knew I had to get rid of the bodies. That wouldn't be a problem. I had planned to bury Jamie in the warehouse before I came to my senses, so I was well equipped to do the job. Only difference now was that I had two bodies to bury. I took off my clothes and put on the pair of overalls I had placed in the warehouse to keep from getting my clothes dirty. I'd have to answer a lot of questions if I showed up at the hotel looking like a homeless person.

I put on a pair of work gloves and used a jackhammer to break up the cement so I could bury my blushing bride and the woman that wanted to be her. Then I remembered my Glock. Parris had stolen it. I had to go outside, find it, put it in the warehouse, padlock it, and drive all the way from San Francisco to pick it up later, since I could never get it aboard a plane. But when I went out to look for the weapon, it was gone; so was Parris' Mercedes. I looked everywhere for the gun. I knew my blackmailer had it, and with it, he had me, too.

Chapter 57

I looked at my watch. One o'clock in the morning. I was going to be late. I had worked up a tremendous sweat using the jackhammer, digging a six-foot deep grave and burying two bodies in it. Afterwards, I changed back into the clothes I'd worn to the warehouse. As much as I wanted to floor it to the hotel, I remained disciplined and drove the speed limit.

After stopping at a red light, I looked at Jamie's purse, which was on the passenger's seat. It had her identification, which I would need later. I picked up the purse, looked inside, and found several vials of cocaine. I shook my head in disgust. It occurred to me that she must have done the same thing when we went on that thirty-day stint to Sydney.

Twenty-five minutes later, I pulled into the Intercontinental Hotel at Chopin Plaza and hurried inside, still perspiring, but not nearly as much as when I was in the warehouse. After checking in, I took the elevator to my room and showered. I had to hustle over to the airport to pick up Rachel Radcliff, and I didn't want anything to look out of the ordinary. Thankfully, the night clerk didn't ask me about my bride.

Rachel didn't know it, but she was going to be taking Jamie's place as my wife. They favored each other. As a matter of fact, I thought Jamie was Rachel when we met. That's why I needed the ring. Poor Rachel. I hated the idea of killing her, and was relieved when I heard Jamie's story and changed my mind. But now, I had to kill Rachel to explain what happened to Jamie.

Now that I was no longer bitter about Jamie and Parris, the whole plan seemed so dirty, so ridiculously senseless. I wondered why people never thought like this before they do the dumb shit they do. When I planned all of this, it didn't seem like I was doing much of anything wrong. Jamie was only getting what she deserved. That's what I thought when my mind was filled with rage.

How in the hell did I ever let it get this far? But what could I do? Go to jail? I planned to show Rachel a lovely time first, spike her drink one night, and then toss her over the side somewhere in the middle of the Atlantic. I'd make sure the authorities found her purse with all that cocaine in it, and they'd figure she fell overboard or something. If I didn't do the unthinkable—kill Rachel—how would I ever explain what happened to Jamie? She thought she was indulging one of my fantasies when she agreed to come on this trip, but I needed a woman who resembled Jamie so I could get away with cold-blooded murder.

I was on my way to the airport when my cell rang. I wondered if it was my blackmailer calling to let me know what the rules were.

"Hello," I answered hesitantly.

"Where are you, lover?" Rachel asked.

"I'm pulling into the airport now," I responded with a sigh of relief. "You ready for a great time on the Atlantic?"

"Most definitely. Is this you pulling up now?"

"Yeah, I can see you. I'll be there in a second. Bye."

I hit the end button.

Chapter 58

I must be a really depraved individual because when I took Rachel back to the Intercontinental, I made love to her—passionately. Imagine that. I had witnessed two murders, buried the bodies in my warehouse, picked up the woman I planned to kill, and entered her body repeatedly. *Damn!* That first night in my hotel suite, I did it because, well, that's what she expected. I mean, she was a prostitute, wasn't she?

But once I got up in it, I forgot all about the murders I'd seen and rode the woman posing as my wife until the sun rose. The things I did to her—decadent. When we reached the suite on the ship, I entered her again. As a matter of fact, we'd been going at it two or three times a day, like a naval officer who hadn't seen his wife in nine months. Sex with Rachel was so good that I'm ashamed I was still contemplating her death and the means by which I would accomplish it.

Rachel and I were on the deck, stretched out on comfortable recliners. She had fallen asleep. I knew she was tired, but she came out on the deck with me anyway. I let her sleep while I thought about the strange truth I'd learned over the last seven days we had been aboard the luxury liner. I learned that people could commit all kinds of evil deeds and justify them with relative ease. I had planned the murder of two women and justified it by allowing bitter thoughts to dominate my mind. Jamie had hurt me, and for that, I had determined she should die for it.

In the span of less than five minutes, I had seen two women murdered right in front of me. Both women had done some horrendous things to me, but looking back on what they had done, did they deserve capital punishment? Of course not, but dead they were, nevertheless. I guess one could argue that since Parris had killed Jamie, she got her just dessert. She was a real psycho, one who thought she was in love with me, but she hadn't tried to murder me. I actually felt sorry for both women, even though they had wronged me.

I now knew I had chosen anger and bitterness, because if I hadn't, I would have walked away from Jamie when I learned of her betrayal. My anger would not allow Jamie to get away with what she had done to my heart. I had been softhearted toward Parris and it cost me half a million dollars. I couldn't let that happen again, could I? She had to be taught a lesson—that's what my anger told me so many times that I was convinced of it. Maybe people use negative emotions as a safety mechanism to keep from experiencing the same hurt again. I don't know.

All I know is that I'm finding it very difficult to kill Rachel Radcliff. During the seven days we've been aboard the ship, I counted at least fifteen times I could have tossed her over the side. We've been all over the ship together. People know us as Mr. and Mrs. Kennard, which is a part of my plan. I don't think I can do it. I don't think I can kill Rachel. I think I have to do the time. I figure they're going to get me for covering up a crime or something like that. Maybe Le'sett can get me a couple of years, out in a year for good behavior. I can't hide this any longer. When I get back to San Francisco, I'm going to turn myself in.

I looked at Rachel, who was still asleep, and smiled. She had no idea how close she was to death. I brushed her hair out of her face, and she woke up suddenly and looked at me.

"Hi," I said.

"Was I asleep?"

"Yes. Ready to go back to our suite?"

Lovingly, she asked, "Are you? I'm here for you, sweetie." She smiled. "You know that, don't you?"

"Yeah, I know. Let's go."

We were halfway back to the room when Rachel remembered she'd forgotten her sarong. She'd taken it off to let the breeze blow on her legs. I could tell she was tired, so I told her to go on, and I'd go back and get it for her.

On my way back to our suite, I heard about five explosions, one right after another. I was afraid for Rachel and started running toward our quarters. People were running and screaming as if we were on the Titanic with no lifeboats and the ship was going down. I wondered what was going on. As I turned the corner, I had to dodge people who were running scared. Then I heard another explosion, saw a bright orange and yellowish light, and I blacked out.

Chapter 59

Several hours later, I woke up in the infirmary with gauze over both eyes and a bandage wrapped around my head. I could hear voices in the near distance, along with stifled groaning—other patients, I suspected. I couldn't fully understand the voices, but as best as I could make out, they were talking about some sort of attack on the ship. Immediately, I thought it was Islamic Fundamentalists. I tried to call out to whoever was in the room, but my throat was dry and sounded scratchy to me. I raised my arms and crossed them several times, hoping someone would see me signaling.

I heard footsteps coming toward me. "Yes, sir," a man said.

"Water," I managed to say.

I heard him pour water into a receptacle, then he placed it in my hand and guided it to my mouth so I could drink it. I took several big gulps and swallowed hard. When I finished the last of the water, I said, "What happened? Were we attacked by terrorists?"

"No, sir. Pirates, sir."

"Pirates?"

"Yes, sir."

"Where's my wife? Is she all right?"

"I'm afraid not, sir. We lost twenty-five passengers to rocket-propelled grenades, sir. Your wife . . . unfortunately was one of them."

"Rachel," I whispered.

She wasn't my wife, but I liked her. I liked her enough to change my mind about killing her. The last thing I wanted was for something to happen to her. Then something strange but encouraging occurred to me. I began to think about the ramifications of her death. With Rachel dead, I was in the clear. Parris and Jamie were dead. I had nothing to do with either of their deaths. Now Rachel was dead, too.

"Rachel, sir?"

When I heard someone say her name, it occurred to me that I had said her real name and not her "stage" name. It was a good thing half my face was covered with gauze because the realization of making that mistake sent a chill down my back.

"Rachel is my wife's daughter. She's at Georgetown studying law." Half truth and half lie. Simple, but effective. I quickly shifted the subject back to Jamie by saying, "Are you absolutely sure my wife is dead?"

"Not absolutely, sir. But we're pretty sure she's dead. I'm told that all but twenty-five passengers are accounted for."

"You don't have a body?"

"No, sir."

"Tell me, sir, is there any chance she fell over the side? Could she be lost at sea with a life raft? Is there any hope at all?"

"Sir, I'm only the ship's purser. Perhaps the captain should be speaking to you about this matter. I'll get him."

I listened as the footsteps faded. About a half hour later, I heard different footsteps coming toward me.

"Mr. Kennard, I'm Captain McIver. The ship's purser says

you wanted to see me about the death of your wife. Please accept my condolences for your loss. I understand you two recently married in San Francisco."

"Yes, Captain. It's true. We were married eight days ago. What can you tell me? What makes your purser so sure Jamie's dead? When I asked him about her possibly falling overboard with a life raft, he ruled the possibility out without even thinking about it."

The captain remained quiet for a few seconds, which felt like minutes to me, since I couldn't see his face or gauge what possible thoughts occupied his mind.

"Mr. Kennard . . . I don't know how to tell you this. . .but the pirates fired rocket-propelled grenades into a crowd of people that ran when they heard the first set of explosions. Several of our passengers were hit by the grenades, and I'm afraid your wife was one of them."

With a genuinely breaking heart, I said, "Are you telling me my wife was hit directly by a grenade, Captain?"

"We have twelve shaken but credible witnesses who say they saw it happen, Mr. Kennard. The witnesses were close enough to see your wife die, but far enough away to avoid any serious injuries of their own. I can't imagine what you must be feeling right now."

As he spoke, one word stayed with me. "Forgive me, Captain, but I'm having trouble believing pirates attacked a luxury liner."

"Yes. Modern day pirate attacks have increased over the last three years. In 2000, there were 469 recorded attacks; 335 in 2001; 360 in 2002. And this year, in 2003, we've had 275 so far."

"You have to be kidding, Captain."

"I wish I were. Normally, they attack freighters, but now they're attacking luxury liners."

As I lay there in my cot, thinking about what Captain McIver had told me, I came to one unmistakable conclusion.

As morbid as it sounds, I was one incredibly lucky man. I almost killed two people back in the fall of 2001 before the World Trade Center Towers came down. I almost killed a second time a little over a week ago, and changed my mind again. If I hadn't, I'd most likely be dead or in prison. I was almost blown to smithereens and survived that, too. The only thing left now was dealing with my blackmailer, who I was sure had tried to reach me by now, but I had turned off my phone after I picked up Rachel.

"Is there anything else I can do for you, Mr. Kennard?" the captain asked.

"Yes. Tell me . . . am I permanently blind?"

It would serve me right if I was.

"The doctor says you'll be fine in another day or so, which is when we'll reach the coast of Florida." He turned and walked away, then stopped and came back. "I forgot to tell you we found your wife's wedding rings. If she hadn't shown them to so many guests, anyone could have claimed them."

He placed them in my hands.

"Thank you, Captain," I said. "Tell me, Captain, how were you able to get away from the pirates?"

"We have an antipersonnel microwave device that disorients would-be attackers. They broke off the attack, and we got away as quickly as we could."

"No military escort?" I asked, hoping they didn't come aboard and start some sort of investigation—not that they'd find anything.

"None at all. They can't protect all the ships at sea and monitor the drug trafficking too. That's why we have the antipersonnel microwave device."

"Thanks for all your time, Captain."

"You're welcome. And again, I'm truly sorry for your loss."

Chapter 60

As the ship made its way back to port, I continued to analyze it all as a myriad of questions harassed me. Like, how did Parris know where I was? How did she figure out I planned to kill Jamie? And who was her accomplice? Why didn't he wait until after they got the first payment before killing Parris? I was still rattled by it all. Nevertheless, I was starting to feel comfortable, too, because I knew my blackmailer wasn't going to the police, which meant I didn't have to worry about them showing up unexpectedly with an arrest warrant.

I had to do some investigating of my own, without hiring someone who would learn too much or ask too many questions. The only real clue I had was Parris. How did she get out of prison so quickly? What kind of deal did she cut?

The first thing I had to do was move the bodies. As long as the blackmailer knew where they were, he could milk me for every dime. I wasn't sure how I was going to do that, though, and where I would put them once I broke ground again and dug them up.

I thought about taking them to the Everglades or something. Or maybe I could dig another ditch not too far from the warehouse. I owned the fifty acres surrounding the place. I planned to go back to Florida and move the bodies as soon as possible. All the equipment I needed was already there in the warehouse.

The attack on our ship made the national news. Fortunately for me, there were other grieving passengers willing to give interviews on camera when we docked. I got off the ship and onto a plane back to San Francisco as quickly as I could, avoiding the massive media coverage. I planned to do some investigating. I had to learn all there was to know about Parris' records and who she may have talked to.

Later that day, I walked into my house and set my bags on the floor. The cruise line promised to forward Jamie's clothes to my home in a couple of weeks. The red light on my answering machine was flashing. Nervously, I went over to see how many messages I had, believing that the black-mailer had left a message or three, threatening to expose my cover. My answering machine was overflowing. Obviously, word had gotten out that Jamie was dead. Perhaps that's why I had over fifty calls. It made me feel good that so many people bothered to let me know they genuinely cared about me.

I hit the play button and heard my mother's voice. She told me she was already working on the funeral arrangements. That hadn't even crossed my mind. My thoughts were consumed with tracking down the blackmailer. Was I really that cold? I guess I was. Perhaps everything takes a back seat to self-preservation. I listened to a few more calls from friends and family, wanting me to call them back. I wasn't planning to do that, not yet anyway.

I didn't have the heart to pretend to be grief-stricken, which was what I would need to do if I returned their calls. The whole thing made me wonder how people who actually carried out their murderous plans faked grief, knowing full well they had killed their wife or husband. How could they be in the same room with the victim's mother and father, their brothers and sisters, their extended family and friends and pretend to grieve? Suddenly, I was grateful I hadn't murdered Jamie.

I listened to the rest of the calls—none from the blackmailer. I wondered why, but only briefly because the last call was from Grace. Her voice was like an oasis in a hot, barren desert. Her message was short and to the point.

Hello, Nelson. Call me as soon as you get this message. She hung up.

She was wondering what I was going to do now that Jamie was dead. At least that's what I thought, because if the situation were reversed, I'd wonder, too. As a matter of fact, I would have been wondering about the previous phone call, the one where I called on my wedding night and told her I wanted to watch *Pretty Woman* with her again and hung up. Her mind must have been turned into a pretzel behind that one, especially since she had called me months earlier out of the blue and invited me over.

I picked up the phone to call her, and then put it back in its cradle. What the hell was I going to say to her now that Jamie was dead? I couldn't tell her the truth, and I didn't want to lie. *Shit!*

My cell rang out the Main Ingredient tune again, letting me know I had a text message. I knew it was my blackmailer. I looked at my cell. I had three messages.

The first one read: GLAD YOU'RE STILL ALIVE.

The second read: I MOVED YOUR FRIENDS.

Cryptic, but I got it. The bastard had moved Jamie and Parris already. He probably made sure I was on the ship and then moved them someplace.

The third message read: DO THE RIGHT THING.

What the hell did he mean by that? Was he saying, "Pay up?" I didn't know.

Chapter 61

"Hello."

Grace's voice was so soothing, so warm and inviting. She had spoken only one word, but one word from her, in my current state of mind, felt more like a thousand soothing words. How come we don't recognize a good thing until after we've completely fucked our lives up?

"This is Nelson Kennard."

"I know," she said sweetly. "How are you doing with all of this?"

I remained quiet. Here I was covering up two murders, and she was wondering about my well-being. Was she the woman King Solomon had written about in Proverbs 31?

Her loving kindness suddenly awakened me to my own wretchedness, and I broke down on the spot. Suddenly, all that I had done, all that I had covered up, all that I intended to do came back to my mind like a ninety-foot tidal wave. It nearly drowned me in the mess I had made, and I wept. I wept like a baby. I mean I let loose of it all. Here I was, a millionaire thirty times over, with everything to live for, and I had totally fucked it all up. I tried to talk, but I just kept crying. I couldn't stop myself.

"I'll be right there, Nelson." She hung up the phone.

Forty minutes later, Grace knocked on my front door, and I let her in. She saw the tears, which were still flowing, still falling out of my eyes like a loving mother at her only son's funeral. Grace came in and closed the door. She didn't say a word; she just embraced me, held me, rocked me like she had carried me in her womb for nine months and birthed me.

Finally, Grace pulled me away from her bosom, looked at me, and wiped the tears from my eyes. "Have you eaten?"

I kinda laughed and shook my head.

"I brought you some food and some movies, if you're up to it."

"Did you bring *Pretty Woman?*"

She laughed. "You know I did."

Later, as we watched movies together, I toyed with the idea of spilling my guts to Grace. It was eating me up inside. I hadn't killed anyone, but I had planned to. It was obvious to me that Grace still wanted me in her life. I wanted to be in hers, too, but I had this thing . . . this terrible weight on my shoulders that had to be resolved as soon as possible. I wasn't sure yet, but I could probably tell her everything after I found out what my attorneys had to say and what my legal options were.

And what about Rachel Radcliff? Who would cry for her? Who even knew she was dead besides me? I had procured her services for the duration of the cruise, and at some point, someone would come looking. I had an idea what I could do, but it would have to wait until later.

I paused the movie and looked at Grace. "Aren't you the least bit curious about me calling you on my wedding night?"

She looked at me. "Yes. Are you ready to tell me about it?"

"How much time can I have?"

"As much as you need. It doesn't have to be tonight. Whenever you're ready."

I thanked her, pushed the play button, and we continued watching the film.

Chapter 62

The next day, I went to Sterling's law offices. I had learned from my previous visits that I couldn't expect my attorneys to suborn perjury. I knew I couldn't tell Sterling and Le'sett the truth, but I could speak hypothetically about the entire episode.

After waiting in the receptionist's area for about twenty minutes, Sterling came out to escort me into Le'sett's office. When my eyes met Le'sett's, I got the feeling she wanted to say, "What the hell have you done now?" We all took our seats, and then they stared at me for a few seconds, waiting for me to spill the beans.

"I have an idea for a movie," I began.

Le'sett and Sterling looked at each other, then looked back at me.

Sterling said, "What's this movie about, Nelson?"

Le'sett sarcastically added, "Yes, please tell us about this movie. We're on pins and needles, wondering how we can help you get it produced."

I said, "Okay, but this is just a hypothetical movie, understand?"

They looked at each other again and fought off their burgeoning laughter.

"There's this guy, see . . . dumb as hell . . ."

They looked at each other again.

Le'sett laughed this time and said, "What did the guy do *this* time, Nelson?"

"Well, now . . . uh . . . this is just a movie, okay? This didn't really happen, okay?"

"We got it, bro. Move on," Sterling said.

"Okay, so this guy finds out that his fiancée is screwing some other guy. But instead of breaking it off with her, because of the baggage he had from a previous relationship, he decides against his friend and lawyer's advice and marries the woman anyway, knowing he was going to kill her."

They looked at each other again—this time, no laughter.

"So, this guy, he thinks of a plan to get rid of the fiancée, who's deeply in debt and has a coke habit, and get away with it. He plans it all out, and plans to do all that he imagines to her before taking her life. But then, the fiancée tells him a credible story that explains it all and he believes every word and changes his mind about the murder.

"The guy decides to annul the marriage and pay for the fiancée's rehab at his attorney's brother's rehab center. The bride and groom are walking out of the warehouse where the murder was supposed to take place, when they see the woman from the previous relationship. She wants this guy back, okay? And she has the groom's Glock. He hadn't changed the locks at his place, and never got the keys from the ex."

Le'sett and Sterling looked at each other again, spellbound by what they were hearing.

"The former lover points the Glock at the bride and puts two holes in her forehead without so much as batting an eye. Then she tells the groom that he has to have sex with her in the warehouse they had come out of, right then and there, and that he also has to marry her. She wants to have his baby and everything else. She tells him if he doesn't agree, she won't turn him in, but she will blackmail him.

"The groom agrees because he doesn't see any other way out of the situation at the time, and she's pressing him for an immediate decision. Besides, with the knowledge she has, she could bleed this poor bastard dry. At the moment of decision, he figures it's cheaper to keep her, as they say. Anyway, as they are about to move the bride's body inside the warehouse, someone with a rifle shoots the ex. Now this dummy has not one, but two bodies to bury. He figures the only way out of this mess is to go through with his original plan."

"Which was what?" Le'sett asked harshly.

"To kill the look-alike on the ship. This guy met a beautiful, high-class escort a year or so earlier in Las Vegas, when his attorney friend took him there to have a party with a bunch of women after he found out the ex was messing around with another guy. He took him there to cheer him up."

Sterling said, "Which woman at the party?"

"Well, the women were dressed like contestants in the Ms. Universe pageant."

"I know that," Sterling said without thinking. Le'sett looked at him and frowned. "Uh, I mean, I figured that's what you meant, but which one of the hypothetical contestants?"

"Ms. America."

"Fuck!" Sterling yelled.

"Is she dead?" Le'sett yelled.

"Guys, come on now. This is just a movie, okay?"

"Is Ms. fucking America dead?" Sterling shouted.

"Yeah."

"Shit!" they both screamed.

"Look, guys, the groom didn't kill her."

Relieved, they breathed, "Oh."

"But she definitely dies in this movie, okay?"

"How?" Le'sett asked.

"Pirates attacked the ship. Ms. America was killed by a rocket-propelled grenade. Plenty of witnesses saw her die."

"Jesus!" Le'sett screamed. "What a way to go."

"Exactly," I said. "Now listen, the groom didn't kill anyone. *Nobody*. But the blackmailer has the Glock used to kill the bride."

"Have you heard from the blackmailer?" Sterling asked.

"Hey, man, I told you this is just a movie. I don't know what the hell you're talking about. But in the movie script, the blackmailer sends the groom text messages to his cell phone. The caller ID is blocked."

"How much is he looking for?" Le'sett asked.

"He hasn't asked the groom for any money yet. His last message said 'Do the right thing.'"

"Well, you can bet he wants something," Le'sett said. "They always want something. He'll be contacting the groom soon."

"Two more things." I continued the true story. "The attorney contacts his brother, who sent the girls to Vegas for the party, and tells him what happened to her. Now, this guy is a big-time drug and gunrunner. This guy's got connections all over the place, okay? This guy can fix almost anything, okay? Anyway, the attorney lets the brother know the groom is willing to make restitution for his loss because it was one of his girls, and he has to handle her disappearance personally. The other thing is . . . how did the ex know the groom's plan in the first place? When the groom asked her how she knew, the ex said, 'I'll never tell.'

"The ex did some time for insider trading. So did the guy she was screwing. I'm thinking he's the blackmailer. We need to—uh, what I meant is I need an ending for this film before I take it to Paramount Studios. How would the groom track down the guy that went to prison around the same time the ex was locked up? I'm betting the groom's attorneys can find all that out easily, can't they?"

Le'sett went to her desk and picked up the phone, and hit a couple of buttons. "Diana, get the Nelson Kennard file and bring it to me right away."

Chapter 63

Le'sett told me it would be about a week before she got the prison files she requested, so I flew down to Florida to check out the blackmailer's story. He wasn't bluffing. When I reached the warehouse entrance, the padlock I'd put on the door to secure it was conspicuously missing. I opened the door and saw that, just as the blackmailer had said, the bodies were gone. All the equipment was missing, too, giving the blackmailer more ammunition. Since I bought them on my credit card, if he turned the tools into the police, they might be able to trace the serial numbers or something, which would lead them to my front door.

A few days after I returned from my Florida junket, I still hadn't heard a peep from the blackmailer, and I had no idea why. He still had my gun, and he knew where the bodies were buried. I was at his mercy. While I waited for him to contact me, I went through with the funeral and the burial, all of it. I had to. It was expected, and I had to cover my ass, which was seriously exposed.

It had to look like I loved and missed Jamie. I did the best I could. Thankfully, nobody asked me a bunch of questions.

Of course, there were the people who tried to comfort me by telling me Jamie was in a better place. I don't know. She might be. In the end, she'd told the truth. I believed her story anyway.

If I was suspected of anything, I couldn't tell. The insurance money went to her daughter, who was determined to get her law degree at Georgetown, so the cops really didn't have a motive—that is, if they even cared about whether I had anything to do with her death in the first place. They had no reason to suspect me of anything because as far as they knew, Jamie was killed on the ship by pirates.

Le'sett called and gave me the rundown on the prison stints of Parris Stalls and Shenandoah Armstrong. Shenandoah was killed within the first six weeks of his prison sentence, which meant it was impossible for him to be the blackmailer. Apparently, a fellow prisoner took his cornbread at mealtime, a fight broke out, and when all was said and done, they found him on the floor with a prison knife in his gut. His killer opened him up like he was a cod, shoving the knife in his lower abdomen and slicing all the way up to his sternum. Nobody knows who killed him. All I can say is that Folsom must make the best cornbread on earth.

I laughed momentarily about the thought of cornbread being so tasty that one man would kill another man for it. But then it dawned on me that I may have played a vital role in my former rival's demise. I had taken from him a woman he loved and that loss bothered him for two decades. It bothered him so much that he felt the need to return the favor and did. However, in his desire for vengeance, he failed to recognize that the fruit was not only tempting, but its offer of sweet nectar was really the venom of a king cobra and equally lethal. I can't help wondering if Shenandoah Armstrong would be alive today if I hadn't gotten involved with the woman he adored.

As for Parris Stalls, at less than five feet tall, she killed three women in prison, and was acquitted by a jury of her peers. The second of the three women had tried to molest her, and Parris fought as if she were a lioness protecting her young, breaking her neck with her bare hands. The women she killed were part of a rape gang that turned other female prisoners into lesbian prostitutes within the first thirty days of their incarceration. I guess the cliché is true. It ain't the size of the dog in the fight, it's the size of the fight in the dog. No wonder she could kill Jamie so easily.

At Parris' trial, several prisoners testified on her behalf, saying that when a woman came to the prison, if she wasn't a part of a gang or didn't join one, that woman was fair game to every prisoner in the cellblock. Apparently, two members of the rape gang went after Parris to avenge their dead sister, and met their dead sister's same fate.

Due to the testimony of her fellow inmates, Parris was acquitted of the murder charges and left alone for the remainder of her sentence. She had been released from prison after doing a year and a half, a true testament to the sway of her sagacious attorneys at Daniels, Burgess, and Franklin. She had to do an additional six months for smart-mouthing the guards, fighting, and taking part in a cafeteria riot.

Unfortunately, no connection could be made between Parris and the identity of my blackmailer. Another dead end. On the other hand, since I hadn't heard anything from my blackmailer, I considered that a good thing because he could have had some kind of freak accident and lost his life. But still, it haunted me daily because at any time, he could contact me again with another one of his impersonal text messages. I guess the thing that puzzled me most was his repeated message. *Do the right thing.* What did he mean by that?

Chapter 64

Three months had passed, and I still hadn't heard a word from my blackmailer. It was the strangest thing. I'm sure some people think I should have moved on and just forgotten about him, but I couldn't. How could I? He held my life in his hands, didn't he? He had seen it all, knew it all, yet he had done nothing. He hadn't asked for money, and he hadn't gone to the cops. Why?

Then it occurred to me that the blackmailer wasn't a blackmailer after all. How could he be? Blackmailers don't wait months on end to collect their dowry, do they? They want their hush money as soon as they can get their greedy little hands on it, don't they? Besides, why would a blackmailer tell me to do the right thing? Doesn't that sound like someone who cares? Blackmailers don't care about their victims, do they? On the other hand, perhaps he was being facetious. Perhaps he saw humor in me being stuck with two bodies that night. Who knows the criminal mind? I don't.

With this new revelation, I began to compile a number of friends I could consider suspects. Why? Well, what if I was wrong? What if my hypothesis was way off kilter? What then?

What if the blackmailer wasn't a friend, but a foe, and the cops nabbed him for something else? A minor offense, something that got him a two-year stretch in Folsom or Chino. If that was the case, he was probably sitting in his cell, counting the days, looking forward to sending me more of those infamous text messages again. So no, I had to know. How else could I feel safe to start a new life with Grace, who had been a godsend in all of this craziness?

I began to write down the names of friends and family members and why they would kill for me. My first suspects were my parents, of course. They loved me enough to kill for me. Between my mom and dad, my dad definitely would kill everything that moved if he thought someone was threatening me. Having served his country and being a crack shot, I couldn't rule him out.

On the other hand, I don't think my dad could have done this and act as if he hadn't done a thing. I think he would either tell me or my mom, or he'd be in a sanitarium, staggering around in pajamas like a zombie, with his thumb in his mouth and a teddy bear tucked safely under his arm as a means of comfort. Besides, if my dad felt that way about Jamie, he never, ever would have attended that sham of a wedding I paid for.

The most likely suspects were Sterling's older brother, Jericho Wise, and his vicious Vietnamese wife, Pin. They were wealthy, high-powered cocaine suppliers and gunrunners. They had been involved in a shootout with the police and had not only won the gun battle, but escaped when they were surrounded. When I attended the wedding of Sterling's younger brother, Will, during the summer of 1999, Jericho and Pin were the hot topics of discussion among the Wise family members.

According to the family, both of them were cold-blooded killers, especially Pin. As a matter of fact, there were several murders at that very reception, and Jericho had been one of the killers that evening. With the money Jericho had at his disposal and the connections he had in high places, couldn't he have gotten rid of the bodies with relative ease? Of course, he could have.

Then, of course, there was Sterling Montgomery Wise. We'd known each other since we were kids, and he was the one who told me about Jamie's "problems" in the first place. Sterling got pretty upset when I mentioned Ms. America, better known in sex circles as the voluptuous Toledoan, Rachel Radcliff, or Plenty. Would he kill Parris? I doubt it. He wouldn't put his career on the line and risk prison for a guy he hardly ever talks to, would he? *Hell no!*

Last but not least was Grace Underwood. She was very upset when I told her I was getting married the day she asked me over for dinner and a movie. Could she be a nut job, too? I don't know. What would be her motivation? Love? I doubt it. But if she were involved, why would she be? I mean . . . what did I really know about her?

I met her at the bank about two years ago. She said she'd had a husband who died, but did she? If her "husband" did die, did she kill him? Was this some Alfred Hitchcock shit or what? Who was she *really*? At least I knew Parris for four years. I slept with Grace the first time we had lunch together. As a matter of fact, I spent the better part of a week with her, didn't I? What kind of woman would do that? As my banker, she was privy to my accounts and has some idea what my net worth was, didn't she?

On the other hand, maybe she felt something for me all along. She had hinted at dinner a number of times, hadn't she? But then she moved on with another guy, just like she said she would, right? I hadn't heard from her in more than a year. Then she called out of the blue. Why? What made her call me out of the blue like that? On yet another hand, I called her home the night of the murders. We had talked on the phone while a naked Jamie dangled.

Damn!

I'm paranoid as hell!

But still, there was a nagging question. Why would any of them get hooked up with Parris? Perhaps they played her for a fool, and let her think they were in league with her on this. I had to believe that Sterling told Jericho about his strong opposition to the marriage. Sterling definitely had no love or respect for Parris. Why wouldn't he put her in touch with Jericho and Pin, since they both wanted the same thing, that being the removal of Jamie Stansfield from my life?

Maybe it was all my suspects working in concert.

Maybe that's why I hadn't heard from the blackmailer.

Maybe they all thought they were looking out for me.

Maybe that was the reason for the text message. *Do the right thing.*

Maybe the blackmailer was none of them.

Maybe the blackmailer was in prison or dead.

Maybe I was paranoid as hell!

Chapter 65

The next day, I decided to start asking questions, and I was going to start with the most likely suspects: Sterling, Jericho, and Pin. Since Jericho and Pin lived in a penthouse on the top floor of the Renegade Casino and Hotel in the Cayman Islands, I was going to start with Sterling. I planned to use the same ploy he'd used to get me to come to his office when he dropped the bomb on me about Jamie Stansfield.

I told him I'd like to take him out for lunch, but I was on the run, and I could meet him at the Carnelian Room, which was a revolving restaurant on the top floor of the Bank of America. Since my office was in the same building, I was a regular there, and I had a taste for their expertly cooked Black Angus beef, which went perfectly with my predilection for fine German sauvignon.

So, there we sat, slowly and almost unnoticeably spinning on the revolving floor, eating great food and drinking fine wine, talking about our past exploits on the hardwood, our success as black businessmen, discussing the 49ers and, of course, women; women we loved, women we lost, and women we wanted but never had. Before long, we were talking about the women in the restaurant. We were having a marvelous time. And then something unexpected happened.

Sterling said, "So, how are you and Grace doing?"

I couldn't have imagined a better opening than that. I offered him a blasé, "Okay, I guess."

"You guess? That woman is head over heels in love with you, man. You better ask somebody."

I looked my friend in the eyes, in hopes of detecting any deception in them. "How would you know?" I said, and faked a hearty laugh.

"I was in the bank she works at one day, doing a little business which required her approval. When she saw my name on the forms, she asked me if I was the Sterling Wise who had played ball with the great Nelson Kennard. I said yes. Then she told me she hadn't seen you in a long time. I detected a flicker of love . . . and you know how I felt about Jamie Stansfield. So, I told her to give you a call. She told me she would call you, but she didn't call you, did she?"

"Yeah, she called."

"Hmpf! I bet you were too tied up into Jamie, weren't you? You shoulda got a piece and maybe you would have left Jamie alone, and everything that happened wouldn't have happened, ya know?"

"Yeah, she called, but I let her know I was getting married," I said, ignoring his revision of "if" history.

"Uh-huh. What did she say to that?"

"She kinda stammered a bit and hurried off the phone."

"I don't mean no disrespect, but, man. . .I gotta tell you. I think you dodged a bullet with Jamie."

When I heard him say "dodged a bullet" spontaneously, I was back on the ship with Rachel Radcliff, retrieving her sarong. People were screaming and running scared. Then I saw the explosions again, like I was actually there, and jumped a bit.

Concerned, Sterling said, "Are you all right, man?"

"It's just that when you said bullet, I thought of what happened to the chick in the movie I told you and Le'sett about. That was a harrowing experience, man. I'll never forget it."

"I understand."

"You remember my movie, right?"

"Right."

"You know the script isn't finished, right?"

"Right."

"You remember the groom's friend that happened to be an attorney?"

"Yeah."

"Do you think his brother may have done the ex in my movie and hid the bodies? I mean, the attorney's brother in the movie is a killer, man. I think it would work in the movie, don't you?"

"I don't know, man. But if the attorney's brother did it in your movie, would he tell his brother about it? Wouldn't he want to keep him isolated on something like that?"

"Yeah, that makes sense, I guess. What if I wrote that the attorney asked the brother to find out for sure, because if the attorney's brother didn't clip the ex, that means the blackmailer could still be out there, right?"

"Why wouldn't the blackmailer contact the groom by this point in the movie? That doesn't make sense, man."

"It would make sense if the blackmailer was in jail on some other charge. I'm thinking that if he would kill someone, he would certainly commit other crimes, wouldn't he? Either way, the groom couldn't rest until he knew who popped the ex, could he? How could he start a new relationship with a really nice lady if he's got a blackmail thing going on that could rear its head at the most inopportune time? He can't, can he? The groom would need to know if his attorney's brother did the deed. If he did, the groom can go ahead with the new woman in his life. What do you think of the movie so far?"

"Captivating. But what would the groom do if the attorney's brother had nothing to do with the hit on the ex?"

"If that were the case, the groom could take a hard look at the other suspects on his list."

Chapter 66

Unfortunately, it turned out that Jericho had nothing to do with any of the murders. That's what Sterling said anyway. Of course, he could have been lying, but I doubted it. Assuming he was telling the truth, that left my dad and Grace Underwood.

I didn't believe for a second that my dad killed anyone. He was a straight-laced guy and raised me to be that way, too. If he had done the deed, he'd be beside himself with guilt. That left Grace and my never-ending questions about her. Who was she? Where did she come from? And how would she know Parris Stalls? The trouble was, Grace was very good to me, and I enjoyed her company immensely. If she didn't do the deed, then that meant my dad or some other crackpot did. Either way, I had to find out. It occurred to me that Sherman, Jamie's pusher and part-time lover could have killed Parris too. If it turned out that Grace was innocent (I was praying that she was), I would have to hunt him down next. Who else could it be? I refused to believe my dad would do something like this.

I felt bad about it, but the first thing I started doing was searching Grace's place for clues. When she took showers or left the room for any length of time, I'd open drawers, hoping to find something that led to her past. I was trying to avoid hiring another private investigator because he could quite possibly dig up more than I wanted him to.

I didn't ask her any questions because if she killed Parris, if she was originally in league with her, she was probably wondering if I suspected her by now. If I did suspect her, I would start asking probing questions, bringing up things about her past, which, if she *was* a murderess, would make her defensive without appearing to be.

Unfortunately, in the limited time I had, I didn't find one clue that would lead me to any concrete conclusions about Grace's complicity in the deaths of Parris and Jamie. I considered moving on with her, but the blackmailer was a constant fixture in my mind. So, I contacted Sterling again and asked him to hire Keyth Perry to investigate Grace Underwood. If she was involved in the murders, I wanted to know why. I wanted and needed to know how she knew Parris.

What Keyth found was shocking to say the least. Grace had been a captain in the United States Army. I obtained a copy of her military record. Her birth name was Anna Grace Benton. For some reason, the name was incredibly familiar to me, though I could not figure out why. She married a major by the name of Rudolph Underwood, who had died from a mysterious disease he contracted in the first Gulf War. Strangely, learning that was comforting. At least she hadn't killed him.

I continued reading her jacket. There was no record of any actual kills credited to Grace, but she was a marksman and a trained sniper. There it was right there. She killed Parris Stalls—at least there was evidence to support any accusation I made.

Was I reaping what I'd sown in my youth or what?

Damn!

How in the hell do I keep picking treacherous women?

I took a deep breath after coming to this conclusion. I was hurt, but not devastated, and I certainly wasn't going to plot her demise. However, the question as to why Grace had killed Parris loomed larger and larger. Was Parris blackmailing Grace? If so, that would explain why she killed her. It would also explain how Parris knew about the warehouse in the first place. It further explained the text messages. Grace knew I would know her voice.

When I talked to her the night of the murders, she must have forwarded her home calls to her cell. I would never know the difference, nor would I suspect her because I thought she was at home when I called and told her I wanted to see her again. Besides all that, the call couldn't have lasted more than thirty seconds, and I was shaken by the new revelations Jamie offered, which prompted my call to Grace in the first place.

Secrets and lies often led to murder. Whatever secrets Grace had must have been awfully bad. What amazed me was that she had killed at least one person, and she acted as if she hadn't killed anyone. I hadn't killed anyone, yet I was paranoid about the blackmailer. Nearly every waking hour, I thought about him and what he could do to me with the information he possessed.

Day after day, I agonized over when the blackmailer would surface and milk me for every dollar, and over the ultimate solution when he finally contacted me—his murder. It would be him or me at that point. Yet, Grace was as cool as a block of ice; no sign of the stress any sane person would have been under, having to carry the guilt of murder. Did she even feel any guilt over what she had done?

It was time to confront Grace with what I had discovered. Since she was cold enough to plot the death of Parris and carry it out with no sign of guilt or compunction, I wasn't about to be alone with her when I confronted her. I could call the police, but if I did, we would both go to prison for a long, long time.

Perhaps she had some incredible story that would help me to understand and put it behind me, but *could* we put it behind *us*? That was a hard one. It should be a no-brainer, but the woman had killed for me and told me to do the right thing. What did she mean by that? What was the right thing? Murder? Moving bodies around in the middle of the night? Hiding murder weapons? How could she tell me to do the right thing when nearly all of her actions were wrong by anybody's standards?

Chapter 67

Iasked Grace out to lunch and let her pick the restaurant. She chose Scoma's family-owned seafood restaurant at Fisherman's Wharf. I eagerly agreed, as I hadn't been to the restaurant in quite some time and enjoyed the quality of their food and the generous portions they doled out. Nevertheless, I didn't know if I'd even eat because of what I had to do, which was let her know that I knew what she had done. I hoped she would fill in the gaps once I confronted her with what I knew.

I got to Scoma's early. As I waited for Grace to arrive, I toyed with a number of ways to broach the subject and put all I knew on the table. As I thought about how I would begin, Grace walked up to the booth.

"Hi, sweetie," she said as she bent down to kiss me.

I spontaneously recoiled a bit. I didn't plan to, but the idea of kissing someone who had murdered Parris right in front of me was distasteful.

"What's wrong?" she asked with lines of concern on her face.

"Please sit down," I began. "We've got a lot to talk about."

Grace slid into her seat, eying me, apparently wondering what this was all about. I can't say I blamed her, because when I spoke to her on the phone, I never let on that I had something serious to talk about.

"You're breaking it off, aren't you, Nelson?"

The waitress came over before I could respond. "Anything to drink before you order?"

"Bottled water," I said.

"And you, ma'am?"

Without looking at her, Grace said, "Nothing for me."

The waitress blended in with the other customers, and we were alone again.

"What's going on, Nelson?"

I had planned to ease into what I wanted to talk about, but when she saw me dodge the kiss I normally longed for, well, that meant there would be no easing into it.

The waitress brought out my bottled water and set it on the table. "Are we ready to order?"

"Give us twenty minutes," Grace said. Again, she spoke to the waitress without looking at her, staring at me with un-blinking eyelids, dauntingly eying me, murderously, I thought.

The waitress said, "Uh, how 'bout I come back in ten min-utes?"

Again, Grace never looked at the waitress when she spoke to her mockingly. "Uh, I believe I said twenty minutes and uh, that's what I meant. Now, leave us for at least that long."

The waitress stared at Grace for a few nervous seconds and blended into the background again.

"What's this all about, Nelson?"

I took in a deep breath and exhaled softly. "It's about you, Anna," I said, firing the first salvo, but she didn't look sur-prised that I knew her real name.

"So, you know, huh?"

"Yes."

"Well, I wanted to tell you a long time ago," she said.

Firmly, I asked, "Why didn't you then?"

"I wanted to see what kind of man you were. I wanted to see if you'd changed. I needed to see if we could have something together."

"Huh?" I said, having no idea what she was talking about.

"I wanted to see if you'd changed," she repeated.

"I heard that, but what are you talking about? The night of the murders, or what?"

Now Grace had an incredibly surprised look on her face. For the first time since she'd arrived, she looked around to see if anybody was paying attention to us.

Then she leaned forward, lowered her voice, and said, "Murders? Plural? What murders are you talking about? I thought you were talking about the night the pirates attacked the ship and your wife was murdered. But you said murders, as in more than one. Did you mean all the people who'd gotten killed on the ship, or what?"

I stared at her, unsure if she was acting or if she was truly oblivious to what I was talking about.

I said, "Let's begin again. I know your name is Anna Grace Benton. I also know you were a captain in the Army and that you were a marksman and a qualified sniper."

This time, she offered a completely different surprised look, like she thought I knew something that I didn't know.

She offered a demure, "You don't know, do you?"

I frowned. Apparently, we were talking about two entirely different things. "Perhaps it would be beneficial if you told me what you think I know, and I'll confirm if I do in fact know it."

Grace leaned back, resting against the booth, and stared at me, gazing past my eyes, looking, if she could, into my mind, into my very soul. She stared at me for a long, long time, neither looking away nor blinking her eyelids. Knowing she was a murderer made the stare downright frightening.

Finally, she spoke again. "I'm Anna Grace Benton-Underwood, Nelson."

I was thinking, *So what*, but instead, I said, "I know."

She exhaled hard and deliberately. "You don't remember me?"

"Uh, am I missing something? Remember you from where? The bank? What?"

She exhaled hard again. "I know you remember Shenandoah Armstrong, don't you?"

I frowned and said, "Are you trying to be funny, or what?"

"You really don't remember, do you?"

I looked at her. I stared into her face, doing my best to remember, but I had no idea what she was talking about or where she was going with this inquiry.

"I used to be Shenandoah's girlfriend until you came into my life."

Chapter 68

And that's when it hit me. Parris had mentioned her the day she'd come to my office to return my Glock at least two years earlier. She'd accused me of being a hypocrite because I had done my share of sleeping with other men's women, insinuating that what I had done had come back on me. I searched my mind in a vain attempt to find her face somewhere in the recesses of my subconscious being, but no picture, no frame of reference revealed itself to me. I had been intimate with the woman sitting across the table from me twenty years ago, spent day after day with her, and yet had no idea we had blended our spirits.

"What's going on, Grace? Are you holding a two-decade old grudge, or what?"

"No, Nelson. As I said, I had to see if you had changed."

"Changed? Why?"

Grace smiled a bit. "Because I had something to tell you."

"What? That you and Parris Stalls were working in concert to blackmail me?"

Grace looked surprised again. "You think I would work with that barracuda against you? Please!"

I leaned forward again and whispered, "I know you killed her, Grace. Don't bother denying it."

"You're serious, aren't you, Nelson?"

I raised my voice a little and said, "Are you going to sit there and deny it?"

A few customers in my periphery looked in our direction. I relaxed a little, leaned backward, and let my upper back and shoulders rest on the firm booth.

Grace offered what looked like a genuine smile before saying, "Let's go to my place and talk about this. I'll tell you everything."

"You must think I'm a fool. I'm not going anywhere with you."

Grace laughed and shook her head. "Let's go outside then."

"Give me your purse," I demanded.

"What?"

"You heard me. I want to see what's in your purse."

She handed it to me and shook her head again. "You're going to be so surprised when I tell you what happened."

I searched her purse and found no weapons. I felt a little safer, but I believed she could probably kill me with her bare hands if she needed to. However, I didn't think she would commit murder in broad daylight with a thousand people around us.

I handed her the purse, put five dollars on the table, and said, "Let's go."

Once we were outside, we found a bench and sat down. Before speaking, I looked deep into her eyes for a moment or two, searching for the truth, whatever it may be, hoping she would come clean so we could deal with what she had done. No matter what, I wasn't going to the police. I just needed to know the truth. Once I knew what happened and why, I could make some solid decisions.

I said, "Now, are you going to tell me you don't know Parris Stalls?"

"I know Ms. Stalls, sure."

"How?"

"I met her at the Metro Theater, remember?" She thought for a moment, and then continued. "Oh, I guess you don't remember because you were out cold when she and I met."

I didn't like the sarcasm, but she had a point. I didn't remember much of anything about that night other than hearing Grace screaming my name, me looking in her direction, and then turning just in time to see Shenandoah's fist clobber me. After that first blow, the rest was a complete blur.

I said, "So, what happened?"

"After a few men pulled Shenandoah off you, after all the hysteria, Shenandoah recognized me and introduced me to Parris as his ex-girlfriend."

"Why didn't you tell me about that?"

"When was I supposed to tell you, Nelson? When you were in the hospital? Or should I have told you nearly two years after the incident, right around the time your wife was killed by those pirates?"

I felt a little foolish when she said that, but didn't let on, continuing with my questions. "So, you're saying you met Parris on a chance meeting at the Metro and you haven't seen her since?"

"That's what I was trying to tell you. She came to see me a month or so before you got married, wanting to know about your personal finances. When I refused to give her the information, she threatened to expose some very damaging secrets."

"Is that why you called me that day? The day I told you I was getting married?"

"Yes."

"So, it had nothing to do with meeting Sterling at the bank?"

"A little. It all happened around the same time, and I had been mulling it all over, but it was Parris' threats that made me call you."

I thought for a quick second, and asked, "So, Parris was blackmailing you because she knew your secrets?"

"Yes."

"And that's why you killed her?"

"What? Parris is dead?"

"Come on, Grace. You know she's dead. You killed her, didn't you? You killed her to shut her up, didn't you?"

"Nelson, I didn't even know Parris was dead until you just told me."

I stared at her, hoping to see some sign of a dark heart, but no sign revealed itself. I decided to bluff her a bit.

Staring directly into her eyes, I said, "Stop bullshitting! You were there that night. You were the only one it could have been. You're a marksman and you qualified as a sniper, Captain. Come on. Tell the truth. You know I can't go to the police."

"Nelson, I have absolutely no idea what you're talking about. None! What night are you talking about?"

"The night I called you, Grace! My wedding night. Don't tell me you don't remember that."

"Yeah, I remember. So what?"

"So what? That was the night you shot Parris in the back of the head and then sent me a text message on my phone. Are you going to sit there and deny that, too? Come on!"

"Nelson, this is crazy! I was at home when you called. I answered the phone, remember?"

"You forwarded your calls, Grace. You had to know that at some point I would figure it all out!"

"Figure all what out, Nelson? I swear to God I have no idea what you're talking about."

I believed her. That meant that either my dad had killed

Parris, or there was a blackmailer out there somewhere waiting for only God knows what.

Desperate now, I said, "Grace, I need to know what Parris had on you."

"Why?"

I lowered my eyes for the first time since the conversation began and said, "Because someone is in the perfect position to blackmail me."

When I finished speaking, someone walked up behind us and said, "I have a gun and I know how to use it."

Chapter 69

Finally, the real blackmailer had arrived on the scene. I was almost relieved, to be honest. This whole thing had my head twisted in a tight knot. I had been wracking my brain, trying to find out who was playing mind games with me, and now I hoped to get all the answers I needed. I thought it strange that with all my deductive reasoning, I wasn't even close to guessing who was going to blackmail me. When I turned around to see who was behind the threatening voice, I saw a woman I had never seen before. She had her hand in her coat pocket. I assumed that was where the gun was.

Is she pointing my own Glock at us?

"Let's go," the woman commanded.

"Where?" I asked.

"Are you going to be a problem, Nelson?" the woman asked roughly. "Because if you are, I have several bullets with your name on them. Now, are you going to be a problem?"

I shook my head.

"Come on then, both of you. We've got some talking to do. Today, we learn everybody's secrets."

Chapter 70

We rode over to Grace's place in her four-door Range Rover. The ride was quiet. I think we were all nervous as hell because this thing, whatever it was, was about to come to an abrupt end one way or another. At this point, I still didn't know what was going on or who was the woman that had a gun pointed at my back as we rode. Apparently, Grace didn't know her either, which solidified my new belief that she knew nothing about any of it.

Sure, Grace had some kind of secret that Parris held over her head, but that was about it. We all had secrets. I had several secrets that I desperately didn't want to get out. I had witnessed two brutal murders and covered them up. I had planned two murders of my own and had escaped murder myself a number of times. I thought Grace's secret had been revealed when she told me who she really was and that we had been intimate in my basketball playing days at San Francisco University. Apparently, she had another secret lurking in the shadows. Whatever it was, I'd soon find out.

Grace parked the Range Rover, and we all walked up the

steps. Oddly, no one was around to tell we were being held at gun point, and as strange as it may sound, a part of me didn't want to be rescued just yet because the mystery still had not been solved. Was there yet another twist to this elaborate tale? I didn't know, but I suspected there would be more truths unearthed before the day ended. I just hoped Grace and I would live to see tomorrow.

Grace opened the door and we walked in. There was a man on the floor, hog tied, with tape over his mouth. His head was bleeding, and his arms and legs were tied together with an extension cord. Grace gasped and fast-walked toward the man on the floor, screaming, "Hayden! Are you all right?"

The woman holding the gun said, "Don't take another step. He's fine right where he is. Don't you dare think for one minute that I won't kill everybody in this room, including myself. I'm prepared to die, if necessary."

Grace stopped in her tracks.

I looked at the man. He looked familiar. If I wasn't mistaken, he was the guy Grace was saying goodbye to when I came to see her the day after I had shown Parris the door, after she had told me how Shenandoah had beaten and raped her. But I wasn't sure because I didn't pay him much attention that day.

What the hell was going on?

Was she seeing him again?

Was he the shooter and the blackmailer?

If he was, who was the woman with the gun on all of us, threatening to kill us and herself?

The woman with the gun forcefully said, "Sit down, you two. One of you will tell me where Parris Stalls is."

Grace and I looked at each other, wondering if we should tell the woman that Parris was murdered months ago.

The woman continued. "Where's Parris, Nelson?"

"Huh?"

"Last time. Where's Parris, Nelson? If I have to ask you again, your son dies."

I flinched before saying, "My son? There must be some mistake. I don't have any children."

Chapter 71

The woman laughed. "Parris said you were a loser, and she was right. What a fool you've been. Tell 'im, Anna!" She laughed a little more.

I looked at Grace and said, "Tell me what?"

Grace diverted her eyes and said, "I was going to tell you today, Nelson. I was. I really was. I just had to be sure."

"Tell me what?" I repeated, on edge, fearing what she was going to say.

"When we were together, I got pregnant. Hayden is our son, Nelson."

"What? You've got to be bullshitting me!"

"No, Nelson, I'm very serious. Remember when I said I had to see if you had changed? Well, you had, and I was ready to tell you about your son. I was going to introduce you two today. I told him to wait here for us to return. She, whoever she is, must have come sometime after I left to meet you at the restaurant."

That was a tough one to wrap my mind around. I had a son. I looked at him, searching for any resemblance to me. Not that it mattered; he was a grown man now. If she wanted child support payments, she could have easily gotten those years ago, but she never said a word. Of all the women who were either after me because of my celebrity status as a basketball player or my money as the co-owner of Kennard Janitorial Services, Grace never asked me for a thing. I wondered what would have happened if I hadn't assumed she was dating my son that day. I don't know, but the murders, the suspicion, the cover-ups, everything could have been avoided.

After briefly soul searching, I said, "Why didn't you ever tell me, Grace?"

"I didn't want to ruin your life or your career. You never cared for me. You just wanted to bed me. I was so taken with you in those days that I would've done anything just to be around you. You were larger than life. Didn't you know that? I was just a little ingénue from Rosemont, Illinois, on my own for the very first time, with no idea who I was and what I wanted.

"At first, I thought it was Shenandoah Armstrong, but I soon learned that he wasn't what I wanted. Then I saw you, and I watched how people responded to you. I wanted to be around you as much as I could. And then I got pregnant and had to go back to Rosemont, where I had Hayden. When I realized I was pregnant, I believed I had gotten what I deserved because of the way I treated Shenandoah. With the help of my parents, I was able to finish school at Illinois State University.

"Then I joined the Army, where I met Rudolph Underwood. My son needed a father, and Rudy was nice enough. He'd been raised well by his family, and he loved Hayden, but it was you that I never stopped longing for. That's why it was so easy being with you after we met for lunch, Nelson.

"When I called that day, the day of your wedding, I was going to tell you about Hayden then. I couldn't keep it from you any longer, but you were getting married, and I saw no reason to complicate your life. That's why I got off the phone the way I did."

I was seriously blown away. I had a son and a woman who had loved me for years after an initial encounter. Here I had been looking for a needle in a haystack, when Grace was right in front of me. How could I have been so blind? I reached out for her and she came to me. We embraced.

With conviction, I said, "I'm going to make it up to you, Grace. I swear it."

"All right, now that we got that out of the way . . ." the woman with the gun began. "Where's Parris?"

"I'll tell you where Parris is, but first tell me how you figure into all of this."

The woman shook her head and said, "You're a real fool, you know that, Nelson? A real dope. A dingbat. A moron. You could've had Grace here, and you fucked that up. You could've had Parris, and you fucked that up, too."

"How do you figure in this?" I repeated defiantly.

"I was a slave at Norrell Prison, and Parris Stalls was my master."

Chapter 72

S lave?
That word conjured up all kinds of images a black man doesn't want running around in his head. When I think of slavery, I think of being beaten with a bullwhip; lynching; hound dogs snapping at ankles; blazing; unrelenting heat; food that isn't fit for animals, let alone human beings; and knowing the Massa is bedding your mother, your wife, and your daughter or maybe all of them at the same damn time.

Was prison that bad?

Was it really?

Did the inmates actually enslave the weaker prisoners?

And this was going on in a women's prison?

I could hardly believe what I had heard. It was so unbelievable to me that law enforcement officers and even regular citizens expected and accepted this kind of behavior as the norm. This kind of thing had become so acceptable that man-on-man rape in prison was now a standing joke, something to be laughed at, and not a thing to be abhorred. And now to learn that women were being brutalized in prison, too? Then I had a disturbing thought. Was this woman here looking for Parris to kill her, or to reunite with her? I really didn't want to know, but I was about to ask anyway when she started talking again.

"When Parris killed the leader of the Double Deuces, I became her property."

I tilted my head forward and shook it. I didn't want to hear anymore. "Spare us your raunchy prison stories, okay? We don't want to hear about it." The woman pointed the gun at me. I recoiled. "How much do you want, lady? Just name your price and I'll get you the money."

The woman lowered her gun. With compassion and longing, she asked, "Where's Parris, Nelson?"

"She's dead. Now, how much do you want to leave us alone? We won't go to the police, I swear."

With renewed anger, she pointed the gun at me again and cocked it. Her voice was full of emotion and shook when she spoke. "Did you kill her?"

"No."

"Who . . . did?"

"I don't know," I said firmly.

"I fucking loved her, man," the woman cried out.

Her outpouring of grief touched me. She had the gun on me and I felt sorry for *her*? Isn't that strange?

The woman continued as quarter-sized tears fell from her watery eyes. "She treated me like a real human being. She didn't even make me go down on her. I had to make her understand that if I didn't do her so everybody could hear, the gangs would kill her and take me back into captivity. With Parris, I was safe. Nobody messed with me, and I only had to do her a couple times a week to keep us both safe. She never rented me out like that bitch Carmen did. I was so glad when Parris killed her and her best friends, Marsha and Stella."

All of sudden, the woman stopped crying and became enraged again, pointing her gun at all of us.

Her voice was still shaking when she spoke. "Now, you tell me which one of you killed her."

Firmly, I said, "Nobody here killed her, lady."

She screamed, "You fucking liar! I know all about the deal she had with Anna. And I know about your plan to kill Jamie. Parris told me all about it."

"What?" Grace said, looking at me. "You planned to kill Jamie?"

I shook my head. It was all coming out now. I didn't want it to happen this way, but there was nothing I could do about it.

I said, "Grace, it's not what you think."

Grace had this incredulous look on her face, and her voice was full of mistrust when she asked, "Did you plan to kill your wife or not, Nelson?"

I exhaled hard and long. As I was about to speak, I noticed the woman with the gun had lowered it and was leaning forward in eager anticipation, resting her head on the palm of her hand. What was going on here? Was Parris reaching out from the grave in one final stab with her daggers of emotional ruin? Puzzled, I stared at the woman for a moment or two, thinking, wondering about that night at my Florida warehouse.

If Grace didn't kill Parris, who did?

My father?

Sterling?

Jericho and his ruthless wife, Pin?

And then it occurred to me that none of them did. The text messages were the key to it all. I thought I knew who had killed Parris. I figured I could get the information out of the emotional woman sitting across the room from me, holding us hostage, seeking to right a wrong for her beloved Parris. I decided to play a hunch.

"What's your name, Miss?"

In a ho hum sort of way, she said, "Why? What possible difference could my name make?"

"None. I just like to know who I'm talking to, that's all."

"Tracy. There, ya happy?"

"Tracy," I began in a cautious, even tone, "did you know Parris wanted to marry me? Did you know after everything that had happened, she still wanted to get back together and have my children? Did you know any of this?"

Tracy became enraged and screamed, "No! You're lying!"

"I'm not lying, Tracy. Deep down, I think you know I'm not lying, don't you?" I watched the wheels begin to turn in her mind. And when I saw her begin to consider my words, I continued the psychological assault. "You mean to tell me that as close as you two were, as intimate as you two were . . . after she had saved your life and allowed you to pleasure her, she never confided in you, not one time? You mean to tell me that you were in love with her, but she never loved you? You mean to tell me that she never told you she loved me and always would?"

Grace was about to say something, but I reached out and touched her hand, silencing her. I knew she was looking at me. I could feel her staring. I shook my head, hoping she would keep quiet so I could bombard our captor with more psychological missiles. It was working, too.

Tracy lowered the gun and appeared to be thinking very deeply about what I was saying to her, and I poured it on, looking for the opportunity to take the gun away from her and call the police. I began the psychological assault anew.

"Did you know that she was still madly in love with me? Did you know she was so in love with me that she shot my wife, Jamie Stansfield, point blank in the forehead right in front of me to ensure that Jamie and I would never be together? Did you know that the woman you were in love with wanted to have sex with me on the spot, not far from my dead wife's decaying body? She wanted me that badly, Tracy. She couldn't wait to get a room. She had to have me there so my wife could be there, too."

Tracy began shaking her head in disbelief. "No! You're lying!" She pointed the gun at me.

I was no longer afraid. I didn't believe she would kill me because I was about to reveal her secret; a secret she had blinded herself to. I knew how she felt because I, too, had loved Parris Stalls once upon a time.

What was it about Parris that drove us all insane?

I began the mind fuck once more. "The woman you wanted most, the woman you had given your heart to, loved me, and you couldn't stand it, could you? She told you she wanted to have my children, and you couldn't stand that either, could you? You weren't going to stand idly by and let her and I have the happiness we deserved, were you? You couldn't, could you? You had so much invested, didn't you? You thought that once Parris got my money, you two would be on easy street, didn't you? What were your plans? Were you two going to fly to Tahiti, or Mexico, or some other exotic locale and lie in hammocks, sip martinis, and make love on the beach? Is that it?"

Tracy was at the breaking point. I had skillfully shaken her, confused her, made her doubt everything she believed, and I wasn't through. It was time for the final assault on that twisted mind of hers.

"Isn't that why you killed her, Tracy? Isn't that why you put a bullet in the back of her head? You saw us lifting Jamie, and that's when you knew what we were going to do, didn't you? You knew because she told you, didn't she? You knew we were going in that warehouse to fuck, didn't you? And you knew I was going to give it to her good, didn't you? She had told you all about me, didn't she? How good I was in bed. And you hated it, didn't you? You never said a word about it, because as you said, she was your master.

"But killing her wasn't enough, was it? You had to come here and kill me and Grace, too, didn't you? It wasn't fair that Parris was dead, and Grace and I were alive and moving on with our lives, was it? Somehow, after killing Parris, you twisted it in your mind that one of us killed the woman you loved. And one of us has to die because you can't stand to see us happy as a family, can you?"

"I killed her?" Tracy said in question form.

"Don't you think you should tell her you're sorry for what you did? If you could have seen the look on her face when she realized you had betrayed her. She couldn't believe you, of all people, would shoot her after all she'd done for you. You said it yourself, she had saved your life. And for that, you took hers. The only question is, how will you atone for what you've done? How can you ever make it up to her?" She was almost there—in Kookville—and I was going to push her through that gated community she lived in. "I think you oughta go to her and apologize for what you've done. She'll forgive you if you apologize in person."

With a totally vacant look on her face, she said, "Yes, I will go to her in person and tell her how sorry I am for killing her."

When I saw her put the gun to her head, I pulled Grace's head to my chest so she would never have to have that visual in her precious mind.

Pow!

Chapter 73

The detectives were satisfied with the story we told them about Tracy Purcell (they told us her last name.) With her prison record and the word of the prisoners at Norrell, they closed the case in a matter of days. As much as the public would like to believe the police are like the cops they see on TV, they aren't. Unless there is strong evidence that something happened other than what it looks like, the cops close a case and move on to the next one. There were too many fresh murder scenes to waste valuable time on a case like the suicide of Tracy Purcell.

In the coming months, I spent as much time as I could with my son. *My son!* He looked more like me every day. He and I hit it off, and I married his mother. It was as if we had been a family all along.

My mom and dad were shocked when I told them about Hayden, but they were totally happy for me. They absolutely loved Grace, and when we told them how everything happened so many years ago, in the days of my misspent youth, they smiled and said, "Love is like that. It's a crazy kinda thing, but we all want it, and most can't do without it."

I agreed with them.

The last couple of years had indeed been crazy, but in a strange way, worth it all. The one innocent person in all of this was Rachel Radcliff, the beautiful temptress from Toledo, Ohio. I felt sorry for her. I hated that she died the way she did. I hired Keyth Perry to track down her family. I wanted to know if her parents were still alive, if she had siblings, grandparents, or someone I could send money to for her death. It turned out that Rachel's family was destitute and living in the Port Lawrence projects, which was one of the worst places to live in Toledo, I learned.

Her parents were deceased, but she had two sisters, both of them good-looking women in their day. They showed me early pictures of the family. Unfortunately, Rachel's sisters, Sherry and Tonya, were both addicted to crack cocaine. They both had small children. Thankfully, neither was born addicted to the drug. The men they'd had the children with were in jail and wouldn't be released for another ten to fifteen years.

No wonder Rachel wanted to go to Hollywood and be an actress. No wonder she wanted to go somewhere other than her hometown and get paid for pretending to be other people. I found it interesting that the same city that had produced Katie Holmes had also produced Rachel Radcliff. I guess all cities are like that. Some people make good choices; others make terrible ones and end up dead, in prison, or on the welfare rolls.

Life sure is strange, isn't it?

I visited with the Radcliff family and told them that I had married their sister and that she was dead. I told them that I had taken out an insurance policy on her, but since I didn't need the money, I was going to get them out of the Port Lawrence projects and into a better home in a better neighborhood, with one stipulation. Sherry and Tonya had to go into rehab and get clean. I told them that they would never see cash money, but I would use the insurance money to pay for not only their college educations, but their fatherless children's educations as well, if they did.

After they agreed, Grace set up a trust fund to cover their expenses. I then flew the whole family out to San Francisco and paid for their stay at the Intercontinental Hotel. I hired a couple of nannies to take care of the children while their mothers were getting the best care in the country at the Wise Choice Substance Abuse Clinic. Sterling's younger brother, Will, owned it.

The children had a marvelous time. Grace and I visited them daily to make sure they were properly cared for. On the weekends, we took them on sightseeing tours to Hollywood, which I found ironic, seeing that my sole reason for being involved with the family was because of their deceased aunt, who left Toledo for Tinseltown. Though she'd visited the famed city, she never made an attempt to become the actress she'd always wanted to be.

Grace and I wanted the children to see something of the world, something other than what a Toledo ghetto offered them. We thought that if they did see something other than what they were accustomed to, they might make different choices.

While much of what we did for the Radcliff family was altruistic, the truth was, we felt as if we owed them something for what I planned to do to their sister/aunt . . . and one other reason.

Chapter 74

It turns out that Tracy Purcell had not killed Parris Stalls after all. My newfound son had. I realized this shortly after Grace told me he was mine and before I started the mind game with Tracy. Who else would send me a text message saying, *Do the right thing?* My son, that's who. He knew his mother still loved me after all those years had passed. She'd told him the day I saw him and her hugging on her porch.

It turns out that Hayden is a Marine captain. And like his mother, he, too, was a marksman sniper, but he had actually killed for his country. Now, my son's a recruiter in the Bay area. He could have been killed in combat, and I would never have known he existed.

When Parris threatened to expose Grace's secret, the lovechild she'd had with me, she was very upset and told him everything, including the fact that I was getting married and that she didn't want to ruin my life. Was Grace in on my son's murderous plot to kill Parris? According to my son, no. I never talked about it with her. What good would it do? Certain things between a husband and a wife don't need to be discussed.

Here's what really happened. After Parris threatened to expose her secret, Grace was crying when Hayden called. She told him about Parris' threats, which launched an idea he had been considering long before Parris threatened his mother. But when he learned that Parris was willing to blackmail someone, he decided to make her his unwitting pawn, because he was planning to blackmail me into marrying his mother.

Using the number Parris gave his mother to call if she changed her mind, Hayden contacted Parris and convinced her they should work together, telling her I owed him, since I was a millionaire and he had to grow up gallivanting from place to place, wherever the Army sent his "dad," like a vagabond with no place to call home. He made up stories about how he never had any friends and how poor his grades were, which made the Armed Forces his only real choice in life. He continued lying by telling her he was going to kill me, his "real" dad. He believed that since Parris had told his mother the truth—that being that she planned to marry me one way or the other—then Parris would also be willing to help him get the money he was entitled to by law.

Parris fell right into his web of lies, which served her right, and she began to follow me, reporting everything to my son. When I was away in San Diego, giving Jamie all the time she needed with her part-time lover, Parris used the key I'd given her, and she and Hayden went into my house, found the DVDs, the receipts for the jackhammer, everything, and figured it all out. They decided to wait until I had killed Jamie and then blackmail me. Hayden was supposed to get five million, and Parris was supposed to get the rest by marrying me.

But when I let Jamie live, they had to improvise. Parris had already planned for that scenario, since she knew I hadn't had the heart to kill her even when I caught her in the act with Shenandaoh. She hoped I'd kill Jamie, but was more than willing to do it if I couldn't. That was why she took my Glock. Parris thought that by killing Jamie, I'd be on the hook for whatever they wanted. Hayden, on the other hand, was willing to take out both of them on the same night to blackmail me into marrying his mother.

If my son told me the truth, and I believed he had, I wasn't about to tell Grace that the son she had carried for nine months loved her enough to kill for her. When I asked him why he waited to kill Parris until the night of the wedding, he told me that he wanted me in an impossible position so he could blackmail me with my Glock and the bodies he'd buried (He wouldn't tell me where). He said that if it ever resurfaced in the future, if anyone ever figured out what really happened at that warehouse, he didn't want me to know anything. When I asked him about my Glock, which I have now reported as stolen, he said he'd melted it down so it would never, ever be found.

My son and I made a pact never to tell his mother the whole truth about what really happened at the warehouse that night before I picked up Rachel Radcliff from the airport, and Grace was wise enough not to ask. Tracy Purcell was a nut job, and she was threatening to kill us all that day at Grace's house. I couldn't let her destroy my family after we had just found each other, could I? I had to protect my son no matter what. What would you have done in my place if you knew your son had killed a woman to protect his mother's twenty-year secret? Would you have turned him over to the police?

What would have happened if my son hadn't killed Parris Stalls? She would have had me and his mother over a barrel for the rest of our lives. It was either that, or tell the police I had planned to kill Jamie Stansfield but changed my mind. And if I told them that much, I would have to tell them everything and risk going to Folsom or Chino. Would the cops believe I didn't kill Jamie with my gun? In any event, wouldn't the district attorney remember that Parris had filed a complaint, alleging that I had broken into her house and threatened to kill her with my Glock?

A much bigger and daunting dilemma was how would I ever explain covering up the death of Rachel Radcliff, who had posed as my adoring wife on the ship? A tangled web indeed.

Since I hadn't actually killed anyone, it didn't make sense to risk prison. Everyone who knew about this elaborate caper and could harm us was dead. I was taking care of the Radcliff family, meeting all of their needs until they could take care of themselves. What more could I do to make up for what I planned to do and for their loss?

Nevertheless, my conscience still feels a pang when I think of Rachel or see her family. She wouldn't be dead if I hadn't planned to kill her. Hopefully, she knows I changed my mind and was ready to go to the police and confess all my sins. I think she forgives me.

As for me and Grace, we plan to have another child or two . . . and live as man and wife.